Cadillac Hubie

By Rad Crews

Dedicated to my Brother,
Paul Hubert Crews

The original Cadillac
Hubie

Edited by: Stacy Lynne Hunt

Cover art by: Jeff Fillbach

Prologue

In The Year Of Our Lord, 1543

Juan de Trevino stood cap in hand with respect before his lord and master, Alferez Melchor de Diaz. The eldest son, Lucas Gonzalez de Diaz, sat next to his father behind the large hand-carved table as he interrogated de Trevino. Trevino had expected this all throughout the long, two-year journey from the New World. Even so, it was almost impossible to accept this sneering fop as one worthy of questioning his unyielding loyalty to the Diaz family. Still, as the eldest son, Lucas would one day take his place as the master of all within eyesight of the magnificent Diaz hilltop Spanish Villa.

A shame, thought Trevino, that the loved and respected second son, Melchor Diaz could not take control of the vast Diaz holdings. But that was not the way, as the first born always inherited the fortune while younger siblings crossed the waters in search of their own destiny. Such a man was Melchor and Trevino had loved him as if he were his own brother. To make things even worse, it was general

1

knowledge that when Alferez de Diaz married Dona' Laureana Diaz Botello, she was already with child. But, such marriages that brought power and alliance to the region were not questioned by those of lower status. To question the parentage of an eldest child would bring the lash if one was lucky. More likely, the noose or the lance would be the reward given to one that stated the obvious.

And so, Trevino stood stoic under the pointed questions of Señor Lucas, as he asked, "Have you actually read this report you bring to us today?"

"*No Señor*, but I am no man of words and the missive has been sealed, as you can see for yourself."

The elder Diaz raised an eyebrow at this disrespectful reply from Trevino, but he remained silent, preferring to let his son ask the questions. He had learned long ago that this was the best way to understand truth.

A very impatient Lucas paced behind the table as he continued to question Trevino. He made no attempt to hide his distain for his brother's valet.

"It is hard to believe that my younger brother could lose his life due to a poorly thrown lance missing a dog that resulted in his being impaled as it stuck into the ground. My brother was the very best horseman and I have never seen better with the lance. If it were not for the report being written by Pedro de Castaneda de Najera, I would take it for an outright lie!"

Trevino hesitated, wondering how to reply to the avalanche of pointless questions. A sharp retort was on the tip of his tongue when the elder Diaz put his hand on his son's forearm, and silenced him with a glance.

Alferez Melchor spoke for the first time that afternoon, saying, "My dear Juan, I know your grief cannot be less than our's to be tasked with bringing this miserable news home. Can it possibly be true that my son was lost in such a pointless manner, after surviving for so long in that hostile place? Please my old friend, tell us what happened. As my son's valet, the true story resides within you and I beg you to tell the story, no matter how awful it may be."

Trevino began, saying, "*Señor* Diaz…." when the elder man abruptly stopped him.

"Please Juan, Alferez will do here. Our families have been as one for many generations. Your father and I were best companions and friends in our youth. Without the Trevino family none of our good fortune would have been possible. This is why I sent you with Malchor as his valet. Please tell us the story so that we may know the truth."

Juan de Trevino turned to look across the patio at the incredible vista before his eyes. He saw rolling hills lush and verdant with life. The sky was the clearest shade of blue he'd ever seen. Trevino had grown up in this place and loved it with all his heart. On a beautiful day such as this one he might think that being home would bring him joy. But the cold stone within his heart removed any kind of happiness. All he knew was the desperate pull of grief in his chest and the bitter taste of regret upon his tongue. How he could go on living was unknown, but the one thing he did know was that the Diaz family deserved to understand the truth and meaning behind their second son's death. And so he began…..

"As you know we left almost five years ago as a part of Francisco Vazquez de Coronado's expedition of exploration and conquest of the Americas. A better Conquistador than Melchor never existed. Your son inspired confidence in his companions and followers, and always maintained the best of order and of diligence among those who were under his charge. For this reason he was placed in charge of the town of San Miguel de Culiacan. It was later in the year 1539 that Fray Marcos returned from the north with stories of the cities of Cibola and the fabulous wealth to found there.

"In November of that year, Viceroy Mendoza placed Melchor in charge of a small expedition to determine the truth of these rumors. This reconnaissance was to be for the benefit of Coronado's grand expedition. But, there was no wealth to be reported and when we finally found the main expedition, we had only the sad report of mud huts and impoverished Indians. I have seen this, *Señores*, and the reports of golden cities are as false as the Unicorn."

As he spoke, Trevino felt the stifling weight of the story yet to be told. A slick sweat was forming on his brow yet he pushed himself to continue.

"It was later in September of 1540 that his excellency, Francisco de Coronado, sent us on our final expedition to find the fleet of Hernando de Alarcon, which was to be the maritime support of the grand expedition. However the fleet was gone, as the ships were being eaten by worms and they were obliged to depart. Melchor determined that further exploration was necessary to provide Coronado with sufficient information of the area north and west of the great inland sea. Although we had Indian support for our group, they were unreliable and hardly could be trusted to tend the sheep and livestock. But there was one young Indian woman with a limited knowledge of Spanish and she became a reliable guide. She was of the *Kumeyaay* people that have inhabited those lands for all eternity, or so it seemed. Her name was impossible to pronounce and so *Señor* Melchor named her "*Sunni.*" He understood that as she was with child and had no mate, it was of the Christian obligation to protect this young woman and perhaps bring her away from the primitive pagan beliefs that plague the New World.

"For many leagues we traveled northwestward until we crossed the area where the great river from the north emptied into the sea. From there, Melchor determined that we would journey southward with the object being to gather further reconnaissance of the western shores. This journey was made with great difficulty, but your son had the respect and obedience of his men and they followed his lead willingly.

"It was during this portion of our travels that Sunni began to tell tales of the original people that inhabited this inhospitable desert from a time beyond memory. At our evening camp fires, she would weave tales of improbable creatures and legends of the old times. She claimed that these ancient peoples could communicate with the creatures of the desert. One story that your son became truly interested with was of a mountain oasis and the magical waters that flowed there. Sunni also spoke of an amulet or artefacto that was made from the fire of the earth and bestowed great power. But, she also warned of some manner of demon creature that jealously guarded this magical garden.

"Melchor confided privately with me of his suspicion that this could be the true location of the Fountain Of Youth that Ponce de Leon had searched for in vain twenty seven years before. And so we continued our journey in search of the rumored canyon that led to the way of finding this place. But as the days of our expedition continued south, we began to lose many of those natives conscripted as porters. Finally, one morning we woke to find only Sunni remaining, as the rest of the Indians had slipped through the night guard and disappeared. She explained to Melchor that the danger was more than the tribesmen could accept and that she was also unwilling to go further.

"Some of the men, overtaken with the lust for treasure, urged your son to bind the Indian woman and compel her to continue as our guide. But he would never do such a thing to a soul that was honest and loyal. She was truly terrified when she pointed the way into this forbidden canyon and that is when Melchor released her with God's blessing. As I watched this woman take her chances alone in the desert rather than continuing with armed fighting men, I wondered what could compel such a choice.

"That very night while camping in the mouth of that vast arroyo we lost several sheep. It was thought to be caused by the mountain puma which inhabit those mountains, but the daylight revealed strange tracks not seen before. That day we traveled ever upward in this canyon searching for the way to the top. In order to protect the dwindling supply of mutton, Melchor set out extra guards and had fires lit to keep away the mountain cats."

At this point of his narrative, Trevino felt a great weariness come upon him, and he began to shake uncontrollably. The elder Diaz immediately came from behind the great table and urged the man to be seated. Lucas wanted the valet to continue, but his father silenced him with a quick wave of his hand as he poured a flagon of wine for Trevino. He gratefully accepted the ruby liquid and in a few moments took up the tale once again.

"It was on this darkest night of all that tragedy struck our little group. It was well after midnight when the sheep began to bleat piteously. Melchor immediately mounted his stallion and called for his lance which I handed to him. The guards began to scream horrifically as Melchor spurred his mount forward, fearless as always. As I followed on foot, the dimming firelight revealed a dusty conflict taking place but clarity of vision was denied me. Then, I heard your son cry out with sharp pain accompanied by the most devilish screech I have ever heard. Believe me *Señores*, if I were to ever hear such an evil sound again, I would gladly lance my own eardrums. I found him on the ground next to his disemboweled horse which was still kicking feebly as it struggled to rise. Your son was gravely wounded in his left leg and groin. His metal cuirass had protected his upper body although it was rent and torn open as if by a steel chisel. He still grasped his shattered lance, or at least the portion that remained. The sharp end was gone as well as the uppermost third of the shaft. It had been snapped as if it were merely a twig. We got him inside his tent and were able to stop the bleeding. Never before have I seen such hideous wounds."

The memory of what happened next shook Trevino to his core. He had to force the words out as they were still unbelievable, although he had witnessed it with his own eyes.

"In the morning light, we found the remains of the two guards from the previous night. One's neck had been slashed so violently as to have nearly severed the poor man's head. The other one was found some distance from the struggle where he had bled to death, his arm having been ripped from the body.

"We found a pool of blood next to the dead horse and it reeked as if a pestilence and was the most foul color black. Although feverish, Malchor asked if we found the demon he had speared and so we told him the thing was surely wounded unto death and was not to be found. He only laughed at this assessment and bade us retreat from this accursed land immediately.

"*Señores* , your son, your brother was the most brave and strong man I have ever known. But a foul venom took his life after ten days of suffering. He is buried there in that cursed desert with only a carved plank of wood to mark the place."

At this last, Lucas Diaz could no longer contain himself and spoke up accusingly.

"Do you expect us to believe this fantasy? Demons? More likely the lion of the mountains or perhaps his own men killed him in order to return to the main expedition. And what of the other men with your group? Where are they, and why does the written report not reflect your outlandish story if you spoke truth to your superiors?"

Trevino was barely able to contain his rage at this insult, nonetheless he composed himself, explaining, "Yes the full story was told to his honor Francisco de Alarcon when we finally returned to the fleet. It was he that commissioned de Najera to write the account. As far as the other's of our small group, I have no knowledge as I did not return on the same vessel. I only know of the rumors containing stories of being lost at sea. As such, I am the only survivor of that nightmare. The report is false and the truth is as I have stated it. My only explanation is that de Alarcon wished the magical spring, the *artefacto,* and the powers it confers for himself. If so, I welcome him to try and take it."

Trevino paused and reached inside his white linen blouse to remove a small leather pouch hanging from a lanyard.

Looking directly at the elder Diaz he said, "But *Señor* Diaz, it is as I have told you. This talon was embedded into the haft of your son's shattered spear. Look closely, this is not from any mountain lion that I am familiar with. Notice the serrated edge of this devil's claw. This is not something that could ever be retracted into a cat's paw. There is no doubt that the sharp end of his spear is now inside the demon that attacked us. Your son gave his life for his men, *Señor* Diaz, and this is the only truth I know."

Cadillac Hubie

1

The Devil's Peak

Pedro Martinez stopped the stolen Honda Quad. He could go no further. The little machine pinged and gurgled as it tried in vain to cool in the overwhelming August heat. Monsoon temperatures along with the chance of gully-washing rain, if the heavens wished it to be, were always a danger this time of year. Today the sky was clear, which did not help to hide the brutal sun, only made worse by the oppressive humidity. Pedro knew however that high above, rain could gather and come rushing with the power of a runaway locomotive down the granite face, funneling into the many arroyos and obliterate anything unfortunate enough to be in the way. Not Pedro. No, he'd grown up in San Felipe and knew the desert and ocean well. He was very familiar with this particular canyon that stood almost hidden in the Eastern shadow of the Sierra de San Pedro Martir, the backbone of the Baja Peninsula.

He sat on the quad, looking up at his ultimate quest. There above stood Picacho del Diablo, the Devil's Peak. Looking straight up at the vertical rock wall, he had the impression that he'd fall over backwards were he not holding onto the handlebars. Although he scoffed at the stories and myths told to the little boys and girls of those that disappeared and gory tales of the night creatures in forbidden places.... the Chupacabra, he couldn't help but feel intimidated looking up at this peak that towered more than ten thousand feet above. He knew the stories, the rumors and also why another name for the imposing mountain was Cerro de la Encantada, or the Hill of the Enchanted, or Bewitched. *She* was said to still be up there. The timeless one. She of rock and sky and spawned from blood bred in this desert before the time of Cortez and his followers. Those Spanish fools, eager to steal that which they neither earned nor deserved. Their bones littered the uncaring desert, a testament to their foolhardy adventurism. There was no gold; only stinging, crawling, biting, creatures hardened by millennia of survival in this harsh landscape. Dark brown, lean, and as wiry as a hungry coyote, Pedro felt more in common with these desert inhabitants than most humans he'd known during his twenty five years.

The tough Mexican got off the Honda and turned to look back down his long and winding path. Not many knew of this way, and that was why he had been tasked with this journey. From this elevation so far above the white sand beaches of San Felipe he could see the peaceful Sea of Cortez spread before him. He hated it. Yet somehow it always called him back, seeming to hold onto him no matter how hard he tried to escape. It reminded him of the wriggling, doomed fish he would haul in for the fat sweating gringos when he worked as a deck hand on the Tony Reyes charter boats. But el Jefe had requested this, and a request from the

Diabolic one was obeyed under penalty of death. Far in the distance, clouds hovered over the mainland of Mexico, delivering their daily monsoon downpours. He knew that from his vantage point, this evening he'd be able to watch the lightning play in the tremendous storms so high as to be seen from over a hundred miles away.

Understanding how quickly darkness would come in the mountain shadow, Pedro began to arrange his humble campsite. From the basket in front of the handlebars and the container behind the seat, he removed his bed roll and the small cooler containing his hand-pressed tortillas and the ziplock package of frijoles to be eaten cold. The tamales he would eat in the morning, also cold. For now, he could only wait. His ascent would not begin until the very first light of the morning appeared.

His bed would rest on the only remaining flat spot off the arroyo floor before the meager trail dissipated into a treacherous goat path. Even though the sky was clear, he took no chances of a flash flood washing his only mode of transportation into oblivion. Pedro vividly remembered as a young boy how Hurricane Katerina had battered San Felipe in September of 1967. Even though it was almost eighteen years ago, any villagers then present never forgot the horrific experience. Besides, it didn't take a hurricane to make the arroyos run. A relatively small cloud burst on the sharp spine of San Pedro Martir could do the deed.

Pedro washed his spartan dinner of beans and tortillas down from a plastic water bottle, taking care to ration it. He had brought plenty of water bottles with him, purchased from the Pemex gas station when he topped off his stolen quad. The care was necessary as he could only carry a limited amount in his pack during tomorrow's climb and he still needed to leave a reserve with the quad. Those that were careless with water in this unforgiving desert did not live long lives.

As the full moon rose above the Sea of Cortez, once again Pedro was struck by the magical quality of that shaft of moonlight so sharp and clear upon the waters that it seemed as if one could walk upon that shining road right to the face of the moon. While still children he and his little sister, Lupita, would play the moonbeam game on the sandy beaches, running to the water then pretending to walk upon the reflected moonlight. As evening gathered, **mamá** would call them in for bed and **papá** would always read a story. Those were the good times Pedro reflected on. Later, only when age and reality crept in did he realize how poor his family was. The fishing was hit or miss for **papá** and the cleaning did not bring in much extra income, although his poor **mamá** seemed to work her fingers to the bone. Rich tourists don't leave tips for hotel cleaning ladies, and the owners paid a pittance. Still, Pedro always wore clean trousers with a crisp white shirt and Lupita her checkered skirt to school. Being poor does not mean a family should not be proud.

The schools in town only reached to the eighth-grade level, and there was no money for university. Pedro was very young and fresh when he found work on the fishing fleet. The sport fishing boats were hard at first, but he picked it up quickly and got very tough, very fast. Later, when he crewed aboard shrimp boats, he learned the true meaning of man's work. And with all that, still hardly enough pesos to fill one hand. And what of little Lupita? She soon tired of selling trinkets to tourists wandering from bar to bar along the Malecon drive defining the edge of town and San Felipe's beaches. She had grown so very beautiful, and the strip clubs and easy money of the border town Mexicali beckoned to so many young and desirable girls. The last Pedro heard, she had been working the houses of lust up north in Algodones.

This place existed on the border of Yuma only to host elderly gringos seeking cheap medications and stinking drunk Marines from the air station close by. The young and bored Marines would be looking for one thing. Pedro hated them, knowing that it was his sister they were seeking.

He hated all of them. All of the rich and careless norteamericanos, safe and sound beyond la Linea. He had tried many times to penetrate the barrier, hoping to find what made life so easy up there. Always it was something. The heartless inmigración federales would stop the farm worker's transport, looking for papers. Could they not understand he only wanted honest work? Or, he'd been turned back at the border trying to cross legally, again not in possession of the precious green card. He had even watched others as they removed their clothing, placing it into a knotted plastic trash sack, then entering the hazardous waters of the New River where it flowed northward into the U.S. They knew the Border Patrol agents would never enter that flesh burning cesspool flowing from the factories dotting the landscape of Mexicali. And who ran and profited from those Maquiladoras enslaving desperate Mexicanos? Once again, it was the greedy gringos or their Japanese counterparts. Low wages, no medical plan, no retirement assistance, and no protection from the various solvents and products of manufacturing that would never have been allowed in the north. And then, to top it off, just dumping the dangerous substances into the river where the only justice was that the toxic waste flowed right back into the north. It was so bad that Pedro had heard of those contracting hepatitis from entering the water. But it was a risk worth taking, since the Border Patrol soldiers would never go in after the immigrants. Some made it, others were damaged permanently.

So it was that Pedro turned away from the border and

dreams of a better life. Like so many others he fell into employment with one of the cartels, always looking for desperate soldiers willing to give all for the cause. He had been a good match for a place with los Diabolico's growing army. The Diabolic one desired to expand his routes of drug supply into Baja as a means of moving the product northward. Pedro's knowledge of the region got him in the door, and he proved himself one ugly morning when the lives and product were taken from a rival gang's panga as they attempted to land their shipment onto a remote Baja beach. His seamanship was noted when he maneuvered his armed panga in such a way as to block the other boat while they were gunned down. Their blood, soaking the burlap covered product was ignored as the shipment was carried up to the pavement and the waiting trucks.

Soon after this episode, Pedro had been called back to La Paz and ordered to take the ferry to the mainland. There, a white Mercedes brought him to the mountaintop headquarters of the Diabolic one himself. A well dressed and manicured secretary interviewed Pedro at length. The young man was obviously educated, well paid, and without a name. It seemed that no person on this mountain top had a name. Many questions were asked of Pedro. He was drilled on the region and geography of San Felipe, with extensive questioning of the San Martir Mountain Range. He answered all questions with authority based on his growing up in the area, although he could not begin to understand why in the world anyone would care. Then his young host asked about the Enchanted Valley and the myths surrounding the Ancient One, the one said to be inhabiting the alpine valley and the protector of the artifact.

Pedro almost laughed out loud, but seeing the serious expression on his interrogator, did not make that fatal mistake. He soberly explained the childhood stories and how the old woman protected the precious artifact, left there from a time unknown and thought to be magical in quality. Everyone knew of this tale as it was a part of the fabric of storytelling that all shared. When asked if he would be able to find this enchanted valley and retrieve the precious item, Pedro knew his only reply could be yes. There was no alternative. El Diabolico believed in the magical protective properties infused in this object and he would have it. Soon Pedro found himself back on the ferry en route to La Paz and Baja. No questions were asked of a lone Mexican man on a bus and that is how he found himself, once again back in San Felipe, a town he'd thought to have left behind.

It was easy enough to steal the quad from in front of the Miramar Bar and Grill on the Malecon. The bar was filled with raucous smoking and drinking gringos, oblivious to all but the beers and tequila shooters in front of them. The Honda was sitting there, still warm with the key in it. Pedro simply drove it away, filled it with gas, and procured supplies and water. Now here he was, at the very root of the Devil's Peak on a quest for something he'd never believed in. But, that was of no consequence. What mattered was his task, and that he'd fulfill it, or die trying.... because to fail was as sure as death itself.

2

Ancient

Dawn was barely a hint on the horizon when Pedro began his climb. The brilliant moon had long disappeared behind the looming peak of del Diablo, but the glow remained and the goat path was clear before him. He had no idea of what he might find, if anything, but up he went nonetheless. He had no rope, no climbing tools, and had never been this high into the unknown before. Fortunately, the path worn into the hard granite by countless hooves gave him the footing he needed. He was grateful for his lace-up desert boots with the lugged soles and the secure grip they provided. Climbing ever higher, he was very cautious to avoid the treacherous cholla cactus. Those pesky segments seemed to leap out at the unwary, inflicting toxic pain that lasted. Pedro knew his Levi's jeans offered little to no protection, so caution was paramount.

After more than an hour of climbing, the sun broke the horizon like a searchlight illuminating suddenly. His shadow appeared instantly on the rock wall in front of his face and the heat began with the first flash of light. Pedro turned his ball cap around backwards to allow some protection for his neck. He paused to un-tuck his white long-sleeve linen shirt in order to provide ventilation, still the pack began to stick to his back and shoulders with insistent pulling weight. Pedro struggled ever upward for what seemed like forever. Even worse, the sun-baked vertical granite surface began to reflect the heat with a vengeance. Pedro was most surely caught between the rock and a hot place with nowhere to go but up. Ever up.

Arriving at a spot where the trail started to switchback, Pedro sat on an outcropping of solid granite and took in the view to the east. He had never seen anything like the vast vista spread before him. Surely the gray line beyond the sea must mean he was seeing mainland Mexico. That must be Rocky Point, he thought as he took another sip of water. His long experience of desert living taught him that it was better to stay hydrated with small quantities over time rather than attempt to slake thirst by glugging the precious water greedily. Sitting motionless while being baked offered no relief, so Pedro began to negotiate the narrow trail as it switch-backed up the face. He noticed that he could no longer see the sharp spike of Diablo's peak. Above, there seemed to be a horizontal line where the switchbacks disappeared. It was tedious, but easier as he climbed left, right, left, up the mountain. Grateful for the vague trail, he knew there would be no climbing this mountain without technical gear, otherwise. It was easy in a way, as there was no choice but to take this route, any decision about which way to go was eliminated. Without warning Pedro came to a sharp 'V' cut into the imposing rock wall that thrust in front of the switchback trail. The young Mexican climber saw steps hewn into the live rock, so without hesitation up he went. He was stunned at what he saw.

Spread before him was a shelf of the mountain with the pointed spike of the Devil as a looming backdrop. What he saw was not really a valley, but a level and lush giant field, verdant with life and ringed with a spiky natural granite wall. Pedro descended the rock steps before him and immediately felt a cool soothing wave of sweet fresh air flush away the heat from his brutal climb. He saw an orchard at one end of the vast shelf, seemingly ripe with hanging fruit. Before him was a corn field and a neat, orderly garden, freshly tilled. Pedro knelt at the edge of the garden and dug his fingers into the rich earth, loamy and thriving with earthworms and life. The bleating of sheep drew his attention to a small corral. He recognized the animals as sheep of course, but different in some way, as if a strain of breeding he'd not seen before. A hint of movement in the sky drew his eyes to an immense eagle as it settled onto the rook perched on the side of the great mountain. He saw the mother give the two small birds there a pair of live rodents so that they would learn the way of life, and death. The great bird looked directly into Pedro's eyes, aloof, arrogant and unconcerned with those chained to the earth.

Below the eagle's nest Pedro saw the reason for such luscious life up here, high above the burning desert rock and sand. Flowing freely from a split at the base of the mountain top was a bubbling spring, clear and fresh. It cascaded into several natural rock catchments which then overflowed gently onto the rich fields. Excess was routed into a man-made earthen pond and the ripples upon the surface told Pedro that surely fish swam there. He knelt at the edge of the first catchment and refilled his water bottles. Then he dunked his head, cap and all, into the refreshing liquid seeking relief from his earlier labors. As he lifted his head from the waters he saw the shadow there from behind. His impression was one of a looming, hulking, horned creature. Startled, he spun around falling on his behind then immediately scooted backwards against the catchment edge. It was only an old and weathered woman wearing a strange woven hat and woolen hand-spun dress. Pedro awkwardly got to his feet. He towered over the old woman but she resolutely held her position, not moving a centimeter.

"Who are you, why are you here?" she asked.

Her accent was unknown and her voice gravelly as if seldom used. More odd than the accent however, was her cadence between words and how the inflection was strange, as if her emphasis came on the wrong end of a word. Beneath the brim of her hat the eyes were sunken deeply into her skull and glinted with a deep and disturbing black. Her face was impassive as she watched Pedro without waver.

"I was climbing, that is all," he said. "The path led here, there was no other way."

"For many there has been no other way," she said. "For many, no return."

The ancient woman turned abruptly on her leather sandals and motioned for Pedro to follow. She led him on a narrow path through the orchard and they came to a clearing nestled up against the mountain face. There was her casa, set into a natural cave and walled to the top with adobe brick. Two windows were set into the adobe wall on each side of a roughly hewn plank door held in place with leather strap hinges. There were no glass panes, only shutters to be closed if needed. The granite overhang provided protection from the elements. She motioned Pedro to be seated on one of two woven grass fan-backed chairs.

"Do you have hunger? Thirst?" she asked.

"*Sí Madre,*" he replied, trying to find some form of respect for this startling woman. "I can work for payment."

"There is no work," she stated simply. "All is provided

for those who watch."

She turned and entered the dark cavern behind the door. Pedro caught a quick glimpse of the interior to see an earthen kiln stove with a large cast pot heating on the surface. Looking up, he could see the smoke exiting through a crevasse above the adobe structure. Unaware of when it had happened, Pedro was now a believer of all the old stories. He knew the artifact was for real. He knew she had it and it was to be his. Suddenly he realized that he would not bring it to the Diabolic one. He craved this thing, coveting it for himself. It was to be his, his alone. Pedro was not able to understand the infection of greed, like a virus that was brought about by close proximity to the thing. He only knew what was.

Of course the ancient woman understood all of this. It was why she was here and had been here from before memory. The pile of rusted Spanish armor and blades stacked in a rotting mound at the edge of her vast field gave testament to the fate of those that would violate the sanctity of this place. It was here, and here it would stay as it always had been. The thing that was left from the original human, from the very beginning. It belonged to those of the earth and sky, of rock and sand and ocean. Those that spoke directly to their brothers that crawled, hopped, swam or loped along on four legs. Even those elder birds from the before time that knew the sky as their domain were aware of the natural state of these things. Silly people and their wooden boats with painted crosses on the sails, or the robed priests trying in vain to change the natural order. And later, the loud steam engines digging and blasting the rock. She had seen so many times where the rain and wind had put it all back. Silly ineffectual people that had forgotten the very meaning of life. But after many, many seasons the old stories had gradually passed on. The newest generations had become more interested in shiny electronic toys and viewing devices to hypnotize and rob their very souls. Limited to the ribbons of road, they buzzed along never aware of the real world beyond their air conditioned chambers.

It had been so long a time since an outsider had arrived. He would be happy with his fresh gift. And the timing could not be better with a bright luna nueva on the rise tonight. Yes, her companion of the night would be very pleased indeed. She only had to bide her time. This one would be offered with a terrified and still beating heart providing the flavor of fear.

Pedro accepted the plate of beans and rice gratefully. She brought a very old brass goblet with strange images and old Spanish inscriptions that were worn with great age. The water contained inside was sweet and refreshing beyond belief. She saw his eyes light up in delight.

"From the spring," she said. It has been told that this is from the center of all things earth, from the very beginning. It flows as needed, no more, no less. And those that drink of it are free from affliction."

Pedro believed her, and wondered how to take it all. She didn't deserve this, only *he* did, and he must have it. He gazed into her piercing black eyes and saw that he was transparent before her. He looked down immediately, filled with shame but still determined to have it. He knew she could see this but it did not matter to him. Only the method of taking was yet to be determined.

The sun set like a closing door. The ancient one brought Pedro inside, warning against night creatures a prowl under the fullness of night light. He felt something deep and sinister in her warning and actually was eager to get behind the security of a closed door. Anyway, would that not make it easier to search the interior for a lust that called out to be satisfied? She brought some kindling and dry grass scraps from a wooden box then used flint and steel to ignite a small fire. Rather than create an oppressive heat in the cave, it drew up into the overhead crevasse and replaced the stuffy air with fresh drawn in from outside. The old woman reached back into the box and withdrew a scarlet silken scarf then took a powder from it carefully. She dashed a small portion of the dust onto the little fire and the room filled with a strange heady sweet scent, like flowers. Pedro relaxed immediately. The woman began to speak in low tones, still with that odd accent. As she spoke, Pedro was lulled into a dull daze. Gradually, he realized she had changed her language to one that made sense of her strange accent and inflections. Yet Pedro could understand her meaning clearly, although not the words. Time was suspended as she spoke of many things. He was told of the giant beasts that roamed the earth and how they were destroyed by the great light that fell from the sky. In her speech he saw the mountains rise and the ocean split the land. He saw how men in boats came with the intention of owning all things. He clearly saw how some were slaughtered in the little clearing right before this adobe wall. They were torn asunder by something she had called. Something dark and terrifying that ripped and slashed with razor claws, tearing men to pieces. His mind saw the pieces being dragged away and the intent to devour was not mistaken.

Pedro struggled to escape from this deep well of terror. He tried to swim upwards and get away but his hands would not work. He kicked out and felt something yield and fall away from him. Opening his eyes, he saw it was the old woman and that she was leaning over him once again and trying to knot the lasso she'd been placing around his wrists. Desperately Pedro kicked out again, knocking the woman away. She stumbled over the small stool and went down. Before she could recover Pedro was on her, landing with both knees squarely in the center of her chest. He heard cracking and she let out an ungodly shriek as her ribcage crushed inward. Her thrusting and bucking nearly threw Pedro off but he managed to stay on while he got the binding off his wrists. Then with a hate and lust he never knew he possessed, even when killing those rival drug runners, he took her by the hair and began savagely beating her head into the unyielding granite cave floor. Again and again but still she struggled, her strength otherworldly. Blood flowed from behind her head as he continued hammering one sickening wet crunch after another. Finally, she was still.

He came to as if from a deep sleep, finally clear headed. The woman was unmoving on the floor before him. His heart was pounding and his hands were a bloody mess. It smelled like the butcher shop at the back of the mercado when young Pedro was tasked with bringing the carne home. He didn't like that smell then, he didn't like it now. He had to get out. No matter the darkness, he'd wait out on the switch back trail if necessary. But first, he had to find it. It called to him, but where? In the end it was surprisingly easy. After knocking over some rough furniture items, he tore an ancient tapestry from the cave wall. There it was, perched in a small alcove carved from the rock. It was tiny, able to fit in his hand as he jealously reached in to take the prize. It seemed warm as he held it, mesmerized by the rough beauty. The pinprick eyes seemed to glint seductively at him. He could feel the love it shared, the message that everything would be safe, secure and always protected. All it asked in return was to be worshiped and loved.

Pedro became aware of the pounding rain outside. A sharp light and the close crash of thunder brought him to his senses. He had to get out, now. Finding his pack in the corner, Pedro thrust the artifact inside and strapped it on his back. He thought of nothing else and headed for the door but something had his pants leg. He turned to see the old witch looking up at him with hate so strong it smelled of death. He tried to pull his leg free but her bony grasp would not release. Pedro pulled backwards toward the door but she tenaciously dragged along with him, refusing to let go. Her bloody head lifted and bounced from the floor as Pedro jerked and pulled his leg. She fixed him with a hateful stare that was the very epitome of evil.

In a clear and strong voice she said, "You are cursed for all time, he will take your soul."

Then she threw her head back and let out a piercing screech that penetrated Pedro's eardrums as if the spines of a cholla cactus had been thrust into them. Then she was finally still, with open eyes that accused Pedro even though the life had gone. Then he heard it, the answering cry from the distance, unmistakable even through the pounding rain. For the first time in his life Pedro knew true panic. He tried to run for the door but the dead woman still refused to give up her grip. He stomped down, again and again, crushing the wrist and fingers, finally gaining his freedom. Bolting into the driving rain, he ran for his life. Lightning struck all around and the resulting thunder deafened him. It was as if the Devil's Peak was drawing all power from the heavens, intent on destroying Pedro Martinez. He reached the 'V' in the granite wall by following his memory as the flashes of lightning illuminated his way. As he stood in the center of the opening he took a look back into the Enchanted Valley. A series of bright flashes in the billowing clouds overhead showed something high up on the vertical rock face of del Diablo. It seemed to look directly at Pedro while gripping a rock outcropping with clawed and scaly feet. The long tail whipped violently, side to side. Evil, hungry jaws were open as were the long arms, stretched wide with grasping claws. Then the image was replaced with darkness, but not in

Pedro's mind. He turned and ran.

3

Chupacabra

Pedro knew not how he survived the harrowing journey downward in the violent, driving rainstorm. He'd torn several fingernails loose and savagely bashed one knee, almost breaking it. Something was watching over him as he fled head first down the switchbacks and finally, the treacherous goat trail. The joy he experienced upon finding the quad unmolested and able to start was indescribable, but he had no relief from the overwhelming panic that drove him forward. There was no uncertainty that *it* was following. Like a frenzied madman, he drove that quad down toward the moonlit ocean and the sweet promise of safety, even though he wondered if he'd ever find a place far enough away. Pedro reached the ABC bus station in San Felipe just after the golden sun popped free of the Sea of Cortez. The next Autobus to La Paz wasn't until noon but the Mexicali northbound service departed at seven-thirty, only twenty minutes away. Fuck Señor Diabolic anyway, Pedro thought, he can't have it, it's mine. But the real reason he went north was simply because it was the next ride out of town. He had to get away, now. The bus driver offered to take his back pack and place it with the baggage in the compartment under the floor. Pedro quickly recoiled backward, desperately clasping the pack firmly against his chest, unwilling to part with the precious contents.

He felt minor relief as the large bus made it's way northward. The soldiers at the checkpoint came aboard but did not inspect anyone's personal baggage. Pedro did not know what he would have done if they had tried to take the pack from his grasp. The rain came down in spurts and fits but not steady enough to worry about a washout. The farther north they rode, the more relief Pedro experienced. He began to think he had escaped the terror filling the back of his mind, God willing. What was he thinking, he wondered? He'd not been in a church for many years. The memory of those services when he was a child flooded into his consciousness and he wondered how he got to be so calloused. He thought of the books of European Cathedrals and the amazing photos showing the magnificent architecture. Nothing like that was to be found in Baja, that's for sure. But then he recalled the photos showing those awful gargoyles perched like devil birds high above the surface, leering greedily down upon any soul passing by. He shivered with the memory of that thing, clinging to the side of the storm swept Devil's Peak. He hoped that's where it had to stay as if tethered to the enchanted mountaintop valley. Even so, Pedro was taking no chances and intended to get as far away as he could.

The bus service being behind schedule in Mexico was a way of life and Pedro didn't arrive at the Mexicali Station until late afternoon. The rain had subsided somewhat, so Pedro took a cab to the border area. He knew of a park where he'd wait until nightfall, then cross over. Many young men were lounging around, trying to keep dry and waiting for darkness with the same intent. He walked along the boulevard toward where that filthy river flowed northward. Stopping at a roadside food cart, he fortified himself with tortillas, beans, rice and rich fat carne. Then he stopped into a mercado where he found the shop clerk willing to sell individual black plastic garbage bags. Turns out they could get more selling them singly than as a package. There was no need to try and hide the purpose as it was a consistent activity.

Pedro waited on the stinking, slippery bank while the light gave up the day. The overcast had helped to hide the blazing sun and now the rain began again in earnest. Maybe that would help to flush out the foul smelling fluid, slowly flowing below his feet. The rain began to come down so heavy that he wondered if it was necessary to even put his soaked clothing in the bag. But of course you wouldn't want that toxic crap soaking into your clothing. You'd have to throw it all away and walk around naked. As Pedro sat there, he started having that same feeling of dread he'd experienced when fleeing the mountain. Why? The feeling only got worse like an inescapable horrible nightmare even though he was wide awake. Pedro looked around nervously searching, but nothing was to be seen in the darkness and driving rain. He decided to make his move. The line had to be crossed, there was no other way. A monster would get him on the south side one way or another... the Devil, or the Diabolic one.

Pedro removed his clothing, hiking boots, pants, shirt, underwear, all of it. He placed it all inside the large plastic bag and carefully tied the opening into a secure, waterproof knot. Climbing down the muddy bank was a nightmare because if he cut his feet he knew a serious infection would surely occur. The smell was beyond awful and he gagged, almost losing his dinner. Where the sewage flowed through to the north side, the gringos had put a chain link fence across to discourage crossing. It never worked however. Too much junk and refuse just piled up against it, including bodies.... many with bullet holes in the back of the head. Besides, bolt cutters had removed it so many times the gringo's just gave up. The rain storm had swollen the river and it flowed freely. Pedro was through easily, just like that. It seemed the ever present border guards must be inside their shelters, protected from the driving rain.

Clambering up the slippery slope was no easy task but he managed it without ripping the bag. Pedro carefully shook the nasty water off the bag before opening it. He set the pack on the ground next to him, pulled on his pants and shirt, then sat down on the wet sidewalk to tie on the boots. As he tightened the laces he had the feeling that something was horribly wrong. The hairs on the back of his neck lifted and his previous terror returned. The dreadful feeling that there was no escape clung to him much like his wet clothing. How could he have come so far only to have this terrible feeling catch up with him? Why was his heart pounding so? And now the storm increased dramatically, just like before on Devil's Peak. Lightning shot all around him and the thunder was again deafening. Pedro looked back across the river of death he had only just climbed out of. A flash of lightning revealed the source of his mounting terror, showing him exactly why his heart had been threatening to leap from his chest.

It was there, looking across the chasm of rushing water directly at poor, terrified Pedro. Then it leaped claws first directly into the flooding river. Pedro heard the splash like a ton of bricks. He ran, blindly and thoughtlessly, his only instinct to get away even though he knew it was futile. It was only a matter of time before those talons tore him to pieces. What the fuck good was it to be on the other side now? It just didn't matter where he was and the realization filled him with cold fear. He had to hide somewhere, anywhere. There was not much of a chance against this relentless pursuit, but flee he must.

The wind and rain tore at him as the intensity increased exponentially. The storms sound became a low howl, a constant moan and the pack was nearly torn from his shoulders. He could barely keep his eyes open and remain standing against the stinging torrential rain. A palm tree toppled over, almost taking him with it as it blocked the street. No matter as there were no vehicles on the road in these conditions. Pedro stumbled across a broad four lane boulevard and saw a sign proclaiming, 'Calexico Motors.' It's lights blinked, then went out along with the rest of the lighting on the street. In the darkness he imagined he could feel the hot breath of the monster upon him. Pedro frantically began trying to open any car door on the lot. No use, all were locked. He came upon one car, a large one that a flash of lightning revealed to be red with a canvas convertible top. Driven by desperation Pedro did not hesitate. His pocket knife was in his hand in an instant and he sliced a large opening into the white fabric. The back pack went through the hole first with Pedro right behind. The car rocked and swayed in the storm but he moved into the back seat and was free of the drenching downpour flowing all over the front seat.

His heart pounded and his mouth was beyond dry. How long would it be until the thing took him? And then, in his panic he wondered if it really was after him. Perhaps, could it be the artifact? He couldn't stand the thought of leaving it behind but might that be his only chance? Pedro reached to the bottom of the rear interior side panel and pulled it loose, just above the carpeting. Reluctantly he removed the precious thing from his pack and dropped it gently inside the open panel then popped it back into place. He lay still while the storm raged, feeling the evil presence all around him. An awful smell was there, making the New River seem like sweet perfume. *It* sniffed, smelling him out. Another flash revealed the silhouette against the convertible top. *It* was here. He was doomed. There was a scrabbling like nails on metal along the outside. Pedro couldn't take it and wanted to scream out if only he could, but time had come to a stand still and he was stuck in an endless loop of terror.

A clawed hand snaked it's way in through the gash created by Pedro's knife. He was frozen with fear, unable to even breathe as the scaled arm fully entered the drivers roof line then aimed directly for Pedro's head. He was petrified, made of stone. The clammy claw caressed Pedro's forehead almost gently then closed around his face. Then the Chupacabra was gone and with it, Pedro Martinez's soul.

4

Fired

Hubie and his friend Bear stood shoulder to shoulder across the four-lane boulevard from Hubie's destroyed blues club. Well, they were almost shoulder to shoulder as Bear towered over the slender six-foot one-inch Hubie by at least five inches. Hubie was wearing his usual summertime garb consisting of t-shirt, cargo pocket shorts, and his trusty pair of huarache sandals complete with tire-tread soles. He pulled absently on his long blonde ponytail as he looked at the ruin across the street. The destruction of the burned out club was complete. All that was left of 'Cadillac Hubie's,' was a smoldering heap of ashes and chunks of burned charcoal. The hand-carved double front doors were a thing of the past and the two large pane front windows were blown to smithereens. The custom marquee from above the entrance was a twisted hunk of metal and neon tubes that still smoked in the afternoon sun which shone down on the wreckage through the gaping hole where the roof had been. A portion of the bar had survived but was destined for the garbage heap and the rows of liquor bottles from the shelves behind the bar had exploded like hand grenades. The large stage where so many famous acts had performed was also burned to trash along with all the furniture, tables, lighting and even the stairway that led upstairs to Hubie's former living quarters.

Hubie stood stunned, his loss for words were understandable since starting a club like this had been a life long dream. Not only was it a complete ruin but all his belongings from the upper living quarters were up in smoke. To make things worse, he'd built the club up from nothing into a sought after venue showcasing the very best of the best blues entertainers from Chicago to New Orleans. Everybody had loved the funky old industrial brick buildings as gentrification transformed the row structures from the Philly doldrums of the seventies into a glitzy, renovated hip hang out for the eighties music scene. Since Live Aid had been featured in Philadelphia only the month before, Hubie had allowed many alternative bands on his stage but his first love had always been the blues. He even included Led Zeppelin in that category as most of their material was pirated from the Delta region. Still, having sets from groups such as Berlin or Bryan Adams didn't hurt the bottom line and after all…. this was a business and a very profitable one at that. Or, at least it had been. It certainly didn't seem like there'd be much to salvage from this mess.

The station Captain approached the pair from across the street and stuck out a soot covered hand which both men shook although it seemed as if Bear's large paw swallowed the Captain's hand whole.

"I'm Captain Clemmons. This was your club, right?" said the Captain.

"Yep," grumbled Hubie. "I guess, 'Was,' is the operative word though."

"Oh yeah it's a total loss, hope you have good insurance."

Hubie replied, "Sure, of course but some things you can't replace. What a bummer." Hubie stood stoic as he catalogued his loss, but inside his disappointment was stifling.

"That's true," said Captain Clemmons. "We see it all the time. Thankful there weren't any injuries or fatalities. That's the rough part of this business. The strange thing I can't figure is there isn't any sign of an accelerant or faulty wiring or any other source of this blaze. I'm already pretty sure arson can be ruled out. This is just preliminary mind you but I'm not sure how to write this one up. I've been stamping out fires for two decades and I've never seen one like it."

Just then a fireman approached the trio saying, "We're about wrapped up Cap. Hoses are rolled and we're ready to go."

"Sure Freddy, I'll be right over. Gimme a minute."

Clemmons continued, "Like I was saying, never seen anything like it. I mean with these old brick structures sharing walls the heat usually spreads to the neighbors. Last time a fire like this happened it took out the entire row. But the adjacent structures… well, they're not even warm. An inferno like this should have ignited fuel in the buildings on either side. And that's not all. There's a Cadillac parked right in front, pretty one too and it's not even touched. Got a white convertible top and it doesn't even have a single smudge on it. But the lenses on the parking meters along the curb are melted." He rubbed the stubble on his chin in contemplation. "Yep, never seen anything like it."

Hubie said, "That'd be mine. It's an advertisement for the club. Can I take it?"

"Sure," the Captain replied. "If it'll start, its all yours. Good luck guys."

Just then the large Pierce Quantum pumper firetruck fired

up with a diesel roar and the Captain took his place in the shotgun seat. As the red and white vehicle pulled away, finally leaving the boulevard unobstructed, Hubie's Cadillac was revealed. Just as Captain Clemmons had described, the beautiful 1959 two-door convertible was untouched. The red, candy-apple finish gleamed as if it was only just sprayed on that very morning. As usual it seemed as if you could reach right into it like liquid. And the white top did not have a bit of smudge or ash spoiling the bright material. It seemed as if the classic ride had only just pulled up in front of the wreckage a moment before. No one would have ever suspected that this vehicle could have been sitting there during the conflagration and remained untouched.

The normally taciturn Bear finally spoke up. "Well Boss, hell of a day, huh? I mean, who'd figure on both of us gettin fired from JFK and then your place burning down the same day. Weird. How about if the Caddy runs, you follow me over to my digs and we'll figure out what's next. I gotta twelve pack of Schlitz left over and some Jager that might come in handy."

*****

Earlier that morning Hubie had barely arrived at the stadium when he'd been promptly called into the General Manager's office. Hubie knew Harold Stiles well and they got along fine. He was a round, compact man with a ruddy complexion. What he lacked in his looks, he made up for with his style. Silk pocket squares matched his ties every day without fail and his gold watch undoubtedly cost more than a down payment on a home. Yet he always treated his subordinates with care and respect. Stiles had always left Hubie alone while he did his job maintaining and running the stadium sound system for various functions. His style of management was to let the guys alone and not get in their business as long as everything went well. Since the Live Aid show had gone better than expected with the sound mixing being perfect, Hubie was expecting a raise. That was not to be however.

Stiles explained it like this, "Well Hubert, you know we have that new Vice President of Entertainment Operations, right?"

"Yeah, the one that's been nosing around and getting into everyone's business lately, Tim something. Osgood right?"

"That's right. Anyway, you know I've always left you floor and sound monkeys alone. Never had any problem with you guys. But someone just dropped a boulder into my placid lake and the ripples have spread far and wide."

"OK," Hubie replied, feeling his face grow hot as he became defensive. "If it's about letting in specials, everyone does that. I've even seen your sister on the sound stage, and I'm bettin she didn't have a ticket."

"Yeah Hubie. Easy now, it's not about that. Upper management has always let that shit slide. No, it's about some questions coming from Madonna's camp. Seems like some crew posing as journalists got into her trailer pretending to be doing a photo shoot for the Live Aid concert and now she wants to know when publication will happen and if she'll be on the cover. That inquiry went to the top of the Entertainment Division and Osgood got a big red face over the whole incident. He was in here yesterday all butt hurt about being embarrassed and how some heads gotta roll."

A light bulb went off in Hubie's brain as he realized what had happened.

"It's my cousin Sheila isn't it," Hubie said as he stared down at Harry's desk top. "I told her not to be asking for autographs."

"Well Hubie, that's not the worst of it. Appears that she hooked up with some photographer and was all over back stage getting autographs and that guy was snapping photos like crazy. The stadium has no connection to any of that, so it's not like someone just got let in with the crowd to enjoy the show. Osgood is all bent outta shape about liability and royalties for photos and everything else the legal staff advised him on. So the investigation landed right on you and your buddy Stanley Mack, the one everybody calls Bear, although I don't know why you guys don't call him Mack Truck."

"Hey Harry," said Hubie, "Bear's got nothing to do with this, I told him to let them in and he didn't have anything to do with the passes."

Stiles put his hand up to quiet him like a child, saying, "Doesn't matter Hubert. The shit has hit the fan and it shows clearly on the admittance log that Bear signed in that gal. We even got a verification about how she bluffed her way through secondary security towing that photographer along with her. Pretty big balls on that chick, I gotta say. So like I said, heads gotta roll and it's not gonna be mine. Mack handed in his I.D. first thing this morning."

The G.M. looked up expectantly and without a word, Hubie slipped his I.D. and lanyard over his head then gently dropped it onto Harry's desk. Then he turned around and started for the door. As he reached for the handle, Harry spoke up one last time.

"Look Hubert, I trust you can empty your locker and find the parking lot without an escort, right? I don't want to end this on a sour note, but you gotta understand my hands are tied." He made an attempt to sound sympathetic towards Hubie, a brief moment of humanity that quickly dissolved. Back to business, he continued.

"Oh, and there's been several calls for you this morning from someone at your club, and the Philly Fire Department.

My secretary has some numbers for you to call, good luck to you."

5

One Proud Hombre

Señora Martinez was on her knees cleaning a toilet and saltillo tiles in one of the guest bathrooms at the Las Palmas Hotel when a shadow fell upon her from behind. Startled, she turned to see the hotel manager, Señor de Jesus standing over her looking very nervous. He was wringing his hands and sweating profusely. The manager turned away from the bathroom doorway to indicate two local police officers standing silently in the bedroom.

"Margarita," de Jesus said. "These officials are here to escort you directly to your residence." The cops looked to be very serious and she felt a cold dread descend upon her.

"Why?" she asked. "What makes it necessary to take me from my work? Am I to be jailed?"

The eldest of the two policeman, a man that knew the Martinez family personally spoke up saying, *"Señora,* please come along immediately and ask no questions, as we are unable to answer that which we do not know."

She took up her satchel which was always close at hand to prevent theft and followed the two officers out onto the balcony overlooking the expansive rectangular pool. The glistening waters of the Sea of Cortez could be seen beyond the brilliant white sand beaches fronting the town of San Felipe. She took a long glance at the view while wondering what could possibly be amiss. Her heart skipped a beat as she began to imagine all manner of difficulties when dealing with the local magistrate and his officers.

She followed the policemen down the outside staircase as they turned away from the courtyard through an arched passage onto the dirt parking lot behind the hotel. The younger of the two men held the back door of the beat up police cruiser open for her as she took her place on the stained bench seat. Although it was still early on this late September morning and relatively cool, the anxious woman began to perspire from worry. To her great relief, the cruiser passed by the station house and turned up the dirt street where the modest Martinez residence sat in a cool grove of mesquite trees.

Parked in the dirt drive of the one story adobe structure was a large black Chevrolet SUV with an imposing looking man standing beside the vehicle. His attention was directed up and down the narrow dusty street. As soon as the cruiser stopped, the younger officer was out of his seat in a flash and immediately opened the rear passenger door. Señora Martinez could not help but notice the deferential manner with which the young cop treated this stranger standing next to the unlikely black vehicle which could not have been more out of place. Then the police drove away immediately as if the two cops had never before been in such a hurry to leave.

The serious man indicated for her to proceed into the residence with a gracious wave of his hand. As she walked behind the imposing car, she saw her husband, Arturo, sitting in the shade of the palm frond covered veranda. Also sitting at the white plastic table was a well dressed young man wearing a loose white silk shirt and dark slacks. The man was movie star handsome with raven colored hair and chiseled features. He exuded the confidence of one that was used to getting his way. His expensive leather loafers looked very out of place as they had taken on the ever present dust that plagued the back streets of San Felipe.

Both of the men stood as Margarita approached and she could not help but see the grim expression on her husband's face. She noticed another serious looking man standing in the shadows behind the table. His face was horribly scarred. The left side of his cheek had been badly mutilated in some manner that had created a deep furrow into his scalp. Whatever had done that ghastly damage also took off the top of his left ear. The left side of his mouth was permanently open revealing teeth and molars. The effect was one of a permanent ghoulish grin. Although his visage shocked Margarita, it did not escape her attention that the man wore a large black firearm at his waist. His untucked shirt had been pulled up and behind the pistol for quick access.

She went directly to her husband who held her briefly and indicated for her to take the chair he had recently occupied. Then, Señor Martinez placed himself between his wife and the man in the corner while never taking his eyes off the younger man who was quite obviously in charge.

"Margarita, do not worry," said her husband. "These men are here merely to ask questions, or so they say." This last part was said directly to the obviously cultured young man still standing before them. The man looked at Arturo as he stood behind his wife with his hands protectively on her shoulders. It was plain to him that Señor Martinez was in no way intimidated by him or his two guards. He saw the corded muscles on the working man's forearms. His hands were toughened by years of hauling up nets full of shrimp from the ocean floor. The ravages from years of sun and salt water were etched upon his lean face.

Even though a soldier of the cartel stood a few steps from this tough man, there was no doubt that his soft young neck could perhaps be snapped by those powerful hands before any intervention might rescue him.

He bowed graciously toward Margarita saying, "*Dona* Martinez, please allow me to introduce myself. I am Enrique de Moreno and I am in the employ of *Señor* Alfredo de Diaz, whom also happens to be my *tío* as I am the son of his sister. If you would not mind, I would much enjoy the pleasure of your husband's company as I ask him a few questions."

Margarita's heart nearly stopped as she realized just who this man worked for. It was common knowledge that the Diaz cartel was intent on expanding the route of product transportation northward along the Baja Peninsula. She also knew that her beloved son Pedro, had fallen in with these unscrupulous criminal men and she nearly burst into tears but for the comforting touch of her husbands firm hands upon her shoulders. She composed herself and stood.

"Certainly *Señor* de Moreno, please excuse me and I will prepare refreshments."

"No need *Señora* Martinez, we will only be a few brief minutes and I assure you all will be intact if only a few honest answers are provided."

De Moreno had a gracious smile and his accent betrayed a formal education in Spain. But his mannerly nature and smile could not hide the serious intent betrayed in his eyes. She knew that their lives could very well be hanging by a thread of this spider's web. Margarita regained her seat.

Moreno seated himself and began, "My gracious hosts, you will be proud to know that your son Pedro has gained an exemplary reputation during his employment. For this reason I have chosen him to perform a very special reconnaissance in this region." As he spoke he moved his hands expressively, effectively emphasizing his meaning. "That for which he was searching is of no importance to this discussion, so I will not divulge it. However, we do know that he did reach your lovely little town of San Felipe and hence embarked on his mission. It is most unfortunate that since this quest began last month, he is now long overdue and I am only hoping to find his whereabouts. It would make this long dusty day much more bearable if you were to perhaps have some information on where I may find your son."

The hard working fisherman despised all cartels and the violence that had been perpetrated as they went about their grim task of claiming territory and corrupting local police, including municipalities throughout Mexico. He made no attempt to hide how much contempt he held for these criminals.

Arturo Martinez lifted his head with pride and said, "*Señor* de Moreno, as I am sure you are aware, my family has worked for our living in the most honorable and honest ways possible for many generations in this area. We take the *pescado* from these waters for the sustenance of our people. It is hard work but good work. I do not know the location of my son but you may be assured that if I did, I would never tell the likes of a man such as you."

The soldier behind Arturo started forward as if to assault him for his insolence but Moreno stopped him with a glance and a wave of his hand. Margarita left her chair to stand beside her husband. Never before had she felt such pride to have been wedded to this marvelous man for so many years. Arturo put his arm protectively around his bride and with proudly raised chins, they awaited their fate.

Moreno stood up. He appraised the pair with admiration

for their grit. As a business man, he knew that violence must only be used when something is to be gained. By the tone expressed in these proud people, he knew that no information was to be found here. Besides, there are always other ways that could be even more effective for obtaining information. He softened his attitude and tried another approach.

"My dear proud compadres, I believe you. I believe that you would never tell me the location of Pedro. It is still unclear if you do know where he is. I assure you, he will be found. One of my two companions will be staying in San Felipe and if your son returns to this *casa*, it is very possible that the outcome will not be to your advantage. Also there is the matter of your lovely daughter, Lupe. Yes, we know of her and how she used to sell trinkets to the drunken and obnoxious *turistas* inhabiting the bars and restaurants along the *Malecon*." A malicious smirk grew across his face as he continued. "Little Lupita has been said to have grown into the most lovely *Señorita* in all of San Felipe. Our investigation has shown that she left the honorable life to dance and perform other services at the bars adjacent to the border in Mexicali. If you wish to change your mind regarding the inevitable conclusion of our quest, it would be wise to speak up now as it would be best for Lupe if we did not find your son hiding with her."

Martinez glared at Moreno with such murderous rage that the young man almost wished he could recruit a man with such resolve. As it was, he felt more than relieved to have two armed soldiers of the cartel providing protection within arms reach of the powerful fisherman.

"*Via con Dios,* or *Via con Diablo.* Make your choice but go now and do not return unless you would enjoy becoming food for the fish at the bottom of my ocean." Arturo took his wife by the hand and guided her into their humble home.

The door shut, the interview was over.

Enrique stepped out into the bright morning sun and his bodyguard handed him his sunglasses as he opened the SUV's rear door. The other guard took his place in the front passenger seat and the big vehicle pulled away from the Martinez home.

"Manny," Enrique said to the driver, "Stop downtown and let Juan out. Juan, you'll stay here and watch over our new friends to see if their son shows up. Get a room, get a car, stay out of sight. If he is to be found, contact the magistrate, *Señor* Gonzales, and have him arrested. This is where the *soborno* money has the best effect in these back road *ejidos*. Have him held until my return." He smoothed back his thick hair as he stared calmly out the window. "Manny, next stop is Mexicali to find that little whore."

Later, as Enrique and his driver cruised northward toward Mexicali, he had time to reflect on his next course of action. Yes his tío, Alfredo de Diaz was el jefe over the growing Diaz cartel. His penchant for violence had worked to place the organization in a position of growth and power. Enrique however, preferred to use a more subtle approach. His best talents were used in gathering information, planning and organization. As such, his uncle had become more of a figurehead while Enrique quietly ran the day to day operations. In his opinion, Señor Diaz had become sloppy with power and was in the habit of making rash decisions. Enrique did not think it was a good idea to take the rival organizations product by force. It was his thought that making alliances would be better for all concerned, not to mention the consolidation of power. As his uncle made mush of his mind by using his own product and spending too much time with the mindless putas that crawled out of the woodwork like roaches, Enrique was formulating great plans. In good time he would take over the entire operation and if done correctly his uncle would never realize what had happened. Dios mio, the idiota actually insisted on everyone calling him El Diabolico. Perhaps an accident or overdose from the poison already going up his uncle's nose in great quantity would be the way.

Yes, Enrique could see the future with great clarity. Bringing the various organizations together would finally give them the power needed to take over the government. No more millions wasted in bribes, no more loss of soldiers in useless gun battles whenever the government decided to show some teeth. At the top of that pyramid he saw himself as the one that could rule with vision and power. But for now, he had to keep his mind on more mundane tasks while the Diabolic one still had control. Chasing after some stupid family myth and wasting time finding the errant Pedro Martinez was the last thing he wanted to do. But for now, the next step was to find Pedro's sister if he had to wade through every bar and brothel in all of Mexicali.

Rad Crews

6

Road Trip

Before Hubie even opened his eyes he knew this hangover was going to be a bad one. At first he wasn't even sure where he was until he recognized Bear's living room strewn with the debris from last evenings drinking spree. A bottle of Jager was on it's side among the array of drained Schlitz beer cans scattered on the coffee table. Hubie remembered getting dizzy and flopping on Bear's couch, but that's about it. As he sat up with his head pounding he thought about how long it'd been since he'd last had the whirlies. His mouth filled with a wave of warm saliva as his stomach cramped into angry knots. Then a wave of nausea sent him stumbling into the bathroom. He almost didn't make it before letting loose into the toilet. At least he felt a little relief, but not much.

He found Bear in the kitchen working over the stove on a combination of scrambled eggs with bacon. A platter of hot cakes was already on the flimsy kitchen table. The aroma almost made Hubie heave once again but he forced the bile down and flopped into one of the canvas folding chairs that made up Bear's dining furniture set.

"Damn Boss, how'd you get so green?" asked the cheerful Bear. Hubie remembered how his massive friend had matched him can for can. His ability to absorb alcohol with impunity was a legend from all the way back to their military days. Nobody could keep up with him and most gave up trying after the first time. It was safer that way.

Hubie had no reply so he just sat there with his elbows on the table holding his head in his hands as he stared blankly out of Bear's second story apartment window. Bear just laughed at him, then he reached up to retrieve one last shot glass full of Jager from the cabinet above the refrigerator along with a bottle of aspirin also hidden there.

"Here ya go. I stashed this last night. Hair of the dog should fix you right up."

Hubie downed the medicine along with a handful of aspirin which almost came right back up but he managed to keep it down. After a few minutes, Hubie began to feel better though he was sure it'd be awhile before he was ready to eat. Bear sat down across from him with a paper plate piled high with eggs, bacon and a generous stack of flappers. He smeared the stack with butter and then drowned the pile with a flood of maple syrup. The plate of food was disappearing fairly rapidly as Bear occasionally paused to wipe his bushy black beard with the kitchen towel.

"So Boss, guess we don't have to worry 'bout goin to work today, huh?" Bear said.

"Guess not," Hubie morosely replied. "First time I ever lost two jobs on the same day."

"Fuck'n A Hubert, that's a first for me also. Now what?"

Hubie pondered that thought for a moment then said, "Well, guess I gotta go over to the Allstate agent and fill out some paperwork." He leaned over the table and began massaging his temples as he thought of all the trouble that had suddenly landed on him like a ton of bricks. "Then I'll call the old man and see if I can get some front money out of the trust. Might as well try to suck poison out of a rattlesnake's mouth but I'll give it a try."

Bear said, "Well, if you weren't such a hippie democrat I bet he wouldn't be so hard on you."

"Yeah but the insurance should refund him the seed money he gave up last year when we started the club. Anyway, I could tell he did like the business plan and it was making some pretty good profit. You know how those Wall Street dudes are, all bottom line and shit."

"Bullshit Hubie, you're just like your dad and his brother." He licked syrup from his finger before pointing it at Hubie. "If I cut off that pony tail and got you into a three piece suit you'd fit right in. All you'd need to do is get rid of that red Caddy and buy one of those Mercedes fancy rides and they'd make you a partner."

Hubie's eyes lit up and he said, "Hey Dude, speaking of the Cadillac, isn't it strange how that car sat right in front of that fire and didn't even get warm? I mean there was ash and debris all over the sidewalk and my ride was clean as a whistle. Not to mention that it started right up. You'd a thought the gas tank would have exploded and the tires melted with all that heat. Weird for sure."

Bear said, "Well, take your luck where you can get it and don't ask questions of a gift horse that can't speak anyway. Hey, maybe it's a sign you know. Like time to take a road trip or something."

Hubie felt a light bulb flicker on at Bear's suggestion. "You know what Dude," said Hubie, "maybe that's a plan. After all, nothing's going on around here since the clubs gone and the weathers gonna turn to shit in a couple months anyhow."

He stood up and gazed out the window as he thought out loud. "What say we head out west, you know check out those bars we used to hang out at. Maybe even see what's up with the blues scene out in California. Might take awhile for the insurance money to come through so why not? Wonder if theres opportunity out there?"

"Just like your old man," said Bear. "Your family can smell a dime at the bottom of a cess pool. But I'm game. Sounds fun and all we need is gas money."

Actually it was just a given that the two men would come up with a plan together. Not only did Bear work as security over at JFK Stadium, but he was the bouncer and door security at the Cadillac Hubie's club. Hubie liked his friend to check I.D.s and keep the riffraff out. There was hardly ever any trouble at a blues club and besides, nobody ever messed with Bear, not ever. Since Hubie worked sound at the stadium, it was easy to get Bear a gig as security over there as well.

The two men had been fast friends since the end of the Vietnam fiasco. Hubie wasn't particularly political, he just couldn't see the wisdom in getting killed for no good reason. His solution had been to join the Navy in order to avoid being drafted into the Army. He got trained as a Navy Medic which seemed safe enough until he discovered that the Marines don't have their own medics. They used Navy guys and that got Hubie's panties all twisted up. Luckily though, after medical training Hubie was sent to Oakland for additional instruction in Psychology. After that he was stationed at the Balboa Naval Hospital in San Diego where he worked in the Drug Rehab Center's Psych Unit. As a counselor he helped to rehabilitate the broken minds of men suffering from PTSD. The lucky sailor never left California, never set foot on a ship, and never heard a single gun shot.

The young Stanley Mack took an entirely different path.

He'd been raised on a farm in the middle of a sea of corn in Kansas and had never seen a hill, let alone a mountain. He'd spent enough time driving a combine to know that wasn't how he wanted his future to pan out. So, on the morning of his eighteenth birthday with the draft looming, he joined the Marine Corps. His mother cried her eyes out and his father couldn't have been more proud of his first born son. His folks dropped him off at the airport for the flight to Perris Island and basic training. As the plane left the ground, he turned to another enlistee seated next to him and said, "Well Toto, I don't think we're in Kansas anymore!"

The tough training handed out by the Marine D.I.s presented no problems for Bear. He was given that nickname on the first day of training and it stuck. He absorbed the military life with gusto and was especially adept during firearms training. Since he was so large, he trained extra with the M-60 machine gun. Nicknamed the 'Pig,' it became his duty to lug that heavy bitch around. When all his training was completed he got assigned to Embassy guard duty in Saigon, South Vietnam toward the end of 1974. It was fairly easy duty until Spring of the following year when Communist forces began closing in on the doomed city. Every person in Saigon, it seemed, was trying to get on a helicopter out of town. Bear and the other Marine Embassy guards were doing their best to keep the frantic South Vietnamese out of the compound. Fortunately for Bear he never had to fire a shot, although he did knock a few heads. When the last helicopter left the Embassy compound only a few remaining guards were on it, including Bear. It was 7:53 on the morning of April 30, 1975 and it was also Bear's nineteenth birthday. After landing on a Naval vessel in the South China Sea, Bear spent the rest of that crazy day helping to push copters over the side in order to make room for others to land.

After arriving back in the U.S., Bear's unit was broken up and he found himself assigned to security duty at the Balboa Naval Hospital. That's where he met up with Hubie. The two young men hit it off and spent plenty of time getting into trouble and embarking on adventures in San Diego as well as cross border in Tijuana. Some of Bear's buddies from Vietnam had been stationed at the Marine Corp Air Station over in Yuma Arizona. They spent occasional weekends over in the desert to partake of the sights, scenes, drinking and the readily available cheap young ladies that worked just across the border in the Mexican town of Algodones.

It was easy duty and both young men stayed with their respective jobs until being discharged only months apart in the spring of 1978. Bear was twenty three and Hubie only twenty four but both had survived the experience none the worse for wear and they went their separate ways. For Hubie, the next stage was a trial run as a broker at his Dad's Wall Street investment firm. To say he was a fish out of water would have been a massive understatement. Bear found himself back on a combine in Kansas bored out of his mind. When Hubie reached out to Bear a couple of years later they'd both had enough and couldn't wait to leave those mindless jobs behind. He helped Bear get a job as security at the JFK Stadium where Hubie operated the sound system. During this period, Hubie was making arrangements to open his blues club. With Bear hanging out in Philly with a job at the Stadium and Hubie planning to open the club, the two men couldn't have been happier. And now, with both those gigs irrevocably ended, a road trip was the next best plan. It was time to head west.

Cadillac Hubie

7

Lupita

Lupita stared at the well-manicured young man sitting across her desk inside the Seguro Insurance agency. He was handsome and although impeccably dressed had the aura of a bandit, almost as if a Harley Davidson motorcycle should be parked outside rather than the overly large black SUV. He was the kind of man she might have been interested in if not for his hideously disfigured personal guard that had ushered every other person out of her office, customers and workers alike. He got no argument as everyone was more than willing to get out of the creepy hombre's sight.

"Señor Moreno," she began again. "I have told you, I do not know the whereabouts of my *hermano.* I have not seen him since I left San Felipe over two years ago. When I have visited *mis padres*, they have made no mention of him. Since it seems to be evident that he is working with your men, perhaps it would be better if I asked of you where he might be."

Enrique Moreno replied in a manner that revealed his diminishing patience, "*Señorita*, gathering intelligence is my first talent. I know many things of which you are unaware. Do not try to play the game you will never win." He calmly stood up and began to slowly pace back and forth in front of her desk, recounting his journey with annoyance. "I have just spent the previous four nights scouring every sleazy bar and whore house in Mexicali. This is how I came to be sitting in front of you now. Our investigation led us to this shitty end-of-the-line border town of Algodones. Your former employer at the Hawaiian Bar needed very little motivation to provide your whereabouts. I know where you have worked, I know what you are and I know exactly how the little *puta* of the evening happened to become an insurance agent."

Lupe abruptly lunged to her feet causing her chair to fall over backwards. Her deep brown eyes blazed with anger and a barely contained rage was displayed in her entire demeanor. Enrique recognized the same flash of anger he'd witnessed five days before when questioning her father. If anything, her metamorphosis only served to make her more beautiful. She was slender and lean like her father but carried the womanly curves of her mother that even her conservative business clothing could not hide. Her rich black hair was piled high on her head and held in place with several long jeweled pins. A most appealing combination in his opinion, however he was here for business and the sooner it was concluded the sooner he'd be away from this miserable hellhole of a town.

"I was a dancer, *Señor* Moreno, not a willing slut like the one you fell from, spawned from an unknown father!" She reached for the letter opener on the desktop but instantly froze as Manny stepped forward displaying a nine millimeter Beretta that had appeared from out of nowhere. The barrel appeared large enough to swallow her whole as he unwaveringly aimed it precisely between her eyes.

Enrique indicated for Manny to step back. This was not going the way he'd envisioned and he hoped to de-escalate that which was rapidly getting out of control. He reached forward and took the letter opener into his hand. Then he walked slowly behind her desk and retrieved the chair from the floor.

"*Señorita* Martinez, please be seated and accept my sincere apologies as it would seem that our insults are now even. My *madre*, like your's, is the most honorable of women." Moreno's expression took on an unusually sarcastic look as he mentioned his mother. "It has also come to my attention that your activities in the bars of Mexicali did consist of dancing and lifting wallets from drunken gringos. I am aware that you moved from bar to bar precisely because you refused to go into the back rooms with eager patrons. It was most amusing to hear the tale of how your employment ended at that Hawaiian Bar around the corner. The image of a drunken Marine staggering back across the border with your hair pin stuck all the way through his wrist is something I would have liked to have seen for myself."

After taking her seat, Lupita said, "*Si*, he was a pig and would not take his hands off me. He got what he deserved and if I only had more time I would have flayed his bacon for *la cocina*."

"I am sure of this, my fiery *señorita*, but back to business please. Is it true that you have many friends among the border crossing guards and that you are allowed to pass *la linea* at will?" He sat down and leaned forward on the desk, his eyes boring into her's with intensity. He scanned her face for truth or deception. "And is it also true that along with your occupation of issuing Mexican Auto Insurance policies that you have a skill for retrieving stolen vehicles from the *norte* here in Mexico? Please answer in the affirmative as this information is already in my possession."

Lupita swallowed hard and nodded yes. She knew there was no alternative as this man was armed with more knowledge than she could have ever imagined. Enrique dropped a business card on her desk then turned for the door. Manny opened it after first checking the area directly outside. Before leaving, Enrique turned for one final comment.

"*Señorita*, as you may imagine I am unable to cross to the north. This should be obvious to you. But you must know that our agents are numerous and the web spreads far and wide. Your brother has something of great value that his employer is eager to regain. He will be found. If it is shown to be true that you have helped him to escape across the border then you and your humble family will cease to witness another sunrise. As is usual, the method of your demise will not be pleasant. However, this thing that your brother has taken will be gratefully received and the person that brings it to *El Diabolico* will be rewarded beyond expectation. There is always room for loyal employees *señorita*. Think of these things carefully Lupita, as much can be your's, or nothing."

Later, Lupita surveyed her ransacked residence. It seemed that Manny had left nothing unturned in her apartment that was located only a few blocks from the insurance office. The place was an absolute wreck. She was in misery. Her older brother had been so close and protective when they were children and she loved him very much. She knew of his frustration with the fishing business and his desire to seek a better life up north. Like so many others he'd fallen under the influence of the Diaz cartel. She would do anything for Pedro, but what? They had not seen each other or been in contact for over two years. If only she knew where he was she'd go to him immediately and warn of his impending doom. Her despair was overwhelming, but there was nothing available for the cure.

*****

As of that very moment, Pedro Martinez was hiding in plain sight. If any of the many Diaz cartel soldiers searching Mexicali had bothered to attend Mass, they would have found him faithfully seated in the front row of the Catedral de Nuestra Señora de Guadalupe every Sunday. Pedro had stumbled into Our Lady of Guadalupe soon after Border Patrol agents of the U.S. had returned him to Mexico. When the owner of Calexico Motors found him shivering and unable to speak in the back seat of one of his prime autos for sale, he felt great sympathy for the young man. Even though the convertible top of the beautiful red Cadillac had been ripped open allowing the rain in, he still felt sorry for the miserable mexicano. On the other hand, the custom interior of the vehicle was sopping wet and ruined. Since the bedraggled immigrant was unable to even talk or explain himself, there was nothing to do but call the authorities. As for the car, there was no choice but to put it up for auction. At least insurance would offset the loss. This is how Pedro found himself wandering aimlessly through the streets of Mexicali.

Pedro knew he had been touched by the very hand of Satan that horrible evening and the stain on his psyche was indelible. Even though he had lost his faith many years before, when he saw that beautiful church he was drawn to its sanctuary. It was in the very corner of the rear pew that Father Macias found the starving Pedro. The haunted look of terror in the man's eyes disturbed the young Priest so he took him over to the Mission de Guadalupe for food and a much needed bunk. Pedro could often be found back at the church, lighting a votive prayer candle in front of the statue of The Blessed Virgin Mary.

As his memory slowly returned, Pedro was filled with grief for his savage murder of the old lady of the mountain. He realized that his penance was to be chased by the Devil himself throughout every dream and waking moment. Certain that he would one day be pulled down into the very heart of Hell for all eternity, Pedro's soul had no rest. His personal demon lurked behind every corner. Although he had not been to confession since childhood, Pedro once again found himself entering that dark confessional.

While waiting in that small dark space, he felt as if it were his coffin. The grief, terror and guilt that consumed Pedro knew no boundaries. When finally Father Macias entered and pulled back the partition, Pedro's relief was overwhelming. His words flooded out in a hurried jumble until the Priest bade him to slow down and compose his thoughts.

"Si Padre," Pedro said. He began again in the correct manner. "Forgive me *Padre*, for I have sinned. It has been many years since I have confessed. How many I do not know as I was only a child then. I have lost my faith and our Lord above has sent the Devil to punish me. By my own hand, I have awakened *el Diablo* and set him loose upon the Earth."

As the story unfolded, Father Macias listened in rapt attention. Since he had been ordained five years prior, the Priest had heard many outlandish stories of sin and guilt. After all, this was a border town and the drug trade as well as the easy ladies and numerous bars and strip clubs available to tempt even the most righteous were beyond count. He heard the same stories from prostitutes, pick-pockets, murderers, drug addicts and all manner of sinners over and over. Yet never had he heard a story such as the one Pedro confessed that stifling September day. It was an outlandish although compelling tale. Was not the Priest schooled in the world of the supernatural? Did not Priests participate in exorcisms? What about saints and miracles? Visions of the Virgin Mary had been ratified by the Church throughout history. But in the end, it was not really important if the Priest actually believed this tormented parishioner. That was up to the Heavenly Father above. It was only necessary to absolve the poor man of his guilt and personal recriminations for his evil deeds.

Father Macias wondered if there could ever be enough 'Hail Mary's,' to absolve a man that had set the Devil loose. In the end, he instructed Pedro to return to the Church and accept a pious way of life. He told Pedro that only through prayer and service could he be made whole again. The Priest took Pedro back to the Guadalupe Mission and there the Nuns set him up with serving God and those in need. In a very short time Pedro felt his footsteps walking on the road to redemption. This is how he gave in to his fate and placed his life in the hands of his Lord and Savior. A great feeling of peace and serenity came over Pedro, his grief and anguish were no more.

That is where Pedro Martinez was when the Diaz cartel caught up with him.

Cadillac Hubie

8

I Feel Free

The huge Cadillac cruised effortlessly down I-40 enroute to Memphis. Both Hubie and Bear were in great spirits as they put the miles and memories behind them. The further the Caddy got from Philadelphia, the better it seemed to run. October first, 1985 was a gorgeous day with a hint of crisp air that teased the onset of fall. They drove with the top down and drank in the day as Hubie's ponytail whipped in the wind. Bear kept his hair close cut, Marine Corp style, but his bushy black beard flew wild as they cruised down the highway. Both men felt a profound sense of freedom as the miles flew by.

With Bear at the wheel, Hubie passed the hours by fiddling with the radio dial. After mixing the Live Aid concert back in July, he'd gotten his fill of the manufactured mainstream drivel that could be heard constantly on AM rotation. If he had to hear Madonna one more time he felt he might hurl all over the pristine interior of his car. It always amazed him to hear polished, professional sound mixing on studio recordings dissolve when an artist got on stage for the real deal. Madonna was a perfect example. Hubie was a magician when it came to sound mixing on the fly. He prided himself for being able to correct bad sound staging from his control booth. There was nothing he could do to fix a bad voice, however, and she had proven to be the worst. As it were, he felt she was the reason he and Bear had been fired from the Stadium, so there was no love lost there.

When the Dire Straits' song, "Money for Nothing," came on for what seemed like the hundredth time, Hubie finally gave up. He switched the radio off with a grunt of disgust.

"What the hell Bear, isn't everybody tired of this stuff yet?"

"Sure Hubie," Bear replied. "But it sells, even if you aren't buying. Better get over it. Maybe time to get into the magic bag, huh Boss?"

Hubie squirmed around on the generous white bench seat and reached into the back. In a moment he came up with an embroidered carpet bag he'd found in a second hand store downtown where all the third generation hippies hung out. It zipped open at the top and had double leather handles. The bottom of the bag was reinforced with leather, but the really cool thing was the embroidery. Somebody had put many hours into needlepointing a great rendition of the Beatles', 'Magical Mystery Tour,' album cover. The rainbow lettering was still bright and vivid. Hubie had to have it no matter the cost. It held his bonanza of self-made cassette tape compilations from his favorite artists. Most of it was blues and he prided himself on having many copies of the original Delta recording artists. His guilty pleasure was having recordings of the British versions. Sure, he knew the Stones, Zeppelin, and others repackaged that music. He didn't really care as the British Invasion of the late Sixties was what got him turned onto music in the first place and of course he had a love of the earlier Sixties music from the U.S. He wasn't that much of a purist.

He dug around in the bag for a moment and came up with 'Fresh Cream.' It was the first studio recording of Cream and was one of the best examples of Brit-revised Delta Blues. Hubie popped the cassette into the player and hit fast forward until he landed on, 'I Feel Free.' He cranked it all the way up, having faith that his custom sound system could handle it, no problem. Jack Bruce sang the song with righteous style:

> I can walk down the street, there's no one there
> Though the pavements are one huge crowd
> I can drive down the road, my eyes don't see
> Though my mind wants to cry out loud

> Dance floor is like the sea
> Ceiling is the sky
> You're the sun and as you shine on me
> I feel free, I feel free, I feel free

That was more like it. He did feel free and realized it had been a long time coming. It had taken several weeks for the insurance issues over his burned out club to be resolved. Allstate tried hard to blame the fire on someone in order to pass off their responsibility. The fire investigators stuck to their guns that the blaze was caused by an unknown source, so Allstate had to pay up. It could have been a lot worse if the adjacent structures had been damaged but they emerged untouched. In Hubie's opinion, Allstate got off lucky.

So now they were on the road, heading west. After a long first day, they spent the night in Knoxville. Today's ride was shorter and they planned to get a room in Memphis. Perhaps they'd hang out for a day or so. After all, the agenda was to head west after a stop in New Orleans that might last awhile. There was no hurry or obligations. Eventually the plan was to cross the border down by Yuma, Arizona and then scoot across the top of Mexico until they reached Tijuana. From there, they'd head north from San Diego with the goal of checking out the music scene on the west coast, then maybe find a venue to start up a new club.

Bear didn't care much what they did as long as he didn't have to ride through the Midwest. He'd seen enough of the endless corn fields in Kansas, Iowa, and the rest to last a lifetime. He liked hills, mountains, the oceans and any kind of exotic environment at all. His brief tour during the last days of American involvement in Vietnam had whetted his appetite for spicy foods, exotic women, and strange tasting beer as long as it was cold. If someone had offered him a ride to Mars, he would've hopped in without a second thought. Being unencumbered by mortgages, wives, and children had many advantages of which spontaneity was only one.

"So," Bear began. "How long do you want to hang around New Orleans?"

"Don't know, maybe a few days so we can check out how the clubs operate down there. You know, look at how they do decor and stuff. Maybe make contact with some blues cats for later. I mean, if we do open a club out west, it'd be a good idea to have some dudes lined up that might be open to touring."

"Well, that'd be the place to find that kind of talent," Bear said.

"Sure, we'll just see what's up and go with the flow. If nothing's going on, we'll blow outta there, that cool with you?"

"Yeah Boss, whatever works. I do want to get back to the old stomping grounds by Yuma. We used to have a blast over there on weekends. Don't think any of the guys we used to hang with are still around, but I bet cross border action is still going on."

"No doubt," said Hubie. "We can get some beers at that old club then head over to T.J. like we planned. Might even check out a bullfight before we cross into San Diego. Should be fun."

Outside the window, Hubie spotted the first tinges of Autumn painted on the tips of the Dogwood trees lining the road on either side. It was a fine time to be alive, the gas tank was full and the road was open before them. There was no doubt that they were going to take fine advantage of it. Hubie realized that Bear had been driving most of the morning and he wondered if his buddy needed a break.

"Hey Bear," Hubie said. "Need a break? I can drive if you want."

"Naw, it's cool." Bear replied. "I'm dig'n driving this boat. Makes me feel like an Admiral."

Hubie settled back in the passenger seat and stretched his long legs out as the miles swept by. The drive, once again, had became long and monotonous. Aside from the small objections that the minor aches and pains his body made, he didn't mind it. The rolling of the wheels along with the soothing quality of the clean fall air streaming by, allowed him to be lulled away to another time and place as Bear operated the impossibly large Cadillac. Hubie reached into the magic bag and selected one of his 60's oldies tapes. He popped out the Cream tape and inserted the new one with a practiced hand. "King of the Road," was just on the last few measures, then "Unchained Melody," by the Righteous Brothers, started up with that famous first verse, and unmistakeable piano intro:

> Oh, my love, my darlin I've hungered for your
> touch,

A long lonely time
And time goes by so slowly
And time can do so much
Are you still mine
I need your love
I need your love
God speed your love
To me

A memory of his childhood suddenly appeared without Hubie conjuring it up on his own. The mind is strange in that way, bringing up old videos that were long since filed away and forgotten. As a boy, no more than ten years old, he would watch his father incessantly. Many children pay little attention to their parents at that age, being consumed by their own confusing thoughts and changing bodies, but not young Hubert. His father was like a God that couldn't be taken down, always moving and shaking, making big decisions with big money. He seemed to be immortal and untouchable.

Then the young boy watched as his father was finally thwarted and toppled like a great tower, crashing down and then crumbling into a million pieces. Hubie didn't understand exactly what had happened, only that it had something to do with his mother and her departure out of their lives forever. He had watched as his father struggled to keep himself stoic and together, but barely hanging on by a thread. He did manage to hold onto his fragile resolve and successfully raise his young son.

As Hubie listened to the music he remembered a moment in time long ago, when he rested on a sofa in the dark, watching his father sing with a range of emotion he'd never exhibited before. The lights in the household were all turned down as his father stood in front of an impressive sound system that was cranked all the way up. His eyes were closed, beer bottle in hand, as he swayed and sang along with Bobby Hatfield on that iconic track. Hubie's dad sang in a lower octave and still couldn't hit the high notes, but the emotion was revealed as if the bandage had been torn from a raw wound.

He was singing away his pain, then exalting in it at the same time. Hubie knew his father was a great lover of music and the young boy had been exposed to many kinds and types of musicians, including singer songwriters from every genre under the sun. This faded for his father later in life as he threw himself into the business of making millions. But in his younger days, before his heart had been broken, it was a conduit for him to expel and express.

The image of the invincible man, singing in the dark, swaying with his pain made an indelible mark on the young boy. He saw the power of music in the flesh and the dangers of love at the same time. As Hubie clicked back to the here and now, he had an epiphany. His entire life he'd never put this together and felt somewhat ashamed for only just discovering it. He'd never been interested in taking a wife or having children. It just wasn't something he had ever aspired to do. He'd had girlfriends of course, some long term and some shorter than a day in December, but never had he loved a woman so greatly that he had to have her from here to eternity.

Many women had berated Hubie for his lack of commitment, taking it personally and storming off with suitcase in hand. He had watched many times as the door slammed angrily and felt nothing but a small sigh of deep-down relief. Now, he understood and equated his subpar luck in love with the deep rooted memory in his subconscious of his heartbroken father in the dark, alone with his son and the ballad blaring as it permeated their ears and hearts.

Hubie's one true love was music. It was reliable, always there when needed and could be neatly put away when it was no longer wanted.... and the slamming door was not included. He never wanted to feel the pain he saw in his father that night in the dark. He feared that kind of pain like a glowing-eyed monster lurking in his closet. An unmovable mountain of a man was brought down by the abandonment of a woman. Hubie never vowed it to himself out loud, it just was. As if seeing himself for the very first time, Hubie realized it had been the invisible credo guiding the entire course of his life.

9

Diabolico

Alfredo Diaz peered over the top of his reading glasses at his nephew Enrique, who was seated in front of the expansive desk. Once again, Diaz reviewed the folder in front of him as if he couldn't believe his eyes.

"So, tell me again how this son of a *puta*, Martinez, was found?"

"*Si, mi tío...* it is as the report states. One of the men in Mexicali stopped by a soup kitchen operated by the nuns of Our Lady of Guadalupe mission. He was simply handing out food to the needy as if he'd never been anywhere else."

Diaz held up both hands in complete disbelief. "Was there a struggle, did he attempt to flee?"

"No Uncle, he simply put down his ladle and went calmly with the men. Who would have thought Martinez would be found in a church?" Enrique began to rub his temple as he explained his journey. "*Dios mio*, I slogged through every dirty whore house in Mexicali and only found out the location of his sister. Even our agents north of the line had no knowledge of his whereabouts. He was hiding in plain sight, if you could call it hiding."

"You say he does not have the artifact?"

"No *Señor*, although he freely admits to having found it. He seems to be a bit dazed, as if reality is not within his grasp. He mostly refers to God as his savior and that redemption will be his."

"Redemption!" Diaz exploded. "I'll bring his *Madre y Padre* here to be flayed alive within his eyesight." His bloodshot eyes bulged from their sockets as he slammed his fist onto the desk, knocking over a lamp. "I want the artifact and I want to know where it is right now. Perhaps Manny should begin removing his toes."

The overweight cartel boss was used to getting his way at all times. His cruel nature was reflected through beady black eyes that were buried in a fleshy, wrinkled face. He was completely devoid of any semblance of compassion. The usual method of persuasion included torture and bloodshed. He thought nothing of the carnage inflicted on innocent bystanders that just happened to get in the way. As such, he was deeply feared by those around him. Enrique watched as his boorish uncle fingered the ugly claw that hung from a thick, gaudy, gold chain around his neck. How many times had he heard the story of this family heirloom being handed down from eldest son to eldest son? Enrique only half believed the legend but didn't really care of its authenticity. He only knew that he was sick of hearing about it. He was also convinced that his uncle's method of maintaining control might create fear, but fear is not the same as respect. Enrique thought there might always be a better way of persuading people. He felt that arrogance and power was not necessarily a good combination. Enrique Moreno saw himself eventually at the pinnacle of power in Mexico. He knew his methods were superior to the slash and burn mentality of his uncle. He only had to bide his time and the time would come, of that he was certain. For now, he had to play the role of subservient and compliant nephew while he was the one that actually ran the operations of the vast organization. When the time did come, he was certain that the members of the huge network would accept his leadership without question.

"Uncle, I beg your patience. When we returned from our interrogation of the man's sister, he was already being held in Mexicali. Manny and I had many hours to speak with him as we drove south to take the ferry from La Paz. As we speak, Martinez is resting comfortably in our carcel. He was offered any manner of comforts but all he requested was the Holy Bible. As you know *mi tío*, he is safe in our security area and we are protected in this mountain fortress. I am certain there is more information to be gained from Martinez. His story seems to be one of fantasy but he does appear to be gaining greater clarity of thought as time goes by."

"But Enrique, how much longer must we wait? I think that Manny's sharp blade might open a way to more information."

"Perhaps Uncle. But I think we may already have an idea of where your precious artifact could be. Manny has spent countless hours with the young man and is beginning to believe his outlandish tale. My bodyguard has been with me for many years and I know him to be a man that is without fear. Now, I am not so sure. He says that Martinez believes he has been touched by the Devil. In this statement, Manny has assured me that our captive does not mean touched in the emotional sense, but literally. He claims to have been chased and touched by the Devil's own hand. Manny believes him and I have seen him reading the Bible with Martinez."

Diaz sputtered, "Bible? Manny? I have seen him cut the guts from a man so that he tripped in his own entrails. I will have him do the same to this Martinez fuck so that we may use them for hanging this traitor!"

"Please, calm yourself Uncle. There is more I have to say, or would you rather I summon your physician and his irritating blood pressure cuff?"

Diaz took a deep breath and sat back in his overstuffed office chair. With a wave of his hand he gave in saying, "Proceed, the day is lost anyway."

"Yes, of course," Enrique replied. "Like I said, Manny has been spending much time with Martinez. When I learned of his pious nature, I had Manny bring him the Bible and read with him. It worked because Martinez is unafraid of any worldly punishment. There is no thing of beauty, or money, or power that affects him any longer. Over the past several days he has come to trust Manny and divulged many things."

"Such as?" asked Diaz.

Enrique sat back in his chair, smoothing the pleat of his pristine slacks as he continued. "Well, he admits to finding the legendary mountaintop plateau. He speaks of the great beauty found there, and of the magical waters that flow directly from the mountain rock. He has also told of finding the old witch, the *Bruja* of the stories. He admits to killing her in a red rage and taking the artifact. Martinez expressed his grief and regret for killing the ancient woman to Manny. He has found his religion and he believes he was corrupted by this thing that creates unnatural compulsions. Now that he is free of it, he only wants to find peace until he goes to be with his God."

Diaz spoke again, "Yes, yes, God. So I am happy for him and will allow him to find his God this very day unless I am told where the thing is."

"Do not worry *mi tío*," said Enrique. "Manny has gained his trust and relates the strangest of all tales."

"Does Manny really believe this?" asked Diaz.

"Manny is not sure but he is certain that Martinez believes it. He also thinks he knows where the artifact was placed."

The patience of Alfredo Diaz was always thin, but at this point he was on the cusp of one of his legendary explosions. Enrique was well aware of the consequences if his uncle reached the boiling point so he continued immediately.

"*Mi tío*, the man has admitted that he freely went north with the artifact. He claims that *el Diablo* himself chased him to the border where he crossed over during a horrible storm. In terror of losing his life and soul, he sought refuge in a used car lot across the border in Calexico. He recalls a bright neon sign claiming 'Calexico Motors,' before the storm eliminated the electricity. There was one vehicle there with a convertible top that Martinez was able to access by knifing a hole through the canvas. It is there that he claims to have hidden the artifact behind an upholstery panel. After that, his story becomes vague but it is evident that he was returned to Mexico by border agents and somehow he stumbled into that church."

"This is maddening, Enrique. I would send you over the line to find this car but you know I cannot take that chance. If the *americanos* were to catch you, my sister would have my balls hanging from her rear view mirror!"

"Yes Uncle, but there is another way. Manny believes this car was a classic Cadillac with red coloring, white top and those big red fins on the back. One such as that should not be very hard to find. I know of one that will have incentive to find this Cadillac and bring it to us. She will do as instructed if she ever wishes to see her brother alive again. I am preparing a package with instructions for Pedro's *hermana* including photos of her brother. Manny will deliver it immediately. I have determined that not only does she have unlimited passage across the line but she is also adept at finding stolen vehicles brought into Mexico. The insurance proceeds from her speciality can be handsome and I have come to believe she is very good at what she does."

"Very well," said Diaz. "You know how important this is to our heritage, to our *familia*. Since I do not have a son of my own, *you* Enrique, will carry this heritage forward. You will take the ancient claw and someday wield the artifact of power in your own time. Just see that it is done quickly."

10

The Task

      Lupe Martinez was both overjoyed and horrified to know her brother, Pedro, was alive. The joy derived from seeing the photos that Manny de Ortega had pulled from a large manila envelope and placed on her desk. The horror came with the knowledge that the feared Diaz cartel had him in their custody and that his life was in grave danger. Lupita was riveted by the images revealed in the eight by ten photographs. Her brother had a peaceful, almost dreamlike quality in his demeanor. She had never before seen such a vision of satisfaction in her brother.

Even the visage of the horribly scarred Manny seemed to be softer than she remembered. He was looking upon the Mexican beauty with a sense of compassion. That look changed his entire aura to one of understanding. It was a major shift from what had previously been a man that exuded ruthless power. When the bodyguard had visited her only a few weeks prior he had not uttered one word. This time, when he spoke she was surprised to hear the softness in his voice.

"*Señorita* Martinez, I am compelled by my employer to bring you this message and instruction. It is true that we have Pedro in our possession and you should know that he is well. It is my fear that he will not remain so for long if you do not proceed as instructed in the package before you."

She pulled the short manuscript from the envelope and swiftly skimmed over the contents while Manny waited patiently. Pulling the loose ends together eluded her as she could not grasp what possible connection her brother would have with a classic Cadillac and why in the hell would Diaz want it? Lupita placed the papers on her desk and looked up at Manny.

"*Señor*, I am at a loss as to the meaning of this. Is it possible to have more information? Why would Pedro have anything to do with such a vehicle? Did it belong to this *El Jefe* Diaz? Was it stolen by my brother? Is he not able to simply tell Diaz where the vehicle is located? I would do anything to help my brother especially if it means his rescue from your organization. Please help me know more so that I have something to work with."

"*Señorita*, I have spent many hours with your brother since he was located in the Guadalupe Mission of Mexicali. I can only tell you that he has become a man of complete faith. It is not within my power to tell you why, or how he became connected with the car. I am only allowed to bring you this message and instruction. We are not able to pass over the line under pain of prosecution by the *norteamericanos*. Even if I could, I do not have the command of English that you possess. You can do this. There is thirty five thousand dollars in the smaller envelope. The money consists of twenties, fifties and one hundred dollar bills. They are not sequential and are not able to be traced. You may use this for travel expenses and to purchase the car. The last known location was at a used car lot named Calexico Motors. It may still be there, if not you will access records and obtain the current whereabouts of this vehicle. Why it is important to my employer is not necessary for you to know. What is important is that if you do not accomplish this task your brother will be killed."

"And if I can find this all important vehicle that *El Jefe* Diaz desires, then what?" She fixed her gaze squarely upon Manny, squinting her deep almond eyes. His chest tightened at her beautiful intensity.

"Then you will bring it to us. You will use the remote route as described in the instruction packet. This vehicle will then be exchanged for your brother and you will be allowed to take him with you. His service will no longer be required and you can have the satisfaction of knowing that you, your brother and parents will be safe from retribution. *Señorita*, I truly regret to say the obvious about what will happen if you do not perform this task. Your *madre y padre* are currently under observation in San Felipe."

Her heart sank deeply. Now, the true intent of these evil men was clearly apparent to Lupita. It wasn't just her brother that was at risk, but her entire family. People that became mixed up with these ruthless men could simply vanish. Their propensity for violence was legendary as the numerous shallow unmarked graves throughout Mexico demonstrated. She had no choice. She knew it. Manny knew it.

"*Señor de Ortega*, I have a Ford F-150 truck to be repatriated to our sister Seguro agency in Yuma tomorrow. I will cross in the morning then journey to Calexico to seek out this automobile. If it has been sold, I will access the current owner and find it. Searching for a VIN number is easy. Countless vehicles are stolen in the U.S. then brought across."

Manny stood up saying, "*Si Señorita*, you will cross, but not in the morning. You will go now." He gave her a final glance, then turned and opened the glass door leading from the Seguro Insurance Agency onto the parched streets of Algodones. He stepped through into the brutal afternoon heat and was gone.

She felt a sick dread fall over her like a pall. Lupita picked up the phone and dialed 001 for international calls. When the dial tone changed, she placed the number for the Yuma agency. If she was going over to Calexico this very day, she needed to arrange transportation to the Greyhound bus station. It was going to be a very long day.

*****

Manny watched the office where Lupe worked from within the air-conditioned pharmacy directly across the street. Several elderly gringos gave him a wide berth as they waited for their prescriptions to be filled. The cheap availability of medicines within walking distance of the border crossing was the main reason Algodones existed. Well, that and the cheap liquor and women of the sporting persuasion, but that was an endeavor for after hours. Within a few minutes he watched as she emerged from her office and locked the door. He felt the same tightness in his chest as he followed her with fixed eyes, observing her turn away and quickly walk down the street in the direction of her residence. Manny had been there before and knew where she was going. The memory of sifting through her most intimate things was indelibly etched into his brain. He began to grin, but quickly stopped. The warm memory was eliminated as he was overwhelmed by a feeling of guilt. Now, all he had to do was wait until she drove by on her way to the border crossing. There was only one direction for crossing and if she was turned back, he'd be able to observe that as well.

A white-haired couple entered the pharmacy and Manny rose to offer the woman his seat. At first she recoiled from his scarred face, but then gratefully took his chair giving her thanks. Manny had no words of English but understood her meaning and bowed his head slightly. He was well aware of how he appeared to people. Even though he was used to the reactions, he preferred to avoid public spaces such as this.

It had been ten years since that sudden gunfight with the federales had left the previously handsome man disfigured. Now in his mid-thirties, he remembered it as if only yesterday. The memory of searing white-hot pain when the bullet tore open his left cheek and carried away the upper half of his ear still burned at times. Back then he was new to employment under Alfredo Diaz as his employer brutally fought his way to dominance in a field of cartels constantly jockeying for control. In fact, it was a certainty that the government troops that ambushed their motorcade were compelled to do so by a rival gang such as the one run by Cesar Pastor. Things like that were routine as the government men were well paid and also could show some progress in the fight against the drug trade. It made for good newspaper copy although these brief flurries of violence did nothing to stem the flow of drugs to the north.

Manny had fought well and bravely that day which did not escape the attention of Señor Diaz. He continued firing his weapon even though gravely wounded. Later, Diaz made sure Manny got proper medical attention although not much could be done to hide his wound. In truth, Diaz did not offer the assistance of plastic surgery for his employee. He recognized the effective intimidation Manny produced from his looks alone. For this reason, Manny was assigned to receive weapons that were smuggled across from the north.

The underground economy flourished as drugs went north and money went south. Then the money went north again when semi-automatic rifles and handguns were smuggled south by your average white turista. Thousands of dollars could be made by the exchange of a few AR-15 military style rifles. Firearms were plentiful in Arizona and Texas and many found their way south for the pleasure of such as Alfredo Diaz. He had set up a small armory where the semi-automatic weapons could easily be converted to fully auto. Manny received such armament from regular crossings at the Yuma, San Luis and Ajo border gates. He had even made the coveted acquisition of a military M-60 belt fed machine gun including several belts of ammunition. Even though the price was prohibitive, Manny's standing with El Diabolico was greatly enhanced.

U.S. Border patrol officers did not search vehicles leaving the norte. It was rare for Mexican border agents to search incoming vehicles. That was not much of a problem as Manny knew when a smuggler was to cross and the incentive to look the other way was well paid for.

Other crossings to the west at Tijuana and Tecate were controlled by rival gangs. Heading east to the crossings in Texas such as Juarez were also inaccessible to the Diaz organization. Even the roads into mainland Mexico were controlled by other criminal organizations. The road south from Tijuana could not be utilized by the Diaz Cartel either. But, there was one route that worked perfectly for their needs. It was a rough road south of San Felipe passing across a barely usable dirt and granite rock path. There was access from the beaches for product to be delivered across the Sea of Cortez to waiting vehicles, then transported north. This was how Diaz planned to outwit his rivals and move product north and money south. The route also allowed access to the mainland because it joined the main highway between San Diego and Cabo San Lucas well south of the rivals territory. It was easy then to take the ferry from La Paz to the

Mainland.

Manny had served his purpose well and when Alfredo Diaz's nephew, Enrique, returned from his schooling in Spain, he was assigned as bodyguard. Diaz instructed Manny to take care of his young charge.

Diaz said, "Even though my nephew is to inherit all you see, I will do nothing if he is damaged in any way. I will simply hand you over to my sister."

That was warning enough for Manny. But fear did nothing to increase his vigilance of protection for Enrique. They quickly became good friends and Manny knew where his future would be as there was no doubt that the young Enrique Moreno was a man that would wield great power and influence. Many times they shared a laugh over the pompous posturing of Enrique's uncle. The fact that the elder man insisted on being referred to as 'El Diabolico,' created no small amount of derision. His constant fingering of the claw attached around his neck and his continual harping about the family legacy had long ago worn thin.

Now, Manny was not so sure that the legend was a fairytale. Even though Pedro's tale was outlandish on the surface, Manny had no doubts that Pedro believed his story literally. Although Manny's family was as poor as they come in Mexico, he had been infused with the Catholic religion from birth. Reading the Bible with Pedro combined with the captive's fervent belief had given Manny much to consider. If the Catholic religion was good at anything, it was good at producing guilt and Manny had much to feel guilty about. He was beginning to consider a visit to the confessional even though he knew he'd be admonished to change his lawless ways.

Something else had recently crowded into his psyche. When first he laid eyes upon the beautiful Lupe Martinez, Manny's heart had become stricken with love. He relished the assignment to bring the task to her with joy, only for the reason he might see her beauty once again and breathe the same air. Now, he began to worry about the safety of her brother and the difficult journey into harms way that Lupita would take. These feelings were new to this man raised upon crime and violence. For the first time he began to feel remorse over things that had never before received a moments thought. Somehow this beautiful and compelling woman reminded him of someone buried deep in his past and of a love that brought more pain than any man deserved.

In his mind he knew that Lupe Martinez would never give a man such as he a chance. One glance in the mirror confirmed that he would never receive a second look from such a magnificent woman. But that was his mind. A man's heart never gives a care for what his mind thinks.

11

Calexico Motors

For Lupita, the day had been brutal and relentlessly long. When Manny told her to cross the border immediately and locate the Cadillac, she knew there could be no argument. Her Seguro office directly across the border was an affiliate of the main office in Yuma. The office manager in Yuma, a tall and lanky man named Juan Macias, was a friend of Lupita's and when she called he understood the necessity of her closing the Algodones office at once. Besides, the stolen Ford F-150 truck she would be bringing across meant a large insurance payout would not be necessary. In actuality, the cross-border Seguro insurance office did not issue many policies as most tourists obtained one before crossing south. So she had simply locked up, then went to her apartment to pack a bag and retrieve the truck from behind the padlocked complex gate. As usual, crossing to the north consisted of a wave through as soon as the customs agents recognized her. No one asked how she found stolen vehicles and it seemed nobody wanted to know. She provided a service that the border agents approved of and she was well known.

After the stolen truck had been checked in, Macias gave her a ride over to the Greyhound station. It was still early enough to catch the westbound bus to San Diego with a stop in Calexico. On the short ride to the station, he asked her what was going on.

"Juan," she said, it's my brother. He's gotten himself mixed up with some cartel business and they're holding him captive. You know I could not discuss these things on the phone, but I am compelled to find a vehicle on the north side this time. It is the only way to help him and I don't know if it will work anyway, but I must try."

Upon hearing the nature of Lupita's task, Macias asked no further questions. The less he knew of these things, the better. He dropped her off at the Greyhound station, told her another agent would operate the Algodenes office and wished her luck. Before he drove away, Macias reminded Lupita that he'd be happy to help with VIN number searches if necessary. He half believed he'd never see her again, but that was something he could do nothing about, so he drove away without a further word.

It was early afternoon when she arrived at the Calexico Greyhound station which was conveniently located directly across from the pedestrian border crossing into Mexicali. She knew the used car lot was close by on Imperial Avenue, so she braved the heat and made the short ten minute walk. Sure enough there it was, Calexico Motors, but she didn't see any Cadillacs on the lot. Normally a sales agent would have accosted her as soon as they smelled a customer, but in the sizzling afternoon temperature nobody was out on the shoe melting pavement. As soon as she entered the small air-conditioned office a pleasant gringo man stood from behind his desk asking how he could help.

"Yes *Señor*," Lupita said. "I am looking for a particular vehicle that was said to be on your lot."

"*Si Señorita*," he said smoothly transitioning into almost accent-free Spanish. "I am Steve Jones and I assure you this is the right place for a killer deal. He was of medium height and very slender with a full head of very blonde hair. Lupita wondered how this middle-aged norteamericano would be speaking such flawless Spanish, but then figured it would be in the nature of his job. Calexico was almost fully bi-lingual being the sister city of Mexicali.

"Which vehicle in particular are you looking for?" he asked. "We have many fine vehicles for sale here and I'm sure we can help you find exactly what is right for you."

"It is a Cadillac, *Señor*, a red one and older with the *grande* tail fins."

"Oh *si*," he replied at once. "That car was a classic and one that was to have made me a very good profit. But, it was damaged in a violent storm some time ago when an illegal cut the convertible top to gain access. I was plenty mad because the water ruined the front seat and carpeting. However, the insurance payout on a salvage title was adequate and it made more sense to go that route. The vehicle was taken to San Diego where it was sold at auction."

Lupita lowered her head in defeat upon hearing this unfortunate news. Her mind swam as she grasped at what to do next. Her time working the club circuit taught her the skills needed to manipulate any situation to her favor, especially those dealing with men. She thought for a moment longer and decided to play this one straight.

"*Señor*, my name is Lupe Martinez." She lifted her hands to grasp them together, pleading as she continued. "The illegal, as you put it, found in the Cadillac was my brother. He was working for the Diaz cartel and if I do not find this vehicle, he will most certainly be killed. I am asking for your help. My brother is not a bad man but was recruited into that evil organization and I must get him out. *Por favor?*"

Reverting to English, the dealership owner frowned as he replied, "Madam, I certainly do not wish to have any dealings with those people. I am assuming that if you are not successful I may be approached by members of the cartel?"

"Very possible," said Lupita, also speaking in English. "I do not know why this car is of interest, or what my brother has to do with it. I only know that *El Jefe* Diaz wants it, so I must find this vehicle."

The salesman began to rub his chin as he thought for a moment then said, "This is the man that is called, *El Diabolico,* is that correct?"

"*Si Señor.*" Lupita could see the man's expression soften.

"Alright Madam, please have a little patience while I call the auction house over in San Diego."

Jones flipped through a Rolodex on his desk until he found the number he wanted and picked up the phone. He then began a rapid-fire conversation with the party on the other end. Lupita tried to follow along, but could only make out some of it. Words like, 'Philadelphia' and 'shipped east' were understandable, but that was about it. Then she could tell that Jones was asking for some additional information. It seemed that he had to convince the other person of the necessity of releasing it, but he soon picked up a pen and began to write on the paper pad in front of him. After hanging up he tore the sheet of paper from the pad and slid it across the desk to Lupita.

"*Señorita* Martinez, this is the best I can do. The car was put up for auction and was listed in the Auto Trader magazine. It was purchased sight unseen from a buyer in Philadelphia and shipped immediately. You can see the name, Hubert Altair, and the address is also there." He briefly paused as he leaned forward. She saw a hint of sadness flash across his eyes. "I am sorry your brother was apprehended by those madmen. I had no choice but to call the border patrol after I found him. He seemed to be dazed, as if he were a simpleton. I wish you luck and in return for this favor, I implore you to leave me and my humble car lot out of this."

"Certainly *Señor* Jones. Now that I have this information there will be no need of additional contact with you. Thank you for your help." With that, she stood and reached out her hand to shake his. The man had been kind enough to help her despite the potential consequences that her task had brought upon him. She asked him for one last favor, knowing he would oblige her. "Would you please be kind enough to call me a cab? I will need transport over to the airport in Imperial."

The cab ride over to the Imperial County Airport only took about twenty minutes. She sat still, pensive, and deep in thought as she stared out the window. The driver attempted to make conversation with her but soon gave up as he realized she was in no mood for idle pleasantries. After getting dropped off, Lupita wasted no time entering the tiny air-conditioned terminal. The airport was located in the middle of a vast agricultural area. Air traffic consisted of private aircraft and crop duster planes but Sky West Airlines, a small commuter service, did have flights in and out of Imperial several times a day. The lobby was mostly empty of passengers and the Sky West ticket counter was directly across from the double glass entry doors. She approached the counter which was devoid of a clerk. Spotting a desk ringer bell on the counter, she dinged it once and the ticket agent emerged from the back room immediately. She was a young, attractive, shapely woman with long honey blond hair. The name tag pinned onto her Sky West polo shirt advertised her as "Sandy."

She smiled brightly at Lupita, saying, "Good afternoon, how can I help you?"

Lupita replied, "*Buenas tardes*, I am wondering if there is a flight to Philadelphia today? It is important that I travel there as soon as possible."

Sandy noted her strong Spanish accent and had a brief thought that she might be traveling illegally. However, the pretty Mexican woman did not seem nervous and was dressed professionally. Sandy didn't give it another thought anyway. Her job was to ticket passengers, get the airplanes out on time and leave immigration matters up to the Border Patrol. Still, she wouldn't be surprised if the lady paid in cash. That happened often with hispanic customers heading over to Los Angeles. The ticket agent did some quick research on her computer terminal and offered a solution.

"OK," she said. "You have two ways to go. We have a flight coming in from Los Angeles on the way to Yuma later tonight. From there, you would go to Phoenix to get an eastbound flight, but you would have to stay over in Yuma. We also have a flight stopping here on the way to Los Angeles early tomorrow morning. It will arrive in LA at seven thirty." As she quickly typed away at her keys, Lupita noted her long, red nails clacking away at lightning speed. "US Air has flights in the morning from LA to Philadelphia. Our flight leaves for LA at six fifteen tomorrow morning and there is a hotel right across our parking lot. Do you have a car?"

"No *Señorita*, I arrived in a cab."

"Well then, our flight in the morning is wide open and since you'll have to stay over one night in any event, I'd recommend taking the flight out to LA early tomorrow. The Rodeway Inn is right across the lot and an easy walk. That's your best bet."

"Then I will take the flight to Los Angeles *mañana*."

The ticket agent told Lupita the price and she immediately opened a fat envelope and paid in cash. After accepting the fare, Sandy gave her the ticket. Then, Lupita stuffed the envelope securely back into her bag and walked across the parking lot to secure a room for the evening. She felt a mild relief that the first part of her journey had gone smooth enough, despite a huge snag. Yet she still felt an urgent pull upon her heart. She looked forward to a hot shower and time to catch her breath.

12

Lost Cause

Hubie and Bear rolled into New Orleans with gusto on Friday afternoon, then crawled out late Monday morning. The ride out from Philly had proved to be long and monotonous and staying a few days in the blues and jazz capital of the world was a much needed reprieve. After getting rooms in the French Quarter, the pair wasted no time hitting the streets in search of music and fun. There was plenty of both to be had, for sure.

Bear was along for the ride and as usual, ready for anything, reaping the benefits that only a single man could. He never missed the comfort of a wife or the joy of a child, for he received his fulfillment in being unencumbered by any emotional responsibility. For Hubie, this was turning into the trip of a lifetime. After his club burned down, his father had tried once again to get Hubie to join the firm. His uncle and father had built a banking business that was thriving on the excess of the eighties. Their bank was selling securities internationally as well as providing huge business loans and they had their fingers deep into politics. As for Hubert, he never had his heart in that kind of lifestyle. Actually, his philosophy leaned way far to the left as far as his extremely wealthy relatives were concerned. He didn't care, for his love of music and the freedom to explore creativity was his passion and he relished it beyond any concerns of making more money. Though he was a top notch businessman, he was an honest person at heart, and was satisfied with feeding his soul in more humble ways.

Bear exhorted him on many occasions about being able to do as he pleased precisely because of his family's wealth. Once again, Hubert did not care. He proved to himself by joining the Navy in order to avoid the draft that he was independent. There was no doubt that the family money could have found a way to keep him from the Army. Hubie knew of other young men from wealthy families that had paid a doctor to provide excuses from service. The family doctor had even offered to write up a medical excuse proclaiming bone spurs in his heels. Although it didn't make sense, Hubie knew he could never take part in that kind of lying cowardice. He wouldn't take that route and was proud about it. It's true that he never left American shores and was stationed in San Diego for his entire enlistment. That didn't have anything to do with family influence however, it was just the luck of the draw. After Bear had returned from Embassy duty when Vietnam collapsed the two men had made good use of being stationed in sunny southern California. Now they were looking forward to returning to where they'd had so much fun.

In the meantime, the three-day weekend in The Big Easy provided exactly the kind of adventure the two young men were looking for. They visited as many blues and jazz clubs as they possibly could. The liquor flowed and the people were warm and hospitable. Their logic was that they were searching for contacts with musicians that could possibly be persuaded to visit their new club, whenever and wherever that might be. The old Cadillac Hubie club back in Philly had many local artists to draw from and Hubie had a load of contacts over in Chicago that were happy to play at Hubie's. The place was gaining a huge reputation in the three years it had been open. Now, all that had gone up in smoke.

Hubie's beloved Cadillac had survived somehow and they were having a ball driving it cross country. Everywhere they went there were thumbs up all around. Hubie's killer sound system blasted beats across the countryside and with the mild, early-October weather, the white convertible top was usually down. He'd gotten a killer deal on the auction for the car and only needed to have the top replaced and the front seat and carpet reupholstered. He loved that car, and it had all been an advertising write off for the club.

Despite the initial shock of losing everything in a flash, Hubie was actually looking forward to starting a new club out on the west coast. He was an eternal optimist, had Trust Fund money, and the insurance payout had been very fair. Also, even though he fancied himself to be a progressive leaning Democrat, he'd inherited the family's business sense and could smell a nickel to be made as accurately as his old man. They'd met a couple of managers in New Orleans that were interested in touring sometime in the future. One long and lean gentleman named 'Too Tall Paul,' who wore an extravagant three-piece suit despite the sweltering bayou heat, had his fingers into a few groups that he was aggressively pushing. Another promoter with an equally colorful name, 'Sideways Slim!' he'd proclaimed jauntily with a soggy cigarillo hanging from his mouth, was also interested in moving his groups around the country. The idea was, since Blues and Jazz hadn't really been introduced on the west coast and a club like that could be unique, which in Hubie's mind meant dollar signs. But the highlight of the weekend was when the duo stopped into the acclaimed BB King's Blues Bar late Saturday night for drinks and BB King himself stepped up to the stage for an impromptu rendition of, "The Thrill Is Gone."

Slightly hungover and with a stack of contact numbers in hand, they were on the road again late Monday morning for the three-day trip across Louisiana, Texas, New Mexico, and all the way to the western border of Arizona. The plan was to stay in San Antonio, then stop at Las Cruces N.M. and then on to Yuma. They planned to stay there Wednesday evening, then cross the border Thursday and journey across northern Mexico to Tijuana.

*****

At that very moment, Lupita was seven hundred miles north of New Orleans flying at thirty thousand feet above the ground, riding in coach on U.S. Airways flight 1430 direct from Los Angeles to Philadelphia. Her first experience riding in an airplane had been that very morning from Imperial, way out in the agricultural center of Southern California, over to Los Angeles International. Never before had she been so frightened in her life! The tiny airplane only held nineteen passengers and didn't even have a flight attendant. As the twin turbo-prop airplane loudly revved up its engines for take-off, she wondered what she'd gotten herself into. Then, when what she considered to be a rattling death trap had left the ground, she was convinced that her demise was imminent. She found herself unconsciously making the sign of the cross at least a half dozen times. The bumpy ride at first didn't help much, either. As the cramped plane gained altitude the ride smoothed out, then after reaching level flight the engine noise decreased considerably and she began to relax a little. The landing, one hour later in LA was frightening, but at least she was back on the ground.

Lupita gratefully climbed out of the Turboprop Metro airplane and followed the other passengers up a stairway into the large terminal building. The ticket agent from Imperial had sold her a connecting ticket to Philly, but she was intimidated by the hustle and bustle of the busy LAX terminal and had no idea of where to proceed. Thankfully all she had was a carry on satchel and didn't need to negotiate the baggage claim area. She must have looked confused because a kindly black gentleman driving a six seater curtesy cart stopped and asked where she needed to go.

"*Señor*, I am not actually sure," she said nervously. Lupita reached into her bag and showed the man her connecting ticket. He glanced at her ticket and recognized it immediately.

"Hop on Miss, your flight's over to terminal three, I'm goin' there now."

She climbed on the cart, holding onto her bag with the money very carefully. Along the way, the driver stopped to pick up a few other passengers lugging heavy bags. Within just a few minutes he deposited Lupita directly at her gate. She wasn't sure about protocol for gratuity so she dug quickly into her envelope without removing it from the bag and handed the man a twenty. He took a look at the bill and recognizing her as someone who had little or no experience with flying, declined the money.

"You just keep that Miss. Buy yourself a drink on the plane, you'll most likely need one."

He tipped his hat to the lovely young woman and drove off silently in search of other needy passengers.

She was grateful for the ride because they had already started boarding her flight. She saw that they were boarding by rows, so she was ready when her section was called. This time, she walked down a large elevated corridor that ended directly at the large airplane's doorway. A smiling flight attendant greeted her at the opening and directed her toward the rear of the plane. This was more like it. There were two seats on either side of the aisle and at least four attendants in charge. As it turned out, the seat next to Lupita was vacant and she was able to place her bag under the empty seat. This large plane was so different from her earlier experience that she felt fairly comfortable. The cabin crew members seemed to be confident and relaxed which helped immensely. The take-off was smooth and did not rattle so much as the earlier flight. Not so bad, she thought.

The only problem was that the child directly behind Lupita kept kicking her seat. When the seatbelt sign was turned off, she transferred to the empty window seat and gazed outside, amazed at the view. After a worried, almost sleepless night and the nerve wracking commuter flight at dawn, she found herself dozing comfortably. She was awakened by an attendant who showed her how to release the button so that her seat back would recline. Then later, to her surprise she was offered something to drink and a couple bags of peanuts.

Refreshed, Lupita began to ponder exactly what her actions might be upon arrival in Philadelphia. She had plenty of money to purchase the Cadillac, but what if the owner refused to sell? There was always the alternate plan to simply steal the vehicle. She even had a pair of Arizona license plates stuffed in the bottom of her bag. Perhaps she could take the car, then have it painted a different color in a discount paint shop like Earl Schieb, or MAACO. Then, with the different plates she might have a chance of getting away. It could work as long as she wasn't pulled over by the authorities because she didn't have the proper registration paper to match the stolen Arizona plates. There wasn't much she could do about it anyway as long as she was riding in this giant jet airplane. At least she had a name and address. Perhaps this gringo, Hubert Altair would agree to sell. She'd just have to take some time to check out the location and availability of taking the car, if it wasn't locked inside a garage, that is. There was always the option to ship the car down to Yuma. But she was sure any legit shipping company would need to see an ownership title. That left one final option to buy a car hauler trailer, then rent a truck to pull it. If she could steal the Cadillac and get it into a trailer without being caught, that might be the safest way to get it home. She'd just have to see what the best plan would be when she arrived.

It was late afternoon in Philadelphia as the airliner taxied to the gate. After deplaning, Lupita found her way to curbside as she held onto her bag very tightly. There was a long line of cabs waiting outside and Lupita walked directly to the first one in line and climbed into the rear seat. She handed the paper with the address across to the driver. After studying it for a moment, he reset the meter and took off like the hounds of hell were up his ass. It was a chaotic scene on the road and the way her maniacal driver was steering, she felt if she was back in Mexicali. Within thirty minutes she found herself standing in front of what was left of Hubie's burned out club.

It was a mess. There was a crew of three men shoveling burned furniture and trash into a large dump container in front of the destroyed structure. She asked one of the men if this was the correct address as written on her paper. He replied that it was, but that he didn't know anything about the owner or any Caddy car. They were just there to make a buck cleaning up.

Lupita went into the store next to the ruined club. It was a trendy clothing and record store with a barber shop in the back. "Summer of 69", by Brian Adams was playing discretely in the background. Lupita glanced around the shop and noticed a young woman who's spiked hair was dyed red with the sides shaved clean arranging clothing on a rack.

Approaching the young lady, Lupita said, "Excuse me, perhaps you might have some information available about the address next door?"

The young woman looked Lupita up and down, then said, "Well, yeah, it burned up. Too bad, it was the coolest club around. If you're lookin for a job it's a little late."

Lupita's patience was wearing as thin as the day was getting short. She composed herself and decided not to wipe up the floor with this dumb bitch.

"*Señorita*, I am interested in finding this *hombre* named Hubert Altair. He has a Cadillac that I have been led to believe could be for sale."

"Oh yeah, that one. It's a weird deal that, because it was right outside the club when it went up. Cadillac Hubie's, get it? Advertisement for the club. And it wasn't even singed by the fire. Not only that, but this shop and the one on the other side weren't touched at all. None of the clothing didn't even get a smoky smell, just Hubie's club, like the finger of God singled him out."

This situation was rapidly looking to be a dead end. Lupita considered her options and decided more information would be most valuable. She pulled a crisp fifty dollar bill from her envelope and held it up for the clerk to see.

"*Señorita*, I would be most grateful if you could tell me where I might find *Señor* Altair."

Spiky red-hair girl looked at the bill for a moment before taking it and stuffing it into the back pocket of her ripped jeans.

"Sure. Just go west, him and Bear left last week head'n for

California. They're driving the Cadillac, the red one you're looking for."

"Bear? *Señor* Altair has a bear?"

"No silly, it's his friend Bear, the bouncer at the club. Or, used to be anyway. Word on the street is they're heading out west to see about opening up a new club out there."

Lupita hung her head in despair. How could she find this Cadillac out on the road? How could she help her brother, Pedro? The weight of the world was upon her shoulder's and there seemed to be no relief.

"*Señorita,*" she said. "Perhaps you would be kind enough to earn some of that money and call a cab, *por favor?*"

"Sure thing. I'll call right away."

Lupita found herself in a daze back out in front of the destroyed 'Cadillac Hubie' club while she waited for another cab. She saw no alternative but to fly back home and admit defeat. She stamped her feet in anger as her rage looked for something to destroy, anything at all.

"*Dios maldita sea!*" she loudly exclaimed to no one in particular out of pure frustration.

13

Fortaleza del Aguila

Manny waited patiently in the lobby for Alfredo Diaz to call him into his opulent second floor office. A guard armed with a formidable looking side arm and a short stock AR-15 sat behind a desk adjacent to the intricately carved double doors leading into Diaz's office and personal quarters. The guard looked impassively at Manny. The two men knew each other well. Security duty was coveted among the members of the cartel. As a result, the soldiers assigned to that duty grew fat and lazy. Manny had never seen him work out or take any practice on the live fire range. The man was a paper tiger and both he and Manny knew it. The only threat he might present was if he shot his own toe off.

Manny, however, approached his duties with sacred reverence. He was proficient with the blade, bullet, and body. His maimed face was a blatant warning to others that he wasn't to be underestimated. For Manny, his injury was a personal reminder of what could transpire in a gunfight if one was not prepared.   And without fail, he was always prepared.

*****

It was a grueling three-day drive back to the Diaz fortress after his meeting with Lupita.   His boss had named it the "Fortress of the Eagle," because of the mountaintop location. Manny thought it could be easily defended because of the strategic high ground. The problem he saw with a place like this was that there was no escape route if a determined foe blocked the roads. He understood that law enforcement and political authorities were well paid, but he did wonder about rival cartels. Manny was not paid to think of such things or voice his opinions, despite how glaringly obvious it was to him. His rough barrio upbringing had taught him to always have a way out. That was a lesson he had learned the hard way, when he was still young and tender. As he waited in the lobby, his thoughts wandered back to a time when a blind alley and no escape route changed his life forever....

The young Manny de Ortega had grown up in a large and very poor family.   As one of the middle children, he was pretty much left to fend for himself. Two older brothers were in prison, an older sister was lost to the world with no trace, and his mother was consumed with supporting his three younger siblings, one of which was a baby girl still in diapers. His father was mostly absent pursuing some scheme or another, which actually meant he was in a bar drinking with his useless, unemployed amigos.   Sometimes his father brought home money obtained from some endeavor that was never mentioned. His mother took in any kind of work she could find such as cleaning, doing laundry, or babysitting as a wet nurse. After completing seventh level at school, Manny's education came to a screeching halt. It was about that time in his life when the family relocated from Mexico City to the tourist haven of Mazatlán. His mother cleaned resort hotels and his father tried to make a living stealing from tourists only to find himself thrown in jail. Manny followed in his father's footsteps with much greater success. Lifting wallets or cutting purses loose provided easy money for the lawless youngster. It was impossible for fat and sweating norteamericanos to chase down the wiry, slippery Manny. He fell in with a cadre of other clever entrepreneurs selling marijuana to the younger hip college students in town for spring break and other holidays. He had money in his pocket, he felt invincible, and that's when he met her.

One bright Sunday morning, he was hiding out in an alleyway after taking a rather large and luxurious tote from a frail gringa. She was clearly a wealthy woman and would no doubt have the funds to replace the bag. His survival was dependent upon having a complete lack of virtue, for it was dangerous to feel remorse or guilt. If he were to survive this cruel life, he'd have no choice but to lie, cheat, and steal…. or so he thought. As fate would have it, directly across the alleyway was the Catedral Basilica de la Inmaculada Concepcion which was the town's main religious building, completely designed in a Baroque revival style. It was large and beautiful, but Manny had rarely given it a second glance as his interest in repentance and God was nonexistent. He was on his own and he was angry, stuck with a constant roiling in his gut that had left him contemptuous of the human race.

As he was digging through the contents of his loot, he carelessly tossed away items that were of no use to him; tubes of garish lipsticks, used tissue, a bottle of aspirin, and other various sundries that a strait-laced gringa would carry with her. He threw aside most of the junk until he found a large billfold. He lit up inside… jackpot! As he began to voraciously open the wallet, a flash of light beckoned him from across the nearby street. He looked up, startled, and saw a group of twittering young girls huddled together on the curb. They had been applying makeup as they shared a single silver compact. The light had reflected off of the mirror and caught his attention.

His guard was always up and any invasive sights or sounds raised his hackles immediately. He began to look away from them, eager to get back to his loot when one of them caught his eye. She was sitting demurely at the edge of the pack, quietly reading and seemingly uninterested in the excited gabbing of the other girls. Manny found he could not look away from the pretty young girl. She had very long and straight black hair that was naturally vibrant. Her frame looked to be petite and she seemed to exude a sort of reverence he'd never seen in a girl of her age before. He thought she must not be older than fifteen or sixteen.

He suddenly stood up and stashed the bag under an empty cerveza crate. He'd have to come back to it later, for now his full attention was on this young lady as he was inexplicably drawn to her. Manny walked to the end of the alleyway and steadied himself against the building, staring at her, mesmerized. She was the loveliest girl he'd ever laid his eyes upon.

At that very moment, as if she could hear his pounding heart all the way across the road, she looked up and gazed directly into his eyes. He felt panic and thought of running for his life, as if being chased by an angry and armed full-grown man, but he was frozen solid. He'd never been stopped in his tracks before and had no clue how to act or where to go from here. The girl's alluring face curled into a smile, flashing perfect gleaming white teeth. Just as he began to regain composure and form a lucid thought, she slowly stood up, smoothed the front of her skirt, and began to cross the road toward him with the book tucked under her arm. It was as if time stood still as she seemingly strode in slow motion, glowing under the brilliant sunlight. As the amazed Manny watched, she confidently walked directly up to the young thief.

"*Hola a todos*," she said with a soft and gentle voice… and the rest was history, perfect and painful. Her name was Carmelina Benavente, and she had seen Manny near the church before. She'd been quite intrigued by this boy and his covert behaviors. She came from a tight-knit Catholic family that had roots in Mazatlán for the last century. They were loving and God-fearing, virtuous and simple. She was never exposed to any sort of disfunction or turmoil and as a result, had an open heart. She was the complete opposite of Manny, but the two were drawn to each other and were all at once, in love.

They would meet near the church when she was able to leave the watchful eyes of her parents, knowing they would never approve, yet she loved him wholly. She taught Manny how to read from her Bible under the cool shade of a palm grove. His heart and mind began to open up to the possibilities of a life he could never have previously imagined. Perhaps a life with potential for escape from poverty and petty crime. Carmelina accepted his past and was forgiving because she was raised to be so. The heart knows no bounds and she gave hers to him willingly. It was an improbable romance that burned bright and fast, reckless and blind.

As fate would have it, Carmelina was not the only one who had their eyes on Manny. Influential merchants had complained to the local magistrate about the petty thievery perpetrated on unsuspecting tourists. This had the potential to cut into their bottom line, so it had to stop. Officers that normally looked the other way had been admonished to come down hard on the unruly street punks. That very morning, when the two lovers had met, unbeknownst to Manny, he was being watched by a young police officer looking to make a name for himself. The cop knew what Manny was up to, but had not caught him in the act, so he decided to bide his time and wait for an opportunity to bust the young thief.

The time that the young couple spent together was painted in the colors of young, urgent love. Everything around them seemed to be bathed in golden light and the world was just and exactly as it should be. For once, Manny didn't mind the squalor of his own home, or the fact he was neglected, for he had Carmelina and she provided him with the missing pieces. She experienced an untethered and freeing escape from the tight grip of her own family, and was able to explore her feelings without guilt or shame. As for Manny, the old habits were hard to shake. Even though he'd fallen deeply in love, he still stole from time to time, just to eat for the day or bring some pesos home to his struggling mother. He felt guilt over it, but necessity called and he kept the truth from his beloved Carmelina.

One morning, on his way to the church to see her, he saw an opportunity he could not pass up. An old woman was sitting on a bus stop bench, chattering away at her frail husband as she nagged him close to death. She was completely unaware of her surroundings. Manny saw her purse sitting there, ripe for the taking. He snatched it in the blink of an eye and took off down a side street that led to the plaza of the cathedral. As he reached the safety of his trusty alleyway, he could see his lovely Carmelina waiting under the shade of a palm tree. He ducked into the alleyway with haste, digging through the purse with urgency while searching for anything of value. He pulled out a thin coin purse and quickly stuffed it into his back pocket. At the exact moment Manny emerged from the alleyway to meet up with his love, the same officer that had been scouting the area for him, locked his sights on the boy. A convergence of improbable circumstance had occurred. He saw him take the woman's purse and toss it into a waste bin as he emerged from the alley. Seeing his chance to take the young criminal down, he watched the boy cross the street toward the church and quickly broke into a run after him.

After crossing the street and reaching for Carmelina's hand, Manny heard a command to halt and looked back to see the cop bearing down on them. Instinctively Manny took off, nearly pulling the confused Carmelina out of her shoes. She quickly matched his stride as her skirt flowed behind and her feet slapped the uneven pavement. With her hand tightly held by Manny, she didn't understand why they were running, but she held on nonetheless as he darted around a corner, which turned out to be a fatal mistake.

Out of breath and finding themselves trapped in a blind alley, Manny tried to boost his love over a tall brick wall. The cop saw his prey about to escape and quickly unholstered his service revolver. Shots were fired and Carmelina collapsed on top of Manny as they both fell to the ground. He cradled her in his arms for a moment as she looked into his eyes. She seemed surprised, then coughed up a little blood as the light in her eyes extinguished. The next thing Manny knew, he was tasting dirt as his hands were cuffed behind his back.

The sequence of jail cell, courtroom, and transport to prison seemed to take only moments. The two and a half years Manny spent in that hell hole taught him many things. It was there that Manny grew into his manhood and gained a reputation as one to be avoided. He also made the contacts that allowed him access into a much more sophisticated level of crime.

His young lover had died that tragic day and he would

never allow conscience or feelings to get in the way of his job again. Love became a burden to be avoided. Feelings were a hinderance to a man of his persuasion. There were numerous unfortunate souls that experienced their last vision to be the face of death as manifested in Manny de Ortega. The first one to die at the hands of Manny was the same cop that had taken the life of Carmelina. Manny stalked the unaware young officer and when the opportunity presented itself he felt the sharp pain of Manny's blade as it invaded his guts. It was a slow death, and Manny made sure the dying man knew his killer.

This was the man that found himself as the personal bodyguard to the heir of the Diaz cartel. Manny mused on these and other things as he waited for his audience with Señor Diaz. He found himself unable to resist the image of Lupita and actually found it impossible to avoid concern for her safety. He'd thought of her constantly during the long and dusty journey from the bordertown dump of Algodones. Sitting in that lobby, patiently waiting, it finally dawned on him that she spawned the long repressed memory of the young and eager love of Carmelina. One love had been lost just as the flower bloomed and the next was doomed to never sprout. This indisputable feeling Manny knew as fact. His would not be the life to ever enjoy the fullness of love. Manny realized that his utter lack of a fear of death came from the knowledge that he had never fully lived life.

Manny had been summoned to this meeting immediately after arriving from Algodones. The road was difficult but Manny had made the journey several times. The costal route between Tijuana and Ensenada was controlled by rival gangs and the same applied to the direct route along the mainland. The remote road was rough as hell, but passable. After the pavement ended at San Felipe, the road became nothing more than a dirt washboard track. Further south it had been blasted out of lava rock as it wound precariously along the coastal ridges high above the shoreline below. An added advantage to this journey was not only were no rival gangs to be found, but lazy federales avoided that difficult route. The advantage of secure passage made up for the three day journey it took to reach the ferry in La Paz.

Diaz's door guard mentioned to Manny that not only Diaz waited for him, but his sister Yolanda as well as her son, Enrique Moreno. He was relieved to know that his trusted friend, Enrique, would be in on the meeting. Yolanda Moreno made anyone in her presence nervous. She was an unpredictable sociopath and any combination of her with her brother in the same room could become instantaneously volatile. Her reputation as a cold hearted and evil woman was widely known. Even the fearless Manny felt uncomfortable in her presence.

After a short wait, the door opened and Enrique nodded to his friend that it was time to enter. Manny followed Enrique into the large and richly appointed office space and took the chair next to Enrique's as indicated. Alfredo Diaz sat behind his expansive desk while his sister, Yolanda occupied an overstuffed leather chair off to one side. Manny nodded in deference to his ultimate boss and bowed slightly toward Yolanda before taking his seat.

The woman looked upon Manny with undisguised lust as she let her eyes roam lavishly up and down Manny's body. Then she uncrossed her legs and recrossed them as she gave Manny a wink. Her short pink skirt left nothing to the imagination as it was grossly apparent that underclothing was not a part of her wardrobe that day.

Manny tried his best to hide the disgust bubbling up from his very core. Yolanda Moreno as about as repellent as a woman could possible be. It seemed as if she did not try whatsoever to make an effort at attractiveness. She was short and fat with a body like a barrel and possessed skinny bird legs that had never felt a razor. Her linen peasant blouse was off shoulder with a scalloped neck line that revealed an absence of cleavage. It only accented the fact that she apparently had no breasts. The elastic bottom of her top stopped short of her skirt to reveal a roll of body fat. Above the triple chin, her fat lips were smeared with an over exuberant application of bright red lipstick that matched her fingernails and the toes that peeked out from her open-toed spiky stilettos. Beady black eyes peered from under her cartoonishly long glued-on eyelashes as she continued to evaluate a very uncomfortable Manny. Her hairline began barely above her wide uni-brow and her short black hair was slicked back as if greased with lard. Yolanda raised an eyebrow at Manny which had the effect of making the entire brow tilt as one.

Alfredo watched his sister's antics as he rolled his eyes at the spectacle. He actually felt sorry for his nephew's bodyguard. He'd seen this behavior before and he'd see it again. As usual, he held his tongue. It was widely known that Yolanda was one of the most vicious human beings on the planet. Even he had no desire to mess with his sister, let alone correct her gross mannerisms. Her predatory sexual desires knew no boundaries or gender preferences. It was all the same to her, boy, girl or group. Worst of all was the rumor of sadistic behavior forced upon the occasional unknown and unwanted pretty boy or girl that fell into her clutches.

It was said that she had a collection of desiccated and dried ears, cut from her victims with earrings still dangling from the female lobes. People disappeared, that is all. Even Enrique had no idea of the whereabouts of his father. He had not seen him since he was a child and barely had any memory of the man. Enrique had learned years ago that any questions about his father were answered with one conflicting lie after another.

Alfredo spoke directly to Manny, "So, I assume your journey to recruit this *coño* was successful and she has the money?"

"*Si Señor,* and she understands the package of instructions that included the photos of her brother. She is north of *la linea* and will surely find the vehicle. It is clear to her that her brother's life depends on this, and she is well know for her ability to find and retrieve stolen vehicles."

Yolanda's pig eyes bored into Manny as he gave his report. "Why not kill this stupid *baboso* now?" she said. "Give him to me, he is not worth feeding."

"*Mamá,*" Enrique implored, "He is still useful. Lupe Martinez cannot contact us from the north. The D.E.A. surely has international lines tapped for all in our line of work. We must be patient and wait to hear from the woman. It is likely that if she's successful and returns with the Cadillac that proof of her brother's life will be required. She is not one to shrink like some wilted desert flower."

*****

Yolanda's son was the only one able to contradict his mother and remain unscathed. That is why his uncle always tried to have him in on meetings such as this one. She gave in with a sigh and studied her fat fingers festooned with double gold and diamond rings on each one, including her stubby thumbs. That she was rapidly becoming bored was evident. The three men in the room were relieved as it indicated a volcanic disruption might be avoided. The fact that she was even in on this meeting was a fluke as her main job was procuring product from the coca fields in Columbia. Her ability to obtain the cocaine at the lowest prices and facilitate transportation was legendary and she didn't seem to mind tramping around the remote mountain farms while avoiding capture by U.S. supported Columbian troops. She welcomed the adventure, thinking of it as a game. As far as the family legend of the artifact and how the claw had been passed down through the Diaz generations went, she thought of it as a stupid fantasy. Her son, Enrique was the next male heir in line to carry the ancient claw, but since she wasn't even sure of his paternal parentage, she thought the whole idea was idiotic. Idiotic, like her weak and soft brother. She was already disinterested with all of this nonsense and couldn't wait to get back to the jungle and lead her armed and efficient team.

*****

Enrique continued, "Manny, in the meantime, *por favor*…. please continue your conversations with Martinez. He is still in confinement and seems content as long as he has his Bible." He paused in contemplation for a moment before he continued. "I recall interviewing him after he proved himself during the attack as we solidified our control of the Baja route north. He was a hardened asset which is why he was tasked with finding the artifact. His rapid transformation to religion and serenity is most curious and we should gain as much information as possible."

"Then get to it," said Alfredo with a swift smash of his meaty fist upon the desk. "I've got many important matters that need attention." As he said this, he fingered the nasty omnipresent claw hanging from around his neck and his black eyes glazed over as his thoughts were swept away by the fantasy of the artifact. The man had an unwavering and faithful belief in the ancient tales of it's power. No matter what needed to be done, the thing was to be his.

14

What Are The Odds?

The sun hung low in the late afternoon sky when Hubie and Bear crested the foothills east of Yuma. It had been a long three day drive from New Orleans along Highways 10 and 8 as they paralleled the U.S. Mexican border. The drive across Texas had been the lengthiest as the enormous state seemed to stretch on forever. They had briefly considered crossing into Mexico at the border town of Juarez, but nixed that idea as it seemed better to cross over by Yuma then take the Mexican route 2 over to Tijuana. At the very least they had a variety of changing scenery to take in. Crossing into New Mexico gave the men a fleeting sense of relief to have gotten that beast of a state behind them, until they found themselves driving across a desolate wasteland, completely devoid of life and beauty. If they had decided to take a more scenic route up north they would have been greeted by the lush landscapes of Taos or Ruidoso perhaps, but the trip at this point was utilitarian and they braved the mind numbing miles into Arizona. With Hubie behind the wheel, they took in the expansive view from the foothills overlooking Yuma and west to the Imperial Valley. The warm October air was like a comforting shroud and a far cry from the scorching triple-digit temperatures of the summer months. They could not have chosen a better time to journey through the Yuma desert.

Bear glanced at his watch and said, "Hey boss, it's only a little after three. What say we just head past town and cross over this afternoon. We can get the insurance in Algodones and check out that little bar we used to go to."

Hubie cocked his head to the side, "You mean the Hawaiian?"

"Yeah, think it's still open? We can park at that lot out back and get rooms. That way we don't have to drink and drive." Bear arched a brow as he said, "Remember those rooms upstairs?"

Hubie grinned openly as he remembered spending time upstairs with more than a few sporting ladies. They'd visited that club many times when stationed in San Diego. As he remembered, not having a command of the Spanish language was no problem at all. Hubie chuckled out loud as he remembered the image of Bear escorting two gals, one held under each arm like crutches, up the steps until he tripped at the top. The girls giggled at the drunken Marine thinking he would be easy money. Bear just grinned foolishly and then proved them wrong.

"Sure Dude, why not?" Hubie said. "We can be at the border by four and make it for happy hour. Might as well stay there instead of getting rooms in Yuma. That town's a dump anyway. Rather be where the action is instead of eating at Denny's and taking a six pac up to the room. Let's do it."

"OK Boss, if we drive over to T.J. tomorrow, we can hang

out there Friday and take in a bull fight on Saturday. Bear shifted excitedly in his seat toward Hubie and said, "Remember the time that one Matador got horned up inside his leg? I thought he mighta lost his balls!"

"Yeah," said Hubie. "That bull was wear'n him like a hat till those other bull fighter guys distracted the beast and he fell off. Gnarly scene, that's for sure. Anyway, we can cross into San Diego from there and head up the coast."

Although weary from the long drive, the two men got excited about prospects for another cross-border adventure. Hubie's Cadillac had been purring like a kitten during the entire journey with nary a hiccup. As they drove down towards Yuma, the vehicle seemed to pick up speed independently. Hubie kept tapping the brakes in order to keep the large vehicle even close to sixty five. Within twenty minutes they were bypassing Yuma and heading across the Colorado River where they passed the old adobe Yuma Territorial Prison. The beautiful curving concrete bridge deposited them on the western side of the river where they at long last arrived in California. It was only a short drive over to the border crossing at Algodones and they knew they'd be enjoying a icy cold brew within the hour.

*****

At that very moment Lupita Martinez was sitting in the Seguro Insurance Agency office just across the border in Algodones. Her mind was in a whirlwind over what to do about her brother. Since the only place where she could track the vehicle had burned to the ground and the car was said to be out on the road, she had no way of knowing where it was. The young woman had been in a daze during the long flight home. This time she flew directly from Philadelphia to Phoenix and spent the night there. The following morning she got on one of those dreaded puddle jumper flights back to the Yuma airport. The flights to Philly and back had cost several hundred dollars and she had nothing to show for it. She knew she had to call the number listed in the package Manny had given her, but she'd stalled all day. To say that these cartel hombres were ruthless would have been a monumental understatement and she was terrified.

Lupita was heartbroken over the probable fate of Pedro if she was unsuccessful. Not only that, but her parents and her own safety were in grave danger. She was considering taking the rough road down to highway one anyway, then accessing the ferry at La Paz, but then what? What could she bargain with for the life of her brother without producing this stupid Cadillac? For the life of her, she couldn't imagine what would be so important about this particular vehicle. Couldn't that idiota, Diaz simply buy another one? In the end, it didn't matter. The only thing of importance was that she needed to find that car and she had no way of knowing where it could be.

It was almost closing time and business had been very slow all day. Before she closed the office the call had to be made. She knew she couldn't put it off any longer and was reaching for the phone when the glass office door opened and was filled with the largest man she'd ever seen. It appeared as if he would need to turn sideways to navigate the opening. The man was well over six feet tall and his broad shoulders narrowed to a slender waist and flat belly. He wore jeans and a tight t-shirt that accented his large biceps and had a jet black beard which covered his entire neck. He smiled warmly at Lupita and only then did she notice his companion, almost hidden behind the massive man. The smaller hombre stepped around his friend and she noted he was also very tall, but seemed shorter next to the big guy. She noticed his long blonde ponytail and piercing blue eyes.

Also wearing a t-shirt, he had cargo pocket shorts and a pair of those ratty *huarache* sandals, the kind with tire-tread soles that surfers and turistas wore.

"May I help you *señores?*" she asked.

"Sure," Hubie said, we just need some insurance for a couple of days."

"Please be seated," Lupita replied, indicating the chairs in front of her desk. Both men took a seat and waited for the agent to continue.

"I'll need to see a drivers license and registration for the auto. And, for how long will you need coverage?"

Hubie continued to speak as Bear openly admired the young lady. She felt his eyes upon her, but his demeanor was not threatening at all. In fact, she felt herself begin to blush under his gaze and was not offended by his admiration.

"So," Hubie said, "We're here for the night, then we're taking the Highway Two route over to Tijuana. We might stop in Tecate after we get into the mountains, so I guess three days should do it. Tonight we're hanging out here. It's been a long drive from Pennsylvania. Do you happen to know if the Hawaiian Club is still open?" Hubie looked at Bear and added, "We used to hang out there a few years ago."

Before Lupita could reply, Bear spoke up without taking his eyes off her and said, "Better make it five days, Boss. We might not cross back to San Diego until Sunday."

Hubie nodded his head in approval. "OK then, make it five days."

Lupe only then realized that Philadelphia was in the state of Pennsylvania as Hubie handed over the necessary certificates. She was just thinking how funny it was that she'd been there only the day before when she looked at Hubie's driver's license. The name, 'Hubert Altair' jumped out at her like a bolt of lightning as she stared at his license, incredulous at what she was seeing. Then she took a look at the vehicle registration and realized Hubie had handed her the paperwork for a 1959 Cadillac. Lupita felt her heart miss a beat then begin to hammer inside her chest. Could this possibly be the car? She almost began to stammer, but clamped her mouth shut as the color drained from her face.

Bear leaned forward and placed his huge hands on Lupita's desk.

"Are you alright miss? You seem a little pale."

"No, no *señor* all is well," said Lupita recovering quickly. Her mind began to race, rapidly shifting into high gear. She needed to stall for time in order to think things through. Very aware of the large man's admiring gaze, she decided to see if there was some influence she could manipulate through him. She coyly lowered her eyes, then smiled warmly at the giant.

"Excuse me *señor*, I am wondering if you have the car here, or have you left it in the parking lot north of the border then walked across?"

"Naw *señorita*," he replied. "It's right outside."

Lupita took an insurance application from her top desk drawer and handed it to Hubie.

"Perhaps you could fill out the necessary application while I check the VIN number of your car. Is it locked?"

"Sure," said Hubie as he dug the keys out of his pocket and tossed them to Bear. "He'll show you the car."

Hubie bent to the task of filling out the Mexican Insurance application while Bear stood and opened the door for Lupita. She made sure to brush against the man, as if by accident when she stepped into the warm October afternoon. The bright red Cadillac was parked next to the curb just up the street from her office. The color was a dead giveaway as well as the white convertible top, now raised up and latched for security. Bear unlocked the driver's side door and opened it for Lupita. She took a pen from the pocket of her button down yellow blouse and a small pad of paper from the rear pocket of her tight khaki slacks. The VIN number was stamped on a small metal tag that was riveted to the rear side of the door jamb. Lupita bent over at the waist knowing that her high heels were tilting and accenting her posterior. It seemed to Bear that she was taking a long time to notate the numbers, but he really didn't mind. When she straightened up and turned around, it was evident that the top two buttons of her blouse had somehow come undone. Once again, he didn't mind.

"Good enough, *señor* ," Lupita said while grinning at Bear. Then, when she stepped up onto the curb she almost tripped on the uneven concrete and stumbled into her escort so that he grabbed her around the waist to prevent her from falling.

"Oh, *dios mio!*" she exclaimed and steadied herself by holding onto Bear's sturdy forearms. *"Muchas gracias señor."*

"No problem little lady," he said as he looked into her eyes while sporting a broad grin.

The two stood there by the curb while Bear continued to support Lupita around the waist and she seemed reluctant to let go of his arms.

"Cuál es su nombre?"

Bear seemed confused so she repeated in English, "What is your name?"

"Uh, Stan... Stanley Mack, but my friends call me Bear."

"I see, *Oso Grande*, perhaps?"

Once again he seemed unaware of her meaning.

"Large Bear, my friend. I am Lupe Martinez, but you will call me Lupita, like all my friends."

Bear started to walk back down the sidewalk, but Lupita held onto his wrist, making him hesitate.

"Señor Bear, did you not say you and *tu amigo* would be going to the Hawaiian Club this evening?"

"Yep, think so, why?"

"Perhaps I might come by and reward you for saving me

with a drink?" She said this as a question while gazing up directly into Bear's eyes. When he seemed surprised she continued saying, "I worked there before taking the insurance job. The bartender, Mikki is a friend and you must know the drinks are way overpriced. May I?"

"Were you a bartender, Lupita?"

"*No señor,* a dancer and a very good one."

She let go of Bear and did a little flamenco move, stamping her feet while twirling in a circle and pretending to snap castanets above her head. She ended with a flourish pretending to swirl her nonexistent skirt about her while laughing out loud at the astonished ex-Marine.

Hubie had just finished the application when Lupita and Bear entered the office, both having a great laugh. He wondered what was going on. All of a sudden the pair seemed to be old friends. He already knew Bear had a weakness for the latinas, so he wasn't all that surprised.

"Boss, ready for some cold ones?," asked Bear. "The Hawaiian is still open, so let's get going."

Lupita took her seat behind the desk and reviewed the paperwork. She took out a schedule and entered the payment amount then handed Hubie his copy. After she told Hubie how much he owed he retrieved his wallet and paid in dollars. She reached into a money bag after unlocking the bottom drawer of her desk and gave him change in pesos.

As the pair left the office, Bear turned and said, "See you later Lupita."

"Looking forward to it, *mi amigo.* Perhaps in an hour or two," as she lowered her eyes demurely.

As Hubie and Bear got back into the extravagant red Cadillac, Hubie asked Bear what was going on.

"No worries, Boss. Gotta date, that's all, and I think she's got friends. Let's get goin, I'm in need of a rain locker and some serious scrubbing."

As the huge car pulled away, Lupita reviewed her copy of the insurance contract. She removed the paperwork from the folder Manny had given her and compared the VIN number she'd received from the Calexico used car dealer. After verifying it was identical she then crumpled up the insurance copy and deposited it into the wastebasket. The main office had no need of retaining any history of this particular vehicle. The Seguro office would be locked up early this day. She had work to do.

Cadillac Hubie

15

Gone

       The Hawaiian Club was within easy walking distance of the border crossing. All the Mexican strip clubs were located adjacent to the U.S. border so that inebriated gringos had the advantage of a short hike to the border and easy access to their vehicles parked on the north side. Customs officers were well versed in dealing with staggering Marines making their way back after a weekend evening of drunken excess. During daylight hours they screened retirees returning to the U.S. with their precious, inexpensive medications and just before the border closed at midnight, a swarm of young Marines sporting stupid grins lined up for access to the U.S. As usual, the California Highway Patrol had a cruiser or two stationed on the access road to Highway Eight, watching for vehicles that needed to be removed from the road. Many a young Marine found himself in front of his commanding officer explaining why he spent a night in jail. The military knew full well what the routine was, but had no way of stopping it.

Hubie and Bear only needed to turn the corner and drive one block from the Seguro Insurance office to reach the Hawaiian's parking lot. They parked their land yacht in back and entered the club from the rear access door. It took a few moments for their eyes to adjust to the cool darkness after being in the white-hot light outside. They both immediately recognized the interior that had not changed one bit since their military days in San Diego. The familiar odor of stale beer and cigarette smoke was omnipresent as always. There was a large L shaped bar commanding one half of the open floor plan. Along the other two sides of the club were bar-level tables and chairs as well as booths with bench seating. Behind the upper seating level were two glass enclosed offices. One room was occupied by at least two burley security men with watchful eyes and the other contained the D.J. and his impressive sound system. This level was raised above the dance floor below. A few tables were placed around the perimeter of the dance floor but moved back from the open area that contained three brass poles securely anchored to the floor and ceiling above. At the moment only a few newly hired gals were present. There would not be dancing until much later, but the newbies were required before hours as window dressing.

As soon as Hubie and Bear entered, a pair of working ladies were all over them like dry on the desert. They were both in full costume, if you could qualify gossamer see-thru fabric and underwear resembling dental floss attached to a two inch triangular piece of cloth as clothing. Stiletto heels completed the ensemble for both young women. Bear got his heavy arms behind one the girls legs and shoulders then lifted her up to eye level. Cheap perfume assailed his nostrils. She squealed with delight as she kicked her feet, sensing easy money. Hubie gave Bear an elbow.

"Hey Dude, knock that shit off, we got all night. Let's get the rooms first." As usual, Hubie could be depended upon to keep an even keel, even at the most trying of times.

"Sure Boss, just coppin' a feel. Nothing wrong with free."

He tried to set the woman down but she wrapped her legs around his waist as she draped her arms across his wide shoulders. She leaned back seductively with a knowing gaze as her tiny, perky breasts were exposed for viewing. Even though she was heavily made-up with ridiculous glued on eyelashes, on closer inspection Bear could tell the professional woman was very young, still in her early twenties. He put her down and sent her away with a fond squeeze of her tight ass. She pouted, but returned with her friend to their booth where they awaited another more promising mark. Later, when the joint was jumping, she'd take her turn on the dance floor to expose her charms while hoping to hook a customer for a trip upstairs to the rooms above.

The men took seats at the bar and ordered two cold Tecates from the bartender. Two bucks each was the happy hour price and the beers were presented with cut wedges of lime already inserted into the bottle necks. Bear considered ordering a shot of tequila, but decided to pace himself and wait until later.

Hubie engaged the bartender saying, "So, we're here for the evening, can we get a couple of rooms?"

"*Si señores*, but the price is one twenty American and there are only two available as the other's will be in use later."

Hubie noted the almost perfect English spoken by the man who was dressed in the standard long sleeve white shirt buttoned to the neck and black trousers. His dark hair was slicked back and he wore an impeccably trimmed pencil thin mustache. He reminded Hubie of a character from some black and white fifties film such as Casablanca. In fact, with the ceiling fans and art deco decor in the bar, it almost seemed as if they were sitting in a movie set. Hubie was thinking, "Home Sweet Home," as he reached into his right pocket to remove a small stack of twenties. He knew enough to keep the larger pack of bills out of sight in his left pocket safe from prying eyes. Peeling off twelve twenties, he placed them on the bar then presented the bartender with an additional twenty.

"Just one night," Hubie said. "And the red Cadillac parked in back, we'd like it to be watched."

"No hay problema amigo, but perhaps something for *la guardia de noche?"*

Hubie presented the man with another twenty knowing full well that the night guard would most likely never see it. Hubie saw a name tag on the man's shirt proclaiming him to be 'Mikki' as he reached under the bar and came up with two keys tagged with small numbered wooden paddles.

"Señor, take the stairs in back next to the *baños. Tus habitaciones* will be at the extreme back where it will be less noisy and more private. This last part was said with a broad wink that imparted no doubt as to the purpose of the upstairs accommodations. Bear was in the process of destroying his second beer while Hubert had barely started on his first. Hubie nodded to the bartender, saying, *"Gracias,* we know the way."

"Hey Boss," Bear started, "Whatya think the chances are of clean sheets?"

"How about zero, Dude," Hubie said with barely disguised disgust.

"Don't really give a shit. I'm gonna get a pack of beer, scrub off the road dirt and get a nap. See ya later."

"Good idea, see ya in a couple of hours."

The rooms, spartan as expected, were accessed by a narrow exterior balcony overlooking the dirty alleyway in back of the club. Hubie noted that by leaning over the railing he could see his ride parked out back. Satisfied, both men entered their individual rooms through ill fitting wooden doors which provided exactly no security whatsoever. The flooring consisted of white tiles that seemed to have been fitted by a one-armed blind man. Each room had a small single bed pushed up against the far wall with barely enough room to accommodate a night table with a single bare lamp, shade not included. The small bathroom contained the shower, sink, and toilet. A mildewed plastic shower curtain was used in place of the bathroom door which made sense as the shower drain was placed in the center of the floor between toilet and sink. It reminded Hubie of the bathroom design on sailboats he'd crewed as a teenager. Oh well he thought, these rooms were designed for a practical use that did not include any need for luxury. Hubie used the shower, turning the temperature as hot he could manage, feeling his tired muscles begin to relax. He then dried himself with the small white towel hanging from a hook next to the vanity mirror. Worn out from the long drive, he pulled the greasy bed cover back and settled in for a nap, assuming Bear was doing the same next door.

He felt he'd only just closed his eyes when heavy pounding on the door woke Hubie from a deep sleep. As he sat up on the bed, the door opened and was filled with the huge form of Bear. Hubie could see around the edges of the man just enough to realize it was full dark outside.

"Hey Boss, get your ass up. I'll be downstairs."

The door slammed sharply and Hubie felt the heavy footsteps of Bear receding as he headed down the balcony toward the landing and stairway to the bar. There was another muffled pounding noise and Hubie realized he was hearing, "Girls, Girls, Girls," by Motley Crue. Hubie smiled as he realized that, after all, they had decided to get rooms at a strip club bar. Suddenly understanding that the joint would be jumping deep into the morning hours, Hubie was glad for the nap. He grabbed his small travel bag from under the bed and pulled out a fresh shirt. After splashing some water on his face, Hubie pulled his long blonde hair back into his standard ponytail and headed downstairs.

Upon entering the bar, he felt the pulsing sound waves as if a strong wind was pushing against him. Hubie saw that it was filled with noisy, laughing patrons of all stripes. Not only was the room filled with at least twenty professional ladies, but there were plenty of short-haired Marines clumped around tables in groups. There were also many Mexican men as well as elderly gringos. Some of the older men were accompanied by gray-haired wives that seemed to be equally enjoying the garish show being put on by three young, nubile, dark-haired women on the dance floor. Each gal seemed to be trying her utmost to outdo the others. One little bird seemed to defy gravity as she spun around her brass pole while hanging upside down, showcasing her impressive strength and agility.

Hubie noticed Bear waving at him from the bar, so he maneuvered around some tables and walked over. Seated on a bar stool next to Bear was the pretty insurance agent, Lupita. However, she was transformed from her professional look and mannerisms of earlier in the day. Whereas before she'd been clothed conservatively, her brightly colored form-fitting full length dress, while covering her adequately, actually left little to the imagination. It was light blue with an embroidered peacock on one side and cut thigh high on the other, exposing a lovely flash of flawless skin. She sat with perfect posture, perched on the bar stool with her red toenails pointing from platform wedge shoes as she smiled openly at Bear. Instead of being piled high in a bun, her luscious dark hair flowed across her shoulders, reaching to mid back. The thinly strapped top was cut low enough to show the swell of her breasts and a tasteful amount of cleavage. That she wasn't wearing a bra was obvious as well as the fact that she didn't really need one.

"*Hola Señor* Hubie," she said as he joined them.

"Hi Boss, what took ya so long," added Bear. "Wanna brew?"

Before Hubie could answer, Lupita put her hand on Bear's forearm and said, "*Señores*, let us get a quiet table in the back and please, allow me to buy the drinks. Mikki charges the local's rate for me."

"Yeah Boss," Bear said. "She used to work here until she stabbed some dude through the wrist for, should we say, inappropriate behavior." Bear jerked his head over toward the bartender. "Her and that guy were talkin about it."

"Not to worry, *mis amigos*," Lupita said, laughing while shaking her long black hair around her shoulders. "No hairpins tonight! Please allow me. Mikki has a very special rum drink that might surprise you."

Lupita then waved a lovely barmaid over and began speaking rapidly in Spanish. Then she turned to Bear and Hubie saying, "Please, my friends, Lola will show you to private seating and I will join you shortly."

The two men followed the petite hostess to a private corner booth set up for table dances. As soon as they were seated, a throng of lovelies approached them hoping for an audition. The barmaid spoke sharply in Spanish and then indicated which one of them could approach. It was obvious that she meant for the girl to sit with Hubie. Then Lola went back to the bar where Lupita was in conversation with Mikki. Hubie was entranced with his new companion who was all over him like hot on the sun. Bear had his attention on the bar where Lupita and the bartender were in what appeared to be a serious conversation. He noticed the bartender looking over in their direction a few times as they spoke. Bear assumed they were haggling over the price of drinks. Finally, Mikki nodded in approval and turned back to his bar duties.

Lupita turned from the bar and walked directly across the dance floor toward the private tables. As she passed one of the brass poles she grasped it with one hand and writhed seductively around the metal as her other hand caressed her breast, side, and exposed thigh. She did this in time with the pounding music while never taking her eyes off of Bear. For him, there was nothing and nobody else in the room. A group of Marines called for her to come to their table but she ignored them as she walked toward Bear, swaying in time to the compelling beat.

Sliding into the booth, she made sure to press her body next to Bear. Then, as he looked down at her, she placed her hand behind his neck and pulled him down for a full wet kiss.

"Did you like my dance, *mi Oso Grande*?"

Bear was stunned. He had nothing to say and Lupita giggled at his astonishment. Just then the barmaid, Lola, appeared with a tray full of drinks. There were two Tecate beers with lime and four shots of Tequila. Besides two weak drinks for Lupita and Hubie's gal, there were also two large glass goblets filled with Mikki's special rum drink. Both glasses were rimmed with salt and had orange slices floating in the dark liquid.

"*Salud*," Lupita proclaimed, taking up her drink as Hubie's companion did the same. Bear downed one of the Tequila shooters in one gulp and chased it with a Tecate. Hubie just sipped his beer knowing he was a lightweight compared to Bear and neither man had eaten anything that afternoon. Lupita encouraged the guys to try Mikki's rum drink. Then, both women got up and began table dancing as if tomorrow were a lie. Hubie sipped his rum concoction while the dancer wound all over him. Lupita's dance routine was not nearly so obviously blatant but actually very sensuous as she performed for Bear. Before he knew it, his drink was empty and another appeared like magic before him.

Lupita continued to dance before Bear as the song, "Tainted Love," by Soft Cell took over the room. He had the most amazing feeling of relaxation as she danced and the song seemed to go on endlessly. The music became slow and distorted, sounding distant and dreamlike. His vision seemed to wane and blur and he attempted to rub his eyes back into focus. Then, Lupita had him by the hand slowly pulling him up as it seemed the booth had him in some kind of gravity well. He vaguely noticed that Hubie had his head cradled on his arms upon the table. Bear thought through a foggy haze that it was strange for his friend to be taking another nap. Then, he seemed to be following Lupita up a stairway that went on forever. The last thing he remembered was being gently pushed down on his bed which welcomed him like his mother's arms.

*****

Hubie found himself staring at a strange ceiling as light flooded around the edges of unfamiliar blinds. It took a little while to understand where he was. He slowly sat up on the bed and felt his head pound as if a jackhammer was trying to escape from within. He felt the unstoppable urge, then bent over at the waist and promptly vomited all over his huarache sandals. Only then did he notice he was still fully clothed. Making his way into the shower room, he kneeled before the toilet and hurled until only a thin brown bile emerged. Feeling only slightly better, he used the shower to wash off his lower legs and feet. His next thought was for his friend Bear and he threw open the outer door only to be blinded by the white-hot light of mid-morning. Hubie felt as if a thousand needles were piercing his eyes and he staggered back into his room to find his sunglasses.

Re-emerging with his eye protection in place, Hubie found Bear already up and leaning over the balcony railing. He looked worse than Hubie felt as he turned his red, bloodshot eyes toward his friend.

"Dude, you look like shit!"

"Speak for yourself, Boss. Did you get the number of that truck that ran over me?"

"Truck, is that all? I'm looking for a runaway steamroller. Did we have fun? What happened?"

"Don't know, but if I barf anymore I'm gonna turn inside out. By the way, did we go somewhere last night? It looks like your Cadillac's been moved."

Hubie leaned over the railing and looked out where his car had been parked the previous afternoon. He couldn't see it. Instinctively feeling for the keys in his pocket he discovered they were missing. Both men immediately stumbled down the exterior stairway into the parking lot. They looked up and down the row where they'd left their car. The parking attendant was nowhere to be seen. Incredulous, Hubie wondered where he'd left the Caddy. At the same time, both men noticed a pair of Pennsylvania license plates leaning neatly against the curb. The Cadillac was gone.

16

Gomez Gomez

Hubie and Bear staggered back into the Hawaiian Bar blinded by the relentless sun blazing outside. Hubie stumbled, as he was almost completely disabled by the pounding inside his skull. He'd have fallen if Bear hadn't gripped his right elbow. Hubie clutched the license plates with a death grip in his other hand. This early in the day only one bartender was in the lounge, wiping the bar down while a bent old woman swept the floor and cleaned tables. Bear felt as if a hand grenade had gone off inside his head.

They approached the bar and the bored attendant looked up at them, then smirked knowingly. Hubie recognized him as the same guy that had been on duty the night before. Bear gently took one of the plates from Hubie and smiled nicely as he addressed the bartender.

"Good morning *señor*," Bear told the smirking Mexican. "Perhaps you have some information about the Cadillac parked outside last night?"

"No, *mi amigo*, I know of no Cadillac, is it lost?

"Stolen, more like it," Hubie added in a raspy voice.

Bear, still smiling nicely turned to Hubie and said, "Excuse me boss, don't get upset."

Then he took the steel plate in his huge hands and bent it in half a couple of times. He looked the bartender directly in the eyes as his smile suddenly dissipated. A frightening grimace replaced the smile as he effortlessly tore the license plate completely in half. Bear looked meaningfully around the bar, taking in the sound system, lighting, and even the stripper poles that were securely anchored around the dance floor. He then turned his gaze fully upon the now very nervous bartender. Bear tossed the ripped plate halves on the bar and his stare left no doubt in the mind of this bartender that what would happen next would not go well for him. As Bear leaned menacingly across the bar his hand slowly reached out as if to grab the man by the neck.

At that moment, Hubie felt a slight touch on his elbow and turned to see a brown and wizened short Native American looking up at him with a soul-piercing stare.

"Perhaps I may be of help," the short man said, still fixing Hubie with that penetrating gaze from his coal black eyes. The man looked like an extra right out of an old Clint Eastwood western film. He was actually wearing flared brown leather pants which covered worn cowboy boots. His shirt was collarless and made from coarse linen material. A faded red and yellow serape completed his ensemble and a small, battered thatch sombrero hung behind his shoulders from a leather strap around his neck.

"You know where our car is?" said Bear as he turned his attention from the bartender who immediately found something else to do.

"Perhaps, *señor*. Might we take this opportunity to sit and speak of this matter?"

Bear and Hubie exchanged a quick glance and Hubie said, "Sure, might as well, I gotta sit down anyway."

The man led the pair to a table in the corner then gave the cleaning lady a few pesos and asked her in Spanish to bring some glasses before shooing her away.

He smiled knowingly at the norteamericanos saying, "So, unfortunate is the road that has brought you to depend now entirely upon your feet. Perhaps I may be of assistance and you for me as well."

The exhausted men were in no mood for riddles and Bear was rapidly losing his patience. Hubie imagined a scenario of destruction and the inside of a Mexican jail cell, so he put a hand on Bear's generous forearm to prevent any sudden reaction.

"Look dude," Hubie said. "If you think you can be of help spit it out before my friend gets serious again. He's not a well man when he's got a headache, nor am I."

"As I said, perhaps I may be of help but first try this elixir, it will be most welcome, I assure you."

He took out a flask and poured two fingers of the clear liquid into each of the three glasses the old woman had placed on the round table. Both Hubie and Bear looked skeptically at the liquid, hesitant to drink. The wrinkled and browned native nodded at the two Americans and downed his glass in one gulp.

"*Señores*, my name is Gomez Gomez and this *agua* is the cure for anything, including your current affliction. You will not be sorry, trust me."

Bear was hesitant but Hubie, uncaring at this particular point of his history followed suit, downing his glass just as Gomez Gomez did. He was cured, instantly. The drug hangover was gone to be replaced by a feeling of well being that was previously unknown in his thirty-two years.

Turning to Bear he said, "Oh my God, your gonna wanna

do this right away, because even if it does kill you, you'll be one happy dead man!"

Still scowling, Bear abruptly downed the clear liquid. Almost instantly, his black eyebrows shot up as his eyes opened wide. He looked at their new acquaintance with awe as a broad smile slowly spread across his face.

"Man, that effing rocks, where'd you get this shit?"

"*Mis amigos*," the short brown man replied, "all is to be revealed to those with time and patience. Unfortunately, at this moment we have neither."

Again Hubie brought up the subject of his missing car.

"Look, man. Thanks for the hangover remedy but if you know something about my car, spit it out. Like I said. If not, we gotta find the police station and report it stolen." Hubie frowned and dropped his head, "As if that would do any good."

"*Si*, I am a member of a community or how we say, *comunidad*, that are those called the original people. We trace ourselves back from a time before any white men came to this land. Even before that, it is said that the long journey from other *tierras* were made by the feet of our *padres* and their *padres* from before memory. The Inca and Aztec and all other civilized peoples of what was called the "New World," sprung from the loins of our greatest *abuelas*, as you would say, grandmothers."

"That's nice," interrupted Hubie. "How about getting to the point, please?"

"As you wish, for time is of greatest importance. Your car is a red 1959 Cadillac with a white top that is the type which can be removed. A convertible... am I correct?"

Hubie and Bear looked at each other with shocked expressions. At the same moment both men had a flash of understanding that this strange man might have something to do with the theft. Gomez Gomez recognized their suspicion and continued without pause.

"*Señores*, the evidence of your concern is plain to see. Perhaps it will be of help for you to understand that I am also hoping to find your Cadillac and retrieve that which was taken from us."

At this point, Bear was once again on the brink of losing his patience. Before Hubie could even begin to make sense of what their new acquaintance was saying, he broke into the conversation.

"OK mister Gomez, here's the deal. Right here, right now speak clearly and make plain what you're talking about. Are you saying that Hubie's car is yours, and that you want it back?"

"Yeah," Hubie said. "That's my car and I have the salvage title in the name of my business. It was an advertisement and tax write-off. It's legal and it's mine."

"No, no, you mistake my meaning," Gomez said. "It is what was hidden inside your car that is of importance to us. Please, let me explain. We know that the *hombre* that took, shall we say…. the *artifact*, crossed the border during a grand storm and placed it into your car. At that moment the vehicle was in a used car sales business. Since it had been damaged in the storm, it was taken to San Diego where it was sold at auction. This is how you came to have this Cadillac. Am I correct in this story, so far *señores*?"

Once again, Hubie and Bear glanced at one another and Hubie said, "OK, you've got my attention, go ahead."

Gomez continued, "This thing that was hidden in your car is that which we call the *artefacto precioso*. It came to those earliest people from the molten heat of the Earth and has great power. The original people have protected this artifact for countless centuries. When our ancestor's witnessed the greed that was brought to our land by the *conquistadores*, we knew it must be hidden. Such power must never be wielded by men such as them and their priests that seek to replace the spiritual world with the yoke of repression."

"Nice story pal, so how did this thing happen to be in my Caddy?"

"The man who committed murder and took it worked for the Diaz cartel. Are you familiar with these drug lords?"

"Yes," Hubie replied. "The war on drugs is all over the news and we hear all about the different cartels and how they compete for influence. Thats about it, though. We're not drug users. I saw the damage done by that shit when I was in the Navy. A good beer buzz is about all I need, although after last night I sincerely doubt I'll be popping another top for a long while."

Gomez directed his piercing gaze upon both men then said, "You were drugged and your car has been taken by the sister of the *hombre* that placed the artifact into your car. This man, Diaz, compelled the thief to find and retrieve it. The cartel has him in custody and tasked his sister to bring the vehicle, or her brother will be killed."

Bear interrupted once again. "You mean Lupita, I get it. But what I want to know.... right now, is how you know all this stuff. I mean, what's your part in all this?"

"My *grande amigo*, we must go and *rápidamente* if we are to make this right. But I will explain to you this so that you will understand. You have been south of the border before, correct?"

Both Hubie and Bear nodded in agreement.

"*Si*, then you will have noticed the people that ply their trade by washing windshields or selling trinkets and *comida*, the type of food which may be consumed while driving."

"Yeah," Bear replied. "They're relentless, like ants. It always pissed me off because they seemed to be nosy as hell, looking in my car and shit when you're waiting to cross back."

"These are the eyes and ears of the original people. We are always there and everywhere. Those that come and go from north and south do not escape our attention. Our network is alive in all places and recognizes no borders. Even inside the cartels, we are watching. It has been this way since our lives were compromised by the guns, germs, and steel that the Spaniards forced upon us. We have never mixed our blood with those conquerors and never will. We are the *Kumeyaay*. It is known how this thief killed the *Bruja* that guarded the artifact and how he was chased, then forever altered by the touch of evil. We sought him but the cartel soldiers found him first. When he told his tale, we also became aware of the story. This is how we know about the journey of your automobile. So, I will ask you one final question, then we must be on our way."

Gomez Gomez turned to Hubie and asked, "So, *mi amigo*, how did you happen to arrive at the Hawaiian Bar and what compelled your journey?"

"Oh, I don't know," replied Hubie. "Lot's of stuff and it just seemed like a good time to take a road trip."

"But *señor*, I am curious, how did you select the way of your journey?"

"I don't know dude, the road just brought us here and besides, Bear used to be stationed over in Yuma, why'd you ask?"

Gomez hesitated then replied, "Perhaps, was a fire involved?"

Once again, both gringos were amazed by the depth of this wizened little man's knowledge. Gomez recognized the truth of his question by the way the two men looked at each other.

"You see, my friends," he continued. "The thing that is in your car is from the lava of the earth and will always revert to heat and fire. It wants to be returned to where it belongs and with great power over men is able to compel such a journey as you have undertaken. It must not be allowed to fall into the hands of such as Diaz. We must pursue the young *señorita* and return it to where it is safe from evil. She has no knowledge of what she is transporting and surely will be killed if she completes her mission, along with her brother."

Bear slammed a huge hand down upon the table, making the empty glasses jump. Then he stood up. "I'm in, where's your car?"

Hubie looked over at his companion and said, "Well, shit. I guess I'm not walk'n back to Philly by myself. Anyways, the Magical Mystery Tour bag with all my cassettes was in that car. That's enough reason to get it back. He also stood and Gomez Gomez joined them.

"*Por favor mis amigos*, if you would please retrieve your belongings, I will be parked outside and our journey may begin.

The two stranded men headed back up to their rooms but first Bear took a look across the dance floor to see if that slimy barkeep, Mikki was around. Hubie recognized his friends intent and was relieved to find the man was nowhere to be seen. No telling what might transpire if Bear had gotten his hands on that asshole.

Both men were surprised, yet relieved to find their things hadn't been rifled through or stolen while they were out cold. Considering that to be a miracle, they grabbed their bags then headed back downstairs and out onto the sun-flooded street where Gomez waited. He was standing beside an ancient weather-worn 1950 Chevy Fleet Line two-door sedan. It was the fast back design with the roofline sweeping back into the trunk and had rear fenders that stuck out like bubbles. The chrome trim was pitted and the paint was faded and worn down to the underlying primer and even the bare steel in places. Seat covers were made from red, yellow, and green patterned serape blanket material. The passenger window sported an old fashioned air conditioning unit. It was the kind that held water which evaporated when the wind stream flowed through the round canister. The old Chevy was lowered a few inches both in front and back.

Hubie looked at Gomez and said, "Please tell me you haven't named this sled, La Bomba."

"No *señor*, the name of my beauty is 'Christine,' even in Mexico we know of Stephen King and his books. The name is perfect. Now, *vámonos*, it is time."

Bear opened the passenger door and threw his bag into the back seat. Hubie climbed into the back with his bag then Bear took shotgun. Gomez hopped into the driver's seat and the engine roared to life. He took off down the dusty street while the powerful acceleration made both gringos wonder what he had under the hood. Soon the little town of Algodones was receding in the rear-view mirror as both Hubie and Bear began to question what they had gotten themselves into.

17

Desperate Journey

By the time Hubie and Bear had risen from their drugged stupor, Lupita had already driven the stolen Cadillac well beyond San Felipe. Earlier, when Mikki and a couple of dancers helped carry Hubie up to his room, Lupita stealthily removed the car keys from his pocket and set out like a phantom in the dead of night. Her body was pulsing with trepidation at the thought of being caught. She could almost feel Bear's enormous hand closing over her arm as she climbed into the driver's seat, yet she knew what had been slipped into their drinks was enough to knock out an animal much larger than he for several hours. Fortunately, the car had a full tank of gas which was more than adequate to reach San Felipe. Lupita breathed a sigh of relief at the sight of the fuel gage. The huge vehicle came to life immediately as she engaged the ignition switch. She then fortified herself with a deep breath and set out on her desperate journey. Her plan was to top off the tank in town before daylight. She knew her family was being watched and the mere thought of it made her sick with cold dread, so any chance of the Cadillac being intercepted must be avoided at all costs. She had but one opportunity to follow through with her dangerous plan. It was going to be a roll of the dice, but worth the gamble to save her brother. That's why she made no attempt to notify Diaz that she'd obtained his coveted red Cadillac. Lupita knew that if she reached the rough desert road south of San Felipe unseen, then her chances of being detected were indeed slim.

Fortunately, the military checkpoints set up to apprehend drug or gun runners were unoccupied so she had not been obligated to answer any questions from bored Mexican Army privates. Those checkpoints along the highway between Mexicali and San Felipe were operated by the military rather than federal or local police units. So many police chiefs were in the employ of various cartels, it was believed the military had a better chance of actually interdicting drug shipments. The only problem was one of manpower and so many checkpoints were operated only occasionally. Today, the lucky young señorita breezed through without being compelled to stop and perhaps fend off inappropriate advances from the young soldiers. After passing the abandoned checkpoint at El Crucero, she knew it was clear sailing thru to San Felipe and beyond.

One strange incident did happen just north of the sleepy fishing village of San Felipe. While driving by the gringo community of El Dorado Ranch, the big Cadillac inexplicably began to sputter and misfire as it pulled to the right onto the dirt shoulder. She had the impression that the car was driving her rather than the other way around. Lupita braked to a halt and turned off the motor fearing that the car might be overheating. She felt a wave of panic as she pulled the under-dash latch that released the hood, then got out and lifted the heavy cover to check the radiator. The engine was warm, but not excessively hot so she closed the hood and got back into the car, shaking her head with both relief and annoyance. She wiped the sweat forming on her brow and realized she was parked at the entrance to Zoo Road. She was very familiar with the location as her family, along with hundreds of other residents, had used it many times to observe the San Felipe 250 off-road race. It was a huge event for the town and brought in many tourists along with their dollars. By following the hard packed dirt route it allowed access through the foothills along Canyon las Cuevitas which led to the vast, dry salt flat of Laguna Diablo. For some reason, Lupita felt a strange urge to drive the Cadillac up Zoo Road and over to the dry laguna. It was as if a magnet was gently pulling her. She resisted, knowing there was nothing and nobody up there. She remembered that her older brother had told her of a canyon he'd discovered during an outing with friends that seemed to lead up to the ten thousand foot mountain of Picacho del Diablo. Thinking of Pedro brought her out of the trance, then she started the car and continued driving into San Felipe where she fueled the gas tank to the brim.

As she drove through town, the glow on the eastern horizon revealed the coming day was upon her. Grateful that she'd gotten this far, she resisted the urge to drop in on her parents. She just could not take the chance after having experienced the crazy circumstance of the car falling into her lap and then being able to escape with it. If it was taken from her now, she had no illusions that Pedro would be lost forever. As far as illusions go, Lupita was well aware that her ability to rescue him was slender to none, but she had to try. Blood is thick in her family, so she grimly set her jaw with determination and continued her journey.

Shortly after leaving town, she came to a "T" intersection.

Continuing straight ahead would lead her to the local airport. Turning left would take her along the beach route known as the 'South Campos,' where many expatriate gringos were building beachfront homes. She turned left and within one mile, the pavement ended and was replaced by hard-packed dirt. The washboard effect made her feel as if her teeth were shaking loose, although the huge car did seem to float well over the bumps and potholes. She stopped momentarily to let some air out of the tires which did soften the ride considerably. Also, to her relief, she saw that the tires were brand new. Good rubber was essential. Lupita was well aware that the next time she'd enjoy pavement would be many hours later all the way over on the other side of the Baja Peninsula. Mexico Highway One was not a good road at all, but at least it was paved and it would take all of the available daylight ahead of her to reach it.

As Lupita continued her journey southbound, the gathering sunlight allowed her to read the various roadside signs advertising the different campos. Just as she passed Campo Adriana, Campo Los Morritos, and Campo San Pedro, the sun broke the horizon and the entire landscape was instantly transformed by the harsh sunlight. It was as if nature had simply turned on a switch. Even though she'd witnessed this countless times as she grew up, the experience was still startling. The foothills to the west came alive with color and while the sun was just above the horizon the folds and canyons there were still shadowed, exposing the beauty as multi-dimensional. Along the road, Ocotillo cactus proudly displayed their brilliant red blooms which seemed to leap from the branch tips like fire. The color matched the liquid candy-red paint on the Cadillac perfectly, although Lupita could now see the beautiful paint job was dulled by a coating of dust. No matter, she thought, as her only task was to deliver the car to the ferry at La Paz and then follow her directions upon reaching the mainland.

Within another hour, the bumpy road entered the small expatriate town of Puertocitos. There was a short dirt runway there as well as a crumbling boat ramp allowing access for fishing boats into the small harbor. Various structures were perched along the hills that had been built by gringos who were drawn to this desolate area. A light breeze blew in from the Sea of Cortez and carried with it the odor of sulphur from the hot springs situated in natural lava rock pools right at the oceans edge. When the tides were optimum, the cool ocean salt water mixed perfectly with the scalding mineral liquid that was boiling from contact with molten lava deep below the rocky surface. Lupita knew that the natural spa was thought to heal everything from arthritis to male sexual disfunction. Since Lupita was inflicted with neither, she only thought of the place as a momentary distraction. Anyway, she didn't enjoy the odor which reminded her of rotten eggs. Her stomach had been ravaged by her unraveling nerves leaving her tolerance for the stench unacceptable. Besides, now was not the time for indulgence, so she continued driving. Little did Lupita know that the artifact hidden behind the Cadillac's rear seat upholstery was spawned from this very same molten-fiery lava, then spewed up from the depths to be found by the original humans many thousands of years before.

Oblivious to the true reason for her journey, she continued southward along the road that now consisted of dynamite-blasted lava and granite rock. Fortunately, she didn't meet any opposing traffic as the one-lane road was often perched precariously along cliffs that dropped vertically onto the beach hundreds of feet below. Beginning to feel the serious effects of total exhaustion from the overnight journey, Lupita felt depleted but knew she had no choice but to press on. She knew she would need to stop for a hot meal at the next area of civilization in Gonzaga Bay. Although she had never been this far south before, Lupita estimated that it would be mid-afternoon before she reached the next town. There was no choice but to continue and hope the huge red car would operate reliably. She knew she had been the recipient of uncommonly good luck so far and could only hope for it to continue. So, she carried on with caution on this dangerously scary thread of a road. There was nothing else to do but go forward.

18

Conscience

Manny sat with a sad stillness and mused on a part of his past that had long been hidden away. He rarely allowed himself to delve into the dark recesses of his heart, for it was too painful to bear. As he conjured up the images of *her*, he felt the shadows being lifted and he began to feel the familiar ache of loss. Why was Carmelina's memory coming back to him now, at this exact point in time? He could only think that it had something to do with Lupita. The thought dawned on him that his conversations with Pedro and the family resemblance caused his feelings to rise up. But, more than that, Manny knew deep inside that the lovely Lupita bore an uncanny resemblance to his first and only love.

He felt the tug in his chest and the shortness of breath as his body remembered what his mind tried so hard to forget. Carmelina had been his first and last love all those years ago in his early teens when an early romance can make or break you. She was a virtuous, patient, and forgiving girl from a good Catholic family. Why she had anything to do with the lowly criminal that Manny was, he had no idea. Yet they had fallen in love at once, during a white-hot summer there in Mazatlán. The smallest hint of a grin crept across his face as he remembered how she taught him to read and from her Bible, no less. She was so gentle and accepting of him, as if she saw the dimmest glimmer of salvation inside, begging to be let loose. Manny's smile turned into a bitter scowl as he thought of the end. Bits and pieces flashed and teased his memories. The frantic chase into a dead-end alleyway with no way out, no escape. He'd dodged the bullet meant for him, but in a cruel twist of fate, it had found his love. The thread of his thoughts invariably led to the only memory that truly haunted the man. His beloved Carmelina had died in his arms on the filthy ground as he watched the light fade from her eyes. Later, he had welcomed his time in jail, feeling it to be the purgatory he richly deserved. Manny aggressively shook his head, as if that would help to empty his mind of the memories. It was just too dangerous to remember.

Manny knew he had important business to attend to. His employer wanted more information from the captive Pedro and these interrogations were Manny's main task for the time being. He made his way to the quarters which held Pedro feeling a slight trepidation. He was having some trouble trying to understand this man whom he felt might be teetering on the brink of insanity. But perhaps, could it be that this madness was actually salvation? As he walked through the corridor leading up to the second floor suite, he made sure to enter with a guarded mind and heart. His earlier conversations with Pedro had opened up a door inside of Manny that had been long since shut off and he was embarrassed to admit he had almost believed Pedro and his ramblings of God and the Devil. It had been easy for Manny to believe that the only real Devil resided inside the hearts of living men. That certainly made it easier for him to reconcile his many brutal acts with a conscience that had been buried deep within. Now, he was not so sure.

He ascended the stairway, taking note of the luxury that was afforded to Pedro by a generous Enrique. Manny respected how his friend and employer utilized more humane tactics to obtain information from subjects in question. Enrique's uncle, on the other hand, was brutish and shortsighted with no patience or finesse when it came to interrogations. His own mother was even worse. The sadistic Yolanda had even tortured prisoners from rival cartels to death simply for the joy of it, without bothering to gather any useful information at all.

Pedro had been put up in the private wing of the fortress that was usually reserved for important guests and visitors. It contained a master suite equipped with a spacious sitting room, a bath area that could double as a small spa, and a wrap-around patio which overlooked the gardens and valley below. This was arguably the best view of the entire fortress. Manny walked past the lone, lazy guard slumped over in his chair, fast asleep. Enrique must have had little worry for Pedro being a flight risk and decided to enlist a more incompetent guard to take watch. He reached the french doors and knocked twice, then three times more to signal to Pedro that he'd arrived. The special knock had been arranged between the two men to grease the wheels and conjure a little trust. Pedro opened the door with a serene smile, greeting Manny with a warm handshake and motioned for him to enter the suite.

"Welcome back, *mi amigo.* Please make yourself at ease and take a seat wherever you like."

Manny nodded and thought to himself that he could and

would sit anyplace, regardless of the polite invitation from this man. Still, he was impressed by his manners despite being a prisoner of the cartel.

Pedro continued, "I've just been sitting on the patio and taking in some sunlight. I have been truly blessed to have a generous view such as this."

He swept his arm as if to display the expansive vista from his quarters. The patio overlooked a lush pine valley that seemed to stretch into forever.

"This is a far cry from the unforgiving deserts and salty sea of San Felipe."

Once again Manny thought of the dangerous location that had no real escape routes. Any encroaching enemies with enough force could possibly take over the fortress with ease. Not only had he been a witness to the brutal tactics of Alfredo and Yolanda, but he'd been a participant. Even though his employer's arrogance blinded them to this danger, Manny knew that all it would take would be for a few other organizations to band together and collectively eliminate the Diaz cartel once and for all.

Manny cast those thoughts aside as he smiled weakly at Pedro and took an Equipale chair, the leather groaning in protest. For the last few days, the two men had conversed mainly about Pedro and his newly found faith in God along with the grace he'd been subsequently awarded. This revelation intrigued Manny, as he thought it might be an easy way out after doing so many dirty deeds assigned to him by Alfredo. It seemed far too easy to hand everything over to God, to surrender the ego and even hope for forgiveness. Could it really be true that he could find the salve to absolve the personal guilt of his immoral actions? Manny listened and felt his closed mind being opened slowly to the possibilities of salvation being real and attainable to all that sought after it. It seemed that this man, Pedro, had the strange power of disarming the large and imposing Manny, not unlike the young Carmelina had done so long ago. Like Carmelina, Pedro's unflinching belief made an indelible impression on the somber cartel soldier.

"Perhaps we should take a walk below in the gardens to fully appreciate this glorious day God has awarded us. Pedro suggested this with a beaming grin. Manny fought back a laugh at this stupid fool's sappy enthusiasm, but agreed.

"After you, *amigo*," he said.

Manny then stood and walked to the patio veranda door to motion their departure down the steep, wrought-iron spiral staircase while being careful to grasp the railing as they descended. The layout was quite impressive. A brightly tiled fountain filled the air with the soothing tones of bubbling water. It really did put Manny at ease to spend time down here, regardless of his company. Alfredo spared no expense when it came to his beloved fortress. Every type of cacti and flora from the region had been used in its landscaping and the gardener could always be seen toiling away. On this day, Manny decided to shoot an imposing glance at him and the man only needed one look at that gruesome face, then disappeared immediately to work elsewhere. There were sculpted concrete benches placed throughout the gardens and many winding paths which showcased the impressive growth.

As always, Pedro had brought his Bible along with him as it was rarely out of his grasp. Scraps of colored paper protruded from the book, presumably marking pages that Pedro deemed worthy of note. This man was unequivocally convinced that he'd been touched, quite literally, by the Devil in the flesh and had lived to tell his tale. Many times had Pedro admonished Manny that since the Devil was real and not some myth, then it must follow that God also was real. One simply cannot exist without the other. Pedro had said this countless times and the complete transition in his behavior and faith was directly attributed to his life changing encounter. Manny grappled with the dichotomy of Pedro being either a textbook madman, or plainly and unabashedly honest. He spoke with such a calm conviction and he seemed completely serene and at peace. A stark-raving lunatic could not function at the level of composure which Pedro displayed. Manny had intimate knowledge of the evil to be found inside the hearts of men. He knew that a metaphysical creature was not necessary to bring this out in humanity. Even so, Manny felt a quiet and still voice inside him, gently persuading him to listen to this man, to *believe* him. So, he did just that, becoming the student rather than the investigator.

As they strolled through the gardens, Manny listened to Pedro insist about the healing power of salvation. He encouraged Manny to delve into the Holy Bible with a clear mind and open heart. Manny realized that he was supposed to be gleaning information about the Enchanted Valley and its magical spring, but most importantly, find out about the artifact. At the moment, those things just didn't seem important compared to the possibilities Pedro spoke of.

Manny abruptly stopped and said with false conviction in his voice, "Pedro, I have done many unforgivable things. God has surely given up on me. It is simply too late for change and I am in no position to abandon this lifestyle."

Pedro peacefully grinned again, saying, "It is never too late for even the most conflicted of souls, *mi amigo*. God will always be waiting to take you into his arms."

Manny found the nearest bench and took a seat. He gazed at the rows of agave that were grown at the fortress for Mezcal production. Alfredo fancied himself a connoisseur of the drink and had it produced right there on the grounds. But Manny did not use the potent drink or even snort his employer's product up his nose. He lowered his head into his hands and began to gently run his fingers over his badly damaged face. He winced as the mangled nerve endings screamed at him in protest. Manny thought of the lives he'd taken and how narrowly he had escaped his own demise numerous times. Could it be that the hand of God was protecting him, or was it merely dumb luck? The concept was too big for him to comprehend and he tried to push the thoughts away.

Pedro took a seat beside Manny and the two men sat in silence for a few moments. A pair of sparkling tailed hummingbirds gently hovered nearby, zipping throughout the shrubbery and flower beds. Manny then looked up at Pedro and came to a sudden realization of the close resemblance he held to his sister, Lupita. His profile had Lupita's likeness, but it was something else. Then it dawned on Manny that it was the smile. It was the same one that Pedro had been flashing at Manny so regularly during their meetings. He hadn't witnessed much emotion from Lupita other than fear and distain when their paths had crossed, but he knew the beauty the woman possessed could be truly unleashed when she smiled. He recognized this deep in his bones and didn't have to be the recipient of a friendly encounter with Lupita to understand it. The woman was simply radiant. With all his heart, he knew a woman like her could never love a man such as himself. And then there was something else again. He had the memory of another radiant creature with a smile so disarming that it could stop a man dead in his tracks. He had lived with the knowledge of his actions causing the death of Carmelina. He asked himself, why would God dangle the unobtainable Lupita before him? Could it possibly be God's punishment for his evil deeds? If so, Manny accepted that he deserved this Hell on Earth as punishment. It was a life sentence.

Manny did find an odd sense of comfort while spending time with Pedro. The man emanated a strange sense of truly knowing Manny from the inside out. As if Pedro could sense a weak spot in Manny's wall, he began to speak again.

"And Peter said to them, 'Repent and be baptized every one of you in the name of Jesus Christ for the forgiveness of your sins and you will receive the gift of the Holy Spirit.'"

Manny turned his head to Pedro and cocked an eyebrow as if to say, 'Oh, really... are you certain of this?'

"Matthew 6:14 *mi buen hombre*. It is never too late to be forgiven and in turn, to forgive yourself." Pedro said this with a glint of sadness in his eyes. He seemed to sense the deep well of turmoil that was brewing within Manny and truly wanted to help his new-found friend. The last few days had forged a sense of trust between the men and he appreciated the patience Manny awarded him. The other guards and cartel lackeys treated him like he was a loco delirante.

"If I can be so lucky as to have escaped a life of filth and greed, then so could you."

Manny stood up again and continued to walk along the garden pathway. Pedro rose and followed closely. They walked in slow silence taking in the sights of doves bathing in the fountain and orange monarchs stretching their wings in the lantana beds while they reflected on the life all around them, unencumbered by the contradictions of being human.

"This is truly a magnificent hacienda I have been afforded, given the circumstances. I do not take this garden for granted in the least," Pedro said. "But I have been witness to a place much greater than that before us. A place so magnificent and pure that you could not even imagine."

Manny knew what he was getting at.

"You mean the place where the artifact came from, don't you? Where Diaz sent you to retrieve it?"

Pedro nodded solemnly then said, "Si, I did not believe it with my own eyes at first. But, *mi amigo*, it is true and it very much exists. Although I am forgiven in the eyes of my Lord, I do regret the life I took and how this most holy of places is now left with no one to protect it." Pedro looked up at the clear blue sky and Manny could tell his next statement was not directed at him. "If only I could be led upon that path once again so that I might devote my life to protecting that which I intended to harm."

Manny knew the tales of this hidden utopia, but was hesitant to fully believe in them. Then again, why would Pedro feel the need to lie or fabricate such details if he had been fully transformed overnight? He'd spoken nothing but the truth since the incident in which he claimed to be touched by the Beast.

Pedro stopped talking and hung his head in shame as he rummaged through his thoughts. Then he lifted his head and began again.

"*Dios mío*, our Lord knows what was in my heart for he sees all. I myself was a victim to it's great powers. The influence it holds is compelling and makes a man do unimaginable things. Unforgivable things."

Pedro continued, "The place of which I speak is untarnished by the dirty hands of humanity and is guarded by an ancient people that have remained unseen for centuries. They have protected the powerful *artefacto* ,knowing fully well what would happen if it were placed into the wrong hands. Now, because of my transgression, it is out there in the world being pursued by evil men that wish to wield it's power to create more death and destruction."

Pedro looked up and straightened his shoulders once again.

"But I have full repentance now, and my Lord and Savior

knows my sins have been washed clean."

Manny gave a slight smile as he nodded knowingly at Pedro. He understood the meaning of sin all too well, but it was the forgiveness part that escaped him. He knew how unrelenting Alfredo Diaz could be when it came to something he coveted. Nothing could prevent his desire and he would pillage and plunder all the way to that mountaintop in order to declare it his. He would still any beating heart that became useless to him, including Pedro and his sister Lupita, once the ancient artifact was in his possession. If anyone could find this fabled red Cadillac and deliver it, Manny knew Lupita would. He also felt a pang of guilt for keeping Lupita's forced conscription secret. He had come to care for Pedro and realized how distressed he'd be if he knew his sister was involved with Alfredo Diaz's obsession over the artifact. Although Manny was unsure about the rumors of power and compulsion manifested within the thing, he knew Pedro believed and would most likely go insane with grief and guilt to know his sister was anywhere near it. Like a heavy, cold stone in his gut, Manny understood there was much more to Diaz's diabolical scheme, but was unsure if he had the ability to stop it.

19

El Clásico

       Cesar Pastor sat at a round table in the conference room at his headquarters in Nogales. Also seated at the table were his most trusted lieutenants and advisors. Pastor had chosen the round table format in order to encourage participation from his inner circle. He knew that sitting at the head of a more traditional table would set him apart from these men and he wanted to foster open participation from all. He treated these men that he had known since childhood as equals, but there was no doubt that he was their leader. Pastor had the look of a vaquero. He had been raised in the saddle by his rancher father and to be astride a good mount was the most natural feeling in the world. As his wealth and power grew, he never forgot his humble beginnings. The border area between Nogales and Agua Prieta was as familiar to him as one's own backyard. When the flow of marihuana and cocaine began to infiltrate into the U.S. through Douglas and Tucson in the sixties,

162

young Cesar Pastor had the knowledge and ability to facilitate the transportation. He was also blessed with an uncommonly keen business sense.

Now in his mid forties, he remembered the lessons he'd gleaned from watching American news broadcasts of the Republican president, Reagan and his philosophy of trickle-down economics. It intrigued him and prompted him to learn English. The idea of supply and demand made perfect sense to the young Cesar and thus his burgeoning enterprise supplied the demand from north of the border. His demeanor was best described as calm, cool, and collected. It was strictly the business opportunity that had motivated Pastor and as far as trickle down went, he spread the growing income equally among his men. They were loyal to a fault and Pastor loved and protected them. The bribes handed out to local law enforcement were as much to facilitate movement of the product as they were to keep his workers out of jail.

Not only did he take care of his men, he was active in the community and provided generous assistance to schools and orphanages. It was for this reason he'd obtained the nickname of, "El Clásico." Children would affectionately sing narcocorridos to him as he passed by on the street, to which he would tip his hat in appreciation. Much of the población under his influence were content with the way the man ran his empire. It was his doting control which held the society together. Stealing, kidnapping, and extortion were almost obsolete under Pastor's reign. He generously gave to the poor, paved roads in dire need of repair, and gave countless members of the community steady jobs. He ruled his empire with an iron fist and used the other hand to comfort and embrace it's inhabitants. Any ruthlessness or unsavory behavior that always accompanied drug trade was well hidden by his immaculate public relations. He was also a fervent believer of Jesus Malverde, the patron saint of Mexican drug trafficking, who was a Robin Hood type that took from the rich to give to the poor. Statues and idols of the saint were placed throughout his compound and he always made sure he kneeled and prayed to his revered saint several times a day.

Cesar Pastor was whipcord lean and ruggedly handsome with the look of a dignified vaquero. He was always impeccably, yet reasonably, dressed in his exotic python snakeskin boots equipped with spurs made from custom handcrafted silver. The man could be heard coming from what seemed to be a mile away. Another trademark of his was a leather bolo tie containing a large scorpion cast in resin. He'd snatched that very scorpion out of a baby's bassinet, and absorbed the sting, before it could harm the innocent child. The child's mother smothered him with kisses and blessings, so he kept the predatory arachnid as a reminder to himself about the importance of taking care of his people.

A weather-beaten straw cowboy hat hid his now balding forehead, but he was still considered a catch by the local señoritas as he'd remained single all these years. He could have been the model for the Marlboro Man advertisement except he didn't smoke, drink, or use any of the product his fortune was based on. It was strictly business as far as he was concerned and excessive violence was not good for business. That was why he had called his trusted compadres to the meeting.

Pastor opened the meeting by saying, "*Mis amigos*, we all know of the disastrous result when trying to include the Baja route for shipping product northward. Five good men were lost, three in the panga and two more when their truck was hi-jacked. Our intelligence has only just found the perpetrators of these murders. As you know, we thought it was the Tijuana operation that thwarted our exploratory mission. Now, it has come to my attention that it was Diaz who blocked our operations and killed my men."

Pastor's demeanor was normally composed and passive. However, it was clear to the seven men sitting around the table that el jefe was mad as hell. He knew the men that had been dispatched for the inaugural foray into the alternative Baja route. There was an expectation that violence could occur, but it was worth the risk because of the vast wilderness of that region and the perception that more than one operation could prosper there.

He continued, "I had thought that an alliance could be maintained with Tijuana and expect product from the mainland to be brought across the border at San Diego could be mutually profitable. Now, his investigation has revealed the tragic loss of men and cargo was done by the Diaz group. I am assured that no person from Arruza's business dealings was involved."

Ismael Glison, Cesar's right-hand man, motioned for permission to speak. Cesar nodded in deference to Glison.

"We must assume that this *imbécil* Diaz, is attempting the same strategic plan but without first making the required connections with Tijuana. It is well known that this *idiota* spends more time sucking coca off the bellies of his whores than using his brain. If this is allowed to continue we will find ourselves overwhelmed with internal warfare."

"This is true," continued Cesar, "but the death of our *amigos* must not be overlooked. If there are no consequences for this insult, we may find ourselves fighting Diaz here in Nogales when he decides to expand into our region. A strong response must be designed that will make further encroachment undesirable."

Cesar looked directly across the round table at his long time friend, Jorge de Jesus. Jorge was a huge bull of a man with a shaved bullet-shaped head and a dark black goatee sprouting from a perpetually scowling visage. This was a man that you did not cross under any circumstances. He was in charge of security and enforcement for the organization. It was unusual for him to speak up during these meetings as he preferred to carry out his orders quickly and efficiently. He had been drafted into the Mexican military at the tender age of seventeen. Later, men of his brigade had been invited to the United States to participate in a cross border relations exercise. He excelled in the Special Forces training which not only included weapons and tactics but advanced classes on leadership and intelligence. The overall plan for this cooperative exercise was meant to bolster Mexico's ability to harness the drug operations south of the border. This training was valuable when he became a master at outwitting the U.S. Border patrol as they attempted to stem the flow of drugs northward.

Cesar Pastor said, "*Capitán* de Jesus, please give us your assessment of the threat and what would be the proper response."

"*Sí señor*, I have already looked into this matter and find the threat to be considerable. Alfredo Diaz has proven himself to be ruthless and unconcerned with risk."

Jorge had a deep rumbling voice and an unnerving way of looking at whomever we was speaking to with an unblinking stare. Cesar was used to it, but most found it easy to look away.

He continued, "In my opinion it will be costly but the head of this *serpiente de cascabel* must be removed. If not, the price tag will only increase as time goes by. My men are well trained and armed. We have plans for a direct assault on this place called *Fortaleza del Aquila*. I have a small group of commandos ready for a reconnaissance mission. But it already appears that while the structure is sound, the security is lazy and a properly equipped force will be able to easily breach the defense."

He slid a large manila envelope across the table toward Cesar saying, "Here is the outline I have prepared for your approval. It provides for a stealth approach and control of the only road into the area. The assault will be sudden and overwhelming. The goal is to eliminate Diaz and his sister along with the other operatives present. We propose to attack just as daylight fades so that maximum confusion will prevail. This timeline also allows our force to retreat under the cover of darkness. We have learned that a sudden and surgical approach such as this will produce the maximum effect with minimum casualties. Since this would be an intramural conflict, the *federales* would not be involved and the possibility of collateral damage is non-existent."

Pastor nodded thoughtfully as he reached for the envelope. His first impulse was to avoid conflict and the resulting loss of life. However, reaching out to Diaz and trying to form an alliance seemed to have a very unlikely chance of success. He knew that there is a cost to doing business and to make a small payment up front was better than being forced to empty your pockets later.

He stood up, signaling the end of the meeting and said, "Alright *mis amigos*, we have much to consider. I will call another meeting within the week to formalize plans. I expect each of you to coordinate with Jorge to determine the logistics needed to support his plan. Jorge, please send in your reconnaissance team. I want no surprises if we decide to go forward."

After his compadres left the room, Cesar sat down again, alone with his thoughts. Things seemed to be getting out of hand. In the early years it had been so easy to move drugs northward. Now, there was aerial surveillance, listening devises, infra-red detection, and a Border Patrol in the north that was more like a disciplined army force. Even so, it seemed as if the greatest threats were now coming from within his own nation. He felt like he was being squeezed from within and without. More than anything he longed for solitude and the days of old on horseback, when his pockets were empty yet his mind was free. His dream was to return to raising fighting bulls for the Gran Corridas de Toros in Mexicali and Tijuana as his father had done. Señor Pastor had a reputation for producing the best toros arrogantes for fighting and it was a source of tremendous family pride. Perhaps he would follow his father's footsteps someday. However, for now he had responsibility for the men under his administration. They have their families, Cesar realized, and I have the responsibility. He knew it wouldn't take much motivation to trade places with any one of them.

20

A Harsh Land

The sun was finally setting as the trio pulled into the Papa Fernandez Campo just north of Gonzaga Bay. It had been an extremely rough ride, for sure. The journey from the border town of Algodones to San Felipe did nothing to prepare Hubie and Bear for what was to come. After topping off the tank in town, Gomez Gomez drove Christine south until the pavement gave way to dirt. He came to a halt briefly, lowered the pressure in all four tires, then set out again like they were in some kind of off-road race. Bear and Hubie glanced nervously at each other and both men were alarmed by Gomez's maniacal driving. He explained that keeping the speed up caused the vehicle to float over the washboard. When Gomez slowed down to provide an example, Bear and Hubie felt as if their teeth were shaking loose. Their driver smiled and nodded knowingly as his weathered face folded in on itself in amusement. He then immediately mashed the gas pedal flat. His passengers had no further complaint as the rooster tail of dust marked their path. At least the dust plume was behind them.

They saw no other travelers on that lonely road, just the occasional lizard running frantically across their path or evil red-headed vultures feasting on some rotting carcass by the road. It was evident to these gringos that death was a way of life in this desolate landscape. The sun was relentless, the heat oppressive, and the primitive air conditioner quickly exhausted it's meager water supply. Gomez Gomez continued forward with an attitude that made it obvious he would remain relentless in his pursuit. The only stop was made at the tiny expatriate town of Puertocitos.

Gomez turned off the main road, if you could call it that, and drove his old Chevy up a winding trail flanked by dilapidated structures that seemed to be mostly abandoned.

"It's the *gringos*," Gomez explained. "They come in the winter season, then flee north from the heat."

He continued driving up the bumpy dirt road that divided the empty seasonal homes. Hubie and Bear could see the small bay on their right, protected from the ocean by the sweeping arm of volcanic rock that they were riding on. As the vehicle topped the rise, a beautiful view of the Sea of Cortez became evident, as well as an overwhelming stench of rotten eggs. Below, at the waters edge was a series of bubbling tide pools emitting an acrid odor of sulfur wafting their way, being propelled by the light onshore breeze.

"Dude," Hubie exclaimed. "That's some odiferous malfeasance, for sure!"

"This *mal olor* is most unpleasant *mis amigos*, but it is the essence of creation. In this place the earth is thin where the fires of creation and damnation flow together. This is where the original people discovered the *Artefacto Precioso*. They soon discovered that it resonates with all that is good and evil. For this reason, it is most *imperativo* that this object be retrieved immediately. Have patience, we will only be a moment."

Gomez stopped the car next to a small rock pathway that led down to the steaming water. The tide was out and there was no doubt that entering those pools at this time would send a person to the hospital burn ward. He walked down the pathway to the edge of the first pool. Hubie and Bear stayed by the car having no desire to be any closer to this portal that belched nasty skank from the very bowels of the earth.

They watched as their companion knelt by the waters and bowed his head. Then he began to speak in a strange language with odd inflection that was almost like a song. He spoke, singing to the earth, then raised his head to the sky while spreading his arms wide and continued the strange cadence. Gomez repeated this ritual a few times. The two men watched this unfold and both recognized they were witnessing something very ancient indeed. For some reason, both Hubie and Bear felt humbled by the experience. Then, Gomez stood up and returned to the car.

"We must go, now," he said. Hubie and Bear piled back into the low rider and off they went.

The trio rode in silence for some time. Gomez had quickly maneuvered his Chevy back through the small port town and then up onto the rough volcanic road that had been blasted through the lava flows. At this point he slowed down to a near crawl at times, explaining that the sharp rock could easily take out a tire. After some time passed, Bear, who was still riding shotgun could no longer contain his curiosity.

"So," Bear rumbled at their driver. "Just what was that all about, really? For a moment I thought you might dive into that water and we'd be having boiled Gomez for dinner."

Gomez Gomez laughed out loud at the thought of diving into a boiling lobster pot. He looked over his shoulder at

Hubie who was sitting behind Bear and decided his American companions deserved a more clear picture of what they were up against.

"You will recall our conversation this morning at the bar, and how you became cured from your afflictions by drinking the water I offered you?"

Both men nodded enthusiastically as they remembered the miraculous cure.

Gomez continued, "My companions, the way of the world in all things is pulled by good and evil. They go one with another, hand to hand and always present. This is something my people have always understood. We have no written word of history. Our experience with books only came to us from the Jesuits who sought to destroy our way of living. Our heritage of knowledge is passed down through generations by word alone. In this way, our truth is not polluted or diminished in any way. We witnessed the arrival of Spanish explorers that were accompanied by Priests and slaves." He paused as his eyes seemed to darken slightly. "Our blood has never mingled with these intruders, and never will."

He stopped talking for a moment as he negotiated a sharp curve in the primitive lava road. On the right, a sheer wall of rock reached toward the cloudless sky. On the left, within a few feet of the tires, the drop fell straight down to the beach at least five hundred feet below. Although unspoken, all three agreed that this was a place for paying attention to the task of driving. The view to the east of the azure-blue Sea of Cortez was a contrast not lost on the men. Beauty and danger were always present in this harsh land.

Presently, the rocky cliffside road descended toward flat terrain interrupted by the occasional dry arroyo. Hubie was greatly relieved, of course, but now they were back on the washboard dirt track so Gomez Gomez stepped on it once again. He raised his voice in order to overcome the constant thrum of vibration as the vehicle sped forward.

"You have heard tales of the Fountain of Youth and the Spaniards that searched for the fable?" Once again his companions nodded with affirmation. "Well, *mis amigos*, you have tasted that very water this morning. We, of the originals protect this place as well as the *Artefacto*. It must not be allowed discovery by those that currently shape destiny. There have been five great extinctions on this earth. The last was caused by a great rock from above. However, not all life perished. The one that dared take it came to know the true face of evil from a world that existed long before the current one evolved. I have told you the story of how the *Artefacto* came to be placed in your Cadillac, yes? And now you must understand that this thing can never be allowed to fall into the hands of Diaz, the Diabolic One. The power is just too great for one such as he to control. It must be returned, then a new human to watch over it will be selected. The Chupacabra assists in this protection. The balance of good and evil, you see? That balance must be regained."

Now that they could keep their speed up, the miles raced by. As daylight diminished, Hubie and Bear began to worry that they'd be driving out there in the darkness. Just as the sun fell below the western mountain peaks, Gomez turned left onto an almost unrecognizable track marked by a small sign proclaiming, "Papá Fernandez." Less than a mile down this dirt road they came upon a small settlement that would be recognized as an oasis by any weary traveler. They stopped in front of a small one-room building constructed of native rock and mortar. There was a covered patio on two sides of the structure with picnic tables indicating it was the local eatery. Huge Piñon trees provided shade. All three men were grateful to exit the vehicle after the bone jarring ride.

As they entered the restaurant, Gomez was immediately

greeted by two short women showing great enthusiasm. One was young and curvaceous, with an inviting smile. She wore a white apron around her middle and her jet-black hair was pulled back into a bun. The other woman was elderly yet spry in her movements. She hugged Gomez tightly then rushed through the door calling out for someone named Gorgonio.

Hubie took in the contents of the small room. It had picnic tables just like outside and there was a kitchen area behind the counter in one corner. Many photos festooned the walls, most reflecting grinning white men holding up prize catches of Grouper, Dorado, White Sea Bass, and Marlin. One photo noted by Hubie featured John Wayne. Also in the picture was a dark Mexican man wearing a straw hat and sporting a pair of black framed glasses. He barely came up to Wayne's breast pocket. Hubie realized the photo must be at least twenty years old, possibly thirty.

The screen door banged open and the very same man from the photo entered. To Hubie's surprise, he didn't look a day older than his image next to the Duke. Gomez and the short Mexican greeted each other warmly while speaking in that unknown dialect. They reverently touched foreheads together, then took seats at a corner table with the expectation of privacy. Noticing this, Hubie and Bear respectfully took over a table on the other side of the room. Without asking, the pretty young gal presented each with an ice cold Tecate, complete with a slice of lime stuck into the neck of each bottle. Before they even finished the first beers, another pair was presented in front of the two men.

Hubie looked up into the smiling face of their waitress. She had loosened her hair which now flowed across one shoulder and down onto her ample left breast. She giggled openly at Hubie then boldly took his long blond pony tail into her hand to examine.

"Dios mío," she exclaimed, *"cuál es tu nombre?"*

Hubie didn't understand her, so Bear told him, "She wants to know your name Boss."

"Oh, Hubie, and he's Bear."

She seemed to understand after looking at the huge man and said, *"Oso grande, muy bien."*

Just then the elder woman spoke sharply from the kitchen so the giggling waitress hurried back to work. In less than ten minutes the two Gringos were presented with refried beans, carne, tortillas, and salsa with freshly fried tortilla chips. As they began to dive in, the young woman poked Hubie in the shoulder, then pointed to herself.

"Rosa," she said matter of factly, then once again returned to the kitchen. She gave a provocative glance at Hubie from over her shoulder as her elder companion rolled her eyes then began to speak rapidly in obvious discontent. Bear laughed at Hubie's embarrassment.

"I guess if we're stay'n here, we'd best get separate quarters, huh?"

"Shut up Bear," Hubie replied. "You're scaring me!"

Just as they were finishing their meal, and a fourth beer each, the man named Gorgonio left and Gomez joined them.

"That was Papá Fernandez. He feels sure that your Cadillac passed by earlier. While it is true he did not directly witness her, he is certain the presence of the artifact was near."

"How could he possibly know that?" asked Bear, with raised eyebrows.

"Because he is one of us," Gomez replied as he placed his hand over his heart. "He has been here for many years. This place was left over from Spaniards that first came exploring in 1746. The well they dug is still supplying water to this *campo*. But the native peoples wanted nothing to do with the Jesuit missionary named Fernand Consag and his soldiers.

They had made slaves of other Native Americans. Papá Fernandez reclaimed the well when he came here to open the fishing *campo*. Later, he brought his family all the way from Loreto in an open rowboat. That *hombre* is legendary, and if he says something is so, then it is the truth."

By now it was full dark and Gomez declared they would be back out on the road before first light. It was his hope that Lupita would push herself too hard and perhaps become stranded on the lonely road ahead. At any rate, he wasn't willing to take a chance on getting foolishly stuck in the night. The elderly woman appeared at the door with a kerosene lantern and beckoned the three to follow her. There were unused cabins close to the restaurant and she led each man individually to his own room. Hubie was reminded of the crude quarters he used back at the Hawaiian bar, only this one had a wooden-plank floor. As far as accommodations went, there was the single bed with nightstand and a small bathroom with toilet and shower together. With no electricity, the room was lit with a candle upon the nightstand. The sheets were clean, so the weary Hubie dropped his clothing to the floor then climbed into bed.

Much later, he was awakened by a soft noise. The door to his cabin was open and he could see that the full moon was up. Then, the doorway was filled with a silhouette that whispered something quietly in Spanish.

"*Es Rosa*," the voice said as she entered Hubie's cabin.

Hubie sat straight up and began to protest but she was already across the small room. She gently placed her hand upon his mouth, pushing him back into his bed.

"*No tengas miedo*," she whispered. She removed her hand from Hubie's mouth and replaced it with her lips. Then she shed her gown by pulling it up and over her head. The moonlight revealed her generous female charms as she pulled back Hubie's covers and slipped into bed with the stunned gringo.   Hubie forgot about his protests and in a few moments even forgot where he was.

21

Recon

The rusty, battered Dodge pickup truck topped the long upgrade and came to a halt in front of a steel double-tube barrier that was chained together in the middle and designed to be folded back for opening. Although the road into the mountainous terrain had been rough and full of potholes, the two men in the Dodge noticed the pavement beyond the barrier was fresh and looked as if it had been recently paved.

In fact, there was no detail that the truck's occupants missed. Their eyes and minds had been keenly trained to operate with laser focus. On the right side of the barrier was a small adobe shack with a shaded palm-frond cover across the front side. The hum of a gasoline powered electric generator was obvious and the long antenna reaching skyward from the shack's roof made it clear there was a method for communication to what was beyond the barrier. In the stifling mid-afternoon air, the odor of marijuana was apparent to both men.

Jorge de Jesus portrayed a silly grin on his face as one guard emerged from the shack and approached the passenger side of the Dodge. The other guard remained seated on the bench in front of the shack and continued leaning against the wall. His automatic rifle, also leaning against the wall remained untouched, just out of his reach. De Jesus immediately recognized the weapon as the Belgian made FN Minimi Squad Automatic with a thirty-round magazine in place. He knew the automatic rifle well as it was a mainstay weapon for the Mexican Army. He also knew the weapon was useless, as it was propped carelessly against the wall, out of reach of the stoned guard who seemed to be barely aware of his surroundings.

Jorge's companion took in every detail as well. The baby-faced young man's appearance of naive innocence hid the fact that he was one of the toughest hombres around. He also put an easy grin upon his face as the guard approached. The man looked into the pick-up bed and saw five hay bales stacked inside, but nothing else. He then looked into the cab and breathed out a vile cloud of stale alcohol stench which wafted over both men. There was no doubt the guard was coming off a heavy night of drinking and was in the throes of a massive hangover.

The young passenger turned his head to the left in disgust. He looked over at de Jesus with an expression on his face that left no doubt as to what he would likely do if the circumstances were different. If the two lackadaisical guards had any idea of whom they were dealing with, they would have most likely already been firing their weapons. Chuy Jimenez was known as El Asesino for his cool manner of taking a life with gun, knife, or garrote. Although barely out of his teen years, Jimenez had been a loyal soldier of Cesar Pastor's organization for many years. It had been his young sister that Pastor saved by snatching the deadly scorpion from her bassinet. The memory of that life saving action was apparent from the scorpion mounted in the bolo tie that Pastor often wore. All members of the Jimenez family would willingly die for Cesar Pastor and Chuy was no different. If El Clásico asked something of Chuy, there were no questions, only action.

"Hey, *Hombres*, the road is closed, *Cerrado*. What are you doing up here, there is nothing for you here," the guard said.

Still displaying his friendly mannerism, de Jesus replied, *"Señor*, we have hay for delivery at *El Rancho Angeles*, but perhaps we have missed the proper *camino*."

"Si, baboso, turn around, there is no *Rancho* here."

The drunken guard stepped back from the Dodge and waved his left arm back down the way they'd come. Chuy noticed that the man's right hand rested on the grip of the Beretta automatic pistol holstered at his hip. Neither de Jesus nor young Jimenez were armed as they had to anticipate the possibility of being searched. This was a reconnaissance probe only, so they turned the truck around and headed back down the mountain. Jorge had discovered all the information needed anyway so it was time to go.

This was not the first time that Chuy had accompanied the older de Jesus in anticipation of an operation. He was once again amazed at the direct manner that Jorge applied in situations such as this one. He had often told his young companion that people usually only see what they want to see. The farmer that sold them his Dodge was more than happy to accept five thousand U.S. Dollars and felt no need to ask questions. Jorge even told the man where he could find the truck later. Now, it was time to return to Mazatlán and brief his strike team that were waiting in various hotels away from the tourist areas. No need to arouse suspicion with a large group of strange men together in one place with several

SUV's.

As they bounced back down the rough road, Chuy began to pepper Jorge with questions.

"Be still *mi hijo*, I know you want first chance at those assholes," said the elder man. "You will lead the team from where we stop out of sight down below. There is plenty of cover and those *idiotas* will be easy for us. When we have completed the task, we'll rejoin the main team and have the advantage of surprise. We must use caution that no message will be sent."

Chuy nodded with consent. He knew the drill.... take out the guards silently, then disable the radio.

Jorge continued, "We'll dump this truck, then assemble the team for briefing. The plan will be approved when we use the satellite phone this evening to contact Pastor. As I see it, tomorrow evening as the sun sets will be the time to strike. Be patient, you and I will be the first in and the guards will be eliminated, quickly and silently."

Chuy Jimenez was satisfied knowing he'd be first in with the commander he loved and respected. The strike would be quick and deadly efficient at tomorrow's twilight. Then, retreat and dispersal would have the best chance of success under cover of darkness. As usual, it was to be a perfect military operation with the outcome firmly in control of de Jesus' trained team.

*****

At that very moment, Lupita waited dockside in La Paz for the cargo trucks to be loaded onto the ferry. Only after they were driven aboard were automobiles allowed. The young woman was reeling with fatigue. She had barely slept during the long drive and that was in the Cadillac's rear seat in the parking lot of a hotel in Loreto. She was unwilling to separate herself from the vehicle except for the few short minutes she allowed to access the luxury of the lobby restroom at the Hotel San Gabriele. Lupita had armed herself with four plastic one-gallon containers of drinking water and a sack full of burritos from a street vendor. The desire to trade the outrageous red Cadillac for her brother, Pedro, was her only thought. That's what kept her going while she drove straight though to La Paz. Her only priority was to gain passage on the ferry across the Sea of Cortez that would carry her to Mazatlán.

She almost didn't get on the ferry at all. When she attempted to purchase her ticket, the official told her the boat was full. Realizing that begging or relying on her feminine wiles would get her nowhere, she produced ten crisp hundred-dollar bills, U.S. from the manila envelope that Manny had given her so long ago, it seemed. The attendant disappeared into the back room momentarily, then quickly returned with her authorization to board the boat. After being directed into the loading area, the ferry gate was closed behind the Caddy. Lupita observed the loading agent in the rear view mirror arguing with a very upset customer that had lost his spot. She didn't care, as she had secured passage on the ferry and that was all that mattered.

After the large eighteen-wheel cargo trucks had been loaded and the pedestrian passengers were all aboard, the automobiles were directed up the loading ramp onto the fantail as the huge ferry rocked gently at its mooring. Lupita's was the final vehicle loaded and as she exhaled a weary sigh of relief, the weight of fatigue fell upon her. Knowing it would be a thirteen hour ride to the mainland and that she'd be arriving long after midnight, she simply rolled over the front seat and promptly fell asleep in the back as if she were a baby in the arms of her madre. She was oblivious to the noise and motion that occurred when the large boat was cast off, the diesel engines roaring with power as they headed out to the open sea.

Lupita was also oblivious to the fact that Gomez Gomez, Bear, and Hubie had only just arrived at the La Paz Ferry loading dock and could clearly see the red Cadillac on the fantail as the large vessel departed. As they forlornly watched their prize leaving it was not lost on the three men how close they'd come to realizing their goal. Gomez was especially distraught and reacted in a manner that his two companions had not yet observed.

"Maldita sea!" Gomez exclaimed vehemently. *"Mierda,"* he added. Then, the compact native kicked one of the iron poles holding a chain which prevented them from driving into the dock area so hard he almost broke his big toe. The pain seemed to calm him down some, but it was apparent that his overwhelmingly distraught condition would not diminish so easily.

All three of the men felt the same way. For Hubie, the sight of his beloved Cadillac with his precious cassette collection heading out to sea created even more frustration. Bear, knowing that Lupita was most certainly aboard that ship and heading into harm's way made him feel as if he would explode from inaction. As for Gomez, the realization that their journey was to become even more difficult and dangerous did not belie the fact that there would be no turning back. It was the wait until the next ferry the following morning which proved to be the worst. It meant they would have no choice but to snatch the Artefacto from within the den of thieves and cutthroats that waited on the remote mountaintop. No matter, it had to be done. If it was to be done the hard way, then so be it. The fact that they had come so close yet were so far weighed heavily on Gomez.

"Mis Amigos," Gomez said. "We have no choice but to wait for *mañana.* For now, all we can do is find rooms and

comida. We will rest and fill our bellies against the next day that will surely test our resolve."

Hubie thought about that for a moment then said, "I guess you mean the plan is to keep chasing that little *señorita* no matter where she goes?"

Before Gomez could reply, Bear spoke up, "Boss, this kicks the shit out of clearing belligerent drunks out of your bar, so I'm in. When have we ever had this much fun anyway?"

Hubie considered Bear's comment about having fun as he reminisced about the bone-jarring three-day drive over the worst road he could ever imagine. He did have to admit that his surprise encounter back at the Papá Fernandez Campo was completely unexpected. It did place a whole new meaning on the word, 'Fun.' In fact, Hubie would have been happy to just remain there for a time. He was finding it difficult to get the smiling Rosa out of his mind. She had a certain way about her, which Hubie found compelling.

Gomez settled it, "*Vamos amigos*, there are many cold *cervezas* waiting. Let us not hesitate."

The three adventurers got back into Gomez's Chevy and set off looking for a bar. Maintaining their throat's dry status would not help the next morning arrive any sooner.

Cadillac Hubie

22

End of the Road

The long ferry journey was just what Lupita needed. She was able to sleep soundly for at least ten hours and was awake and ready when the vessel docked in Mazatlán just before daybreak. Lupita wasted no time driving the bright red car through town as quickly as possible. Her only stop was at a Pemex gas station in order to top off the gas tank. She knew the outrageous automobile would attract attention and she saw no need to encounter curious policía, federales, or any greedy criminales vying to capture such a prize as the car represented.

After leaving Mazatlán, she found a secluded place off the road and consulted the map included with the instructions Manny had provided her. She saw that taking route 40D would lead up into the mountainous terrain east of the resort town. At a small village named Chirimoyos it would be necessary to take a side route up into the very remote area where the headquarters named Fortaleza del Aguila were located. Lupita felt immense dread and anxiety over what could happen if she did not complete her task. She had no choice but to try her best to ignore the fear and continue no matter what the future might bring. Even if she turned around and ran, she knew Enrique and Manny would eventually find her. In that case, it would be a certainty that her brother would die as well as her mamá y padre. The young woman was not so naive as to think Pedro would be released and that they would just continue on their merry way, but at least she had to try. Her only hope for success was that Enrique and the hardened Manny would honor the agreement. At any rate, the journey from Mazatlán would only take two hours and then all would be revealed. She pressed on with a determination she didn't really feel.

After leaving the main highway at Chirimoyos, the road became a rough winding mess as it continued ever higher toward her destination. Lupita slowed considerably in order to prevent a blowout or some other calamity such as going over the side of the steep and dangerous trail. She'd come so far without disaster and was so close that she was unwilling to take any chances. As it was, even with slowing down, she topped a rise and came to a halt in front of a steel barrier by mid-morning. Two armed guards immediately emerged from their shack and approached the Cadillac. By their manner, it was obvious to Lupita that she was expected.

One man carried an evil looking military rifle which he pointed menacingly at the car as he took up a position behind it. Lupita was not going anywhere. The other guard, armed with a holstered sidearm, swiftly moved in front of the vehicle to the driver's side and immediately reached in across Lupita's body to remove the ignition keys.

"*Señorita,*" he said, you are Lupe Martinez, no? You and your vehicle will remain here for now."

He then returned to the guard shack and Lupita could see through the doorway that he was using a radio microphone to call someone. She could also see that the man was very excited as he spoke. He seemed to be very pleased with himself. After completing the call, he walked swiftly to the barrier and opened both sides wide. He then took up position in front of the car as he waited.

In a short while, a large black Chevrolet SUV approached from beyond the open barrier. It slid to a halt and Manny emerged from the driver's side as Enrique appeared from the other. Enrique grinned broadly but Manny seemed to be taciturn and serious as always.

"Greetings, *Señorita Martinez*," Enrique said as he opened her door and graciously motioned for her to get out. *"Muchísimas gracias*, I will take this one, you will ride with Manny."

Manny took Lupita firmly by her elbow as he led her to the open passenger door of the SUV. He quickly turned the SUV around and started back up the paved road while Enrique followed with the Cadillac. At this point, Manny seemed to soften a little.

"Lupita, may I ask, how was your journey?"

"Long, rough and tiring, but I must inquire, is my brother well?" she cooly replied.

"*Si*, he is fine, but unaware of your travels. We speak often and I am thinking you will see that your brother has experienced many changes."

"What have you done to him?"

"Nothing, nothing at all. You will see for yourself and I believe you will find his story to be most interesting."

"So, now what will happen to us? Will we be released as you've promised?"

Manny turned serious again. He seemed unwilling to look directly at Lupita. She had noticed that when Manny seemed to be relaxed, his horribly scarred face was not so menacing. Now, his fiercely frightening countenance returned. He looked directly through the front window and seemed to be fighting some inner conflict.

"Lupe," he said, "My one regret is that these decisions do not belong to me."

The man remained silent until they turned a sharp corner then arrived at the Fortress. In front of the imposing building was a large, round, stone-paved drive that featured a huge fountain as the centerpiece. It was extremely gaudy with trumpet-blowing angels and a huge stone eagle at the top with water flowing from its open beak. Manny drove around the left side of the fountain as Enrique maneuvered the Cadillac around the right. Both vehicles came to a halt, nose to nose, in front of the broad stone stairway leading up to double hand-carved wooden doors. The large building was constructed of carved stone blocks and had the appearance of a fortress. Above the doors on the second floor, Lupita noticed a large balcony overlooking the approach to the building. A man and a woman watched from above. Lupita also noticed armed men on the parapet that surrounded the perimeter of the building at the roof line.

From above, the man nodded at Enrique and Manny as he motioned them to come up. Then both he and the woman disappeared from view. With Lupita between the two men, they mounted the stairs and a guard opened the massive wooden doors for them. Directly inside was a large foyer filled with statues and various oil paintings. Across the large space a curved stairway beckoned. At the top was another set of doors which the guard had already opened.

Behind the expansive desk that was centered in the room the man rose and gestured for Lupita, Enrique and Manny to enter. The female sat in an armchair to the side of the desk and did not rise. The woman stared at Lupita with a look that made the younger woman extremely uncomfortable. She felt like a small fish in front of a very hungry Barracuda.

"*Bienvenida Señorita Martinez,*" the man said. "I am your host, Alfredo Diaz and this is my sister, *Señora* Moreno. You have already met her son, Enrique and our accomplice, Manny. Please accept my eternal gratitude for bringing my prize." He smiled widely, revealing teeth capped with gold. Lupita began to feel sick inside.

Diaz turned to Manny and told him, "Go and get that *idiota* and have him show you where it is hidden."

Manny seemed to hesitate as he took a long look at Alfredo and Yolanda, then he abruptly turned and exited the room. Enrique offered Lupita a seat as Alfredo sat down, but she refused.

"I have been sitting a long time *Señor*, so perhaps it is better to remain standing until you present *mi hermano* and we will be on our way." Lupita also wondered what *"it,"* was that was hidden but kept it to herself. All she wanted was for her and Pedro to be away from this wretched place.

"Be patient my dear, you will join us for dinner and tomorrow we will discuss what is to be done with you and your brother. Perhaps you may wish to be compliant as it will have much to do with your dispensation."

From the way Diaz looked at her, she could not mistake his meaning. One glance at his appalling sister was enough to make her skin crawl. Lupita was tired, scared, and unsure of her fate, but her father's blood began to boil within her veins and a sharp retort was impossible to resist.

"*Suficiente pendejo,*" spat from her mouth before she could stop it. Her dark eyes flashed with anger and she said, "I want to see my brother now, I have done as you asked, let us go!"

This was not the way that a reasonable person would speak to El Diabolico, but he merely smiled as he rose from his desk once again and motioned Lupita to join him on the balcony. Below, he indicated the parked vehicles and Lupita could see Manny along with her brother leaning into the back seat of the Cadillac. Before she could cry out to Pedro, Diaz roughly jerked her back inside.

"You will see your brother when I decide and not one moment before. Do you understand my little spitfire? It will be you that is tamed, not me." Diaz turned to his sister, Yolanda and said, "Take this little *loba* to her quarters, see that she is washed and dressed appropriately for the evening."

Before standing, Yolanda slowly uncrossed her legs offering Lupita a vision she could have done without. Then, the gross little woman took her by the arm with surprising strength and marched her out of the office and down the hallway to another set of guarded doors. The room was a large suite with its own balcony, but the doors were barred and Lupita realized there was no escape. Yolanda took her time before leaving while she indicated the closet and bathroom were complete with all manner of female appointments for bathing and makeup. When Yolanda opened the closet door, all Lupita saw hanging within was a black negligee with sheer outer robe. Little spiky-heeled slippers were on the floor. Lupita jumped when the leering woman pinched her bottom and ran an unwelcome hand over her breasts. The guard watched lavishly from just inside the doorway and there was nothing for Lupita to do but accept the abuse.

"Listen to me, my little *bitch*," said Yolanda. "You will observe the proper attitude for my brother, and for me, if you expect to see your brother and depart our domain alive."

Then the horrible woman pulled Lupita close and licked her slimy tongue up the side of her neck and into her left ear. Before Lupita could pull away, Yolanda spun her around and pulled the long needle-sharp pin from the barrete which held her hair up. Her only weapon was gone. The door slammed and Lupita was alone at last. She fell upon the bed and sobbed silently for a time before gathering herself for what was to come. Her only thoughts were of Pedro and how they could escape this place. She began to resolve herself with the knowledge that she would not go down easily and whatever it took, these people would pay for what they had done to her familia.

23

Confluence

Gomez Gomez, Hubie, and Bear were first in line for the ferry in the morning. The previous evening had been uneventful, with only a few beers being downed and dinner in the hotel dining room. Gomez excused himself early, telling his companions he had contacts to make. Hubie and Bear weren't sure what he meant, but dismissed it as something mysterious as was usual for Gomez. As they waited to drive onto the early morning ferry, Gomez informed them that he had been made aware of the Cadillac's journey and that Lupita would reach the fortress within a few hours.

"How do you know this?" Hubie asked in astonishment.

"Remember, *mi amigo*, I have told you of the ones that watch. These ones, my people, are aware of our journey and our mission. Even though they have been unable to intervene, their resources for gaining knowledge are vast. Your Cadillac was observed departing the overnight ferry early this morning. There is only one place it can possibly be going. That will be what is called, *'Fortaleza del Aguila'.*"

"What do you know about this place?" Bear asked.

"Yeah," said Hubie, "*Fortaleza* means Fortress, right? And these cartel dudes are no bullshit, so it's a pretty safe bet that the thing is defended, right?"

Gomez nodded in the affirmative, then said, "There is more to be revealed *mis amigos*, so calm your worries. The ferry will not dock until late this afternoon then we will arrive at the Diaz *campo* just as dark falls. Our fate is one of destiny, be not concerned."

Gomez hesitated a moment as he drove his battered Chevy up onto the ferry. Then he said, *"Un hombre que corre con un cuchillo puede cortar mil gargantas."*

That statement was way out of the range of Hubie and Bear's limited understanding of Spanish and Gomez recognized their blank stares immediately.

"It is an old saying, my friends. It means simply that one running man with a knife may cut a thousand throats."

Again Hubie worried about what he'd gotten himself into. Bear seemed unconcerned, perhaps even happy to be in the thick of things once again. Hubie was well aware of Bear's stories about the fall of Saigon and being on the last helicopter to leave the U.S. Embassy compound. He'd related what things looked like that day as he sat in the open doorway. The other Marines had their M-16 rifles at the ready and Bear kept that heavy machine gun on his lap. The helicopter gunner had his belt-fed door gun at the ready, but they were not targeted as they flew out to the bay and the safety of the U.S.S. Blue Ridge. Bear and his companions never pulled a trigger, not once. After landing, Bear and his squad helped push Hueys over the side to make room for more landing helicopters. One South Vietnamese pilot landed on the deck, then after his passengers got out he took off again and ditched the Huey right into the water along side of the huge Navy ship. The pilot swam away from the sinking chopper and was retrieved. Bear was amazed at the courage of the man.

He used to tell Hubie, "God Damn, I mean the size of the balls on that guy. You'd have thought the weight of them would have taken him straight to the bottom!"

The story was almost certainly related after the trash can was full of empty beer bottles and Bear would always laugh uproariously as he reviewed the scene inside his head. Now, as the large ferry craft left the dock and began to move in sync with the ocean, Hubie wondered if he could ever find that kind of courage. It didn't matter much at this point as there was no turning back. In thirteen hours they'd be arriving in mainland Mexico and that gave Hubie way more time than he needed to ponder his thoughts.

*****

Time was up for Lupita. She had been served lunch in her quarters but now the day was getting long. Shadows stretched towards her from the corners of the room, as if trying to pull her into the darkness. The young lady attending to her would answer no questions whatsoever about her brother. All she got out of the woman was that her name was Maria and that she was from Mazatlán. She divulged that the pay was good and she was content to be left alone after being told to mind her own business. It was apparent to Lupita that this was a better occupation for the young woman than cleaning rooms at the beach resorts and fending off unwelcome advances from fat drunken gringos.

As dusk gathered Maria returned to help Lupita get ready for the evening. She insisted that Lupita bathe and added fragrant oils and salts to the bath water. The water temperature was perfect as Maria pushed Lupita against the slanted end of the tub and washed her long, dark hair. Under other circumstances it would have been a very luxurious experience. As it were, Lupita was trying to find her strength to survive what was next. She'd already resigned herself to do what was necessary to secure the release of Pedro.

Lupita's helper combed out her hair as it dried. When that was complete, Maria painted Lupita's fingernails and toes a bright shade of red. She then encouraged her charge to make use of the makeup supplied in the suite's master bath. Lupita hesitated, then gathered her resolve and applied a little mascara and some eyeliner. She also applied a small amount red lip gloss, but kept it simple. When Maria led her back into the bedroom, Lupita saw her clothing was laid out on the large king-size bed.

She felt as if she were back in Mexicali working as a dancer in one of those sleazy strip clubs. There was a red satin bustier designed to cinch her waist tight while accentuating the upper part of her chest. Skimpy black panties and a set of thigh-high black stockings completed the outfit. The tiny high heeled slippers were on the floor next to the bed. They had black feather trim attached just above the open toe design. Lupita almost laughed out loud at the spectacle. It was garish, simple, and seemingly designed for the fantasy of some pubescent school boy. Maria brought her a sheer robe to help cover up. From the look on Maria's face, Lupita could tell that she was not enjoying this task at all. After Maria helped her put on the robe, she pulled her hair back to fall across Lupita's shoulders. At that moment, Lupita wished that her ever present hair pin had not been taken away. She remembered lancing that drunken young Marine through his wrist and although she'd lost her job for it, never regretted it for a moment. Now, she literally felt quite naked.

At that moment the door to the suite flew open and Yolanda strode into the room, unannounced. The detestable woman came to a sudden halt as she appraised Lupita openly. As Yolanda licked her lips salaciously, Lupita already felt defiled.   Not once had a room full of inebriated yet appreciative men ever made her feel this way when she danced in the clubs.

Yolanda took Lupita by her upper arm and said, "It is time, *pequeña querida*, my brother is waiting."

She marched Lupita swiftly out the door and turned up the hallway toward the anxiously waiting Alfredo Diaz.   There was no way out.

*****

Manny felt terrible about all of the conflicted feelings he was experiencing.   He'd been so relieved that Lupita arrived safely with the sought after car.   Even though he'd hoped that Diaz would let her and Pedro go, he knew deep inside it was not to be.   If only he could have ripped that Artefacto from the Cadillac, given it to Enrique then driven away with Lupe, he would have done so.   That was not the real world however, at least not the one Manny lived in.   Besides, he knew she would never leave her brother behind.   Diaz was crazy smart that way and what he had up his sleeve was something Manny did not care to think about.   The fact that he knew a woman like Lupita would never have feelings for him did nothing to diminish the emotions he'd already developed.   His thoughts were scattered all over the place. At once he felt a deep desire to protect Lupe and at the same time was experiencing deep rage about the unfairness of it all.

When Manny brought Pedro to the Cadillac to retrieve the thing, he began to pepper Manny with questions but he sidestepped them and bade Pedro to produce it immediately. It only took a moment for Pedro to pull back the interior upholstery panel and present the stone idol to Manny.   It felt heavy in Manny's hand and strangely warm as if the inanimate object had a heartbeat deep within. He hefted the weight of it and had the strange feeling that the stone was appraising him. He shook off the feeling quickly as he had other pressing matters to think about. After taking it up to Alfredo's office and handing it over, it seemed as if Diaz went into a trance. His nephew, Enrique, also looked lovingly at the thing. Neither man noticed as Manny and Pedro backed out of the office. As he left the room, Manny noticed that Alfredo caressed the evil claw hanging from around his neck.

"It's true, *sobrino*," Diaz remarked to Enrique in a reverent whisper. "All the stories passed down about Melchor Diaz and his death at the claws of this creature…. all true. And now my nephew, it is ours."

Manny felt a wave of disgust as he watched this exchange. He and Pedro looked at each other with a glance of mutual agreement. Pedro had already come to grips with the true nature of this unnatural lust and now Manny understood it as well. All the things he had learned from his time with Pedro became crystal clear as he absorbed the teachings exhibited in reality. The two men went back to Pedro's quarters. The guard was still gone as Manny had dismissed him when he brought Pedro to the car.

Now, once again Pedro began to question Manny about how the vehicle arrived all the way up here at the fortress. Manny didn't have the heart to give the truth to his friend because he knew the knowledge of his sister being in the clutches of these heartless people would cause an anguish the serene Pedro did not deserve. Manny did not have the luxury of innocence and his mind began to think of possibilities previously impossible. He stood up and reached under his shirt to retrieve the ever present Beretta automatic from it's holster nestled in the small of his back. Manny pulled the slide back enough to confirm the first round was chambered, then he made sure the safety was on and replaced the pistol.

Pedro couldn't help but notice the hardened look on Manny's face as he wondered what was going through the man's mind.

Manny looked at his friend and said, "Pedro, no matter what happens, remain here. Be prepared to run. Things are going to change very quickly, *mi amigo.*

*****

It had been a very long day for the three men riding in the Chevy Fleet Line. They had recently spent so much time bouncing around in the ancient vehicle that the rough water during the ferry crossing felt like being rocked in a cradle. After negotiating the streets of Mazatlán, Gomez headed directly up into the mountains rising to the east. That the man knew where he was going was evident, so there were no questions to be asked and none to be answered. Hubie still felt uneasy but Bear exuded confidence and Gomez left no doubt that the task at hand would be addressed, no matter the outcome. Hubie remained alone in the back seat with his thoughts as they headed ever uphill.

When they came to the small village of Chirimoyos, Gomez turned off the main road and drove a short distance up a dirt road that ended in front of a meager residence made of crumbling adobe brick with a palm thatched roof. Chickens pecked in the dirt and a wooden corral off to the side held a few goats and ewes. A small, very dark man wearing woven wool clothing immediately emerged from the shack. He came directly up to the driver's side of the car and began speaking with Gomez in the unknown language that was most definitely not Spanish.

After a few moments of rapid-fire conversation, the two

men touched foreheads together in a reverent manner. Then the small man looked at the huge gringo in the passenger seat and Hubie in the back. For the first time he spoke in Spanish.

"Ve con Dios," was all the man said to both Hubie and Bear. Then he turned and disappeared into his humble abode.

Gomez drove back onto the main track then continued up the extremely rough road toward the fortress.

"What the hell was that all about?" asked Bear from the passenger seat.

Gomez thought that over for a moment then said, "We have a saying…. If it is bad news, make it good… If it is good news, be cautious."

An overly stressed Hubie could no longer contain himself and blurted out, "What the fuck, dude? What's going on?"

Gomez adjusted the rear-view mirror so he could look directly at Hubie who was sitting on the right side of the rear bench seat.

"Mis amigos, you must now know that there are reports of a storm gathering between rival cartel organizations. It is known to us that the *hombres* in control of the border-smuggling operations into Arizona at Nogales have reached their limit with the foolhardy adventurism of the Diaz cartel. An armed group of men have been observed in this area and it appears some sort of action is imminent. It seems plain to all but the *idiotas* up at the so-called Eagles Fortress. The dice have not rolled yet, so our number is unknown."

Bear pointed up the road as he looked back at Hubie. "Let's do this boss," he said.

Hubie moaned slightly as he held his head and looked down at his feet.

"God damnit," was all he could think to say.

It was getting dark as they drove up the poorly maintained road. Gomez was reluctant to use the headlights but knew he'd have to soon enough. Then suddenly, they topped a rise and came to a guard shack. There was a barrier but it was open and the place seemed deserted. Bear looked at the open door of the shack and noticed a pair of feet that were obviously attached to a person inside lying face down. He looked left then right and not seeing anyone, got out of the car. Gomez also got out and entered the shack behind Bear. Hubie stayed right where he was, seemingly glued to his seat.

There were two dead men inside. The one lying on the floor rested in a pool of drying, coagulated blood that came from his cut throat. Flies buzzed around his body. Bear stepped across the puddle and lifted up the head of the second man who was seated in front of a shortwave radio. Cut wire dangled from the hand-mike grasped in his dead fist. He had been bludgeoned so hard on the side of his head that his left eye hung from the socket. A stunned look of surprise and betrayal was frozen onto his lifeless face.

Gomez and Bear looked very grim as they returned to the Chevy containing the waiting Hubie. After they got in, Bear looked over at Gomez as if to say, *now what?* Just then a shocking hail of gunfire erupted from ahead where the pavement led. Gomez Gomez nodded slightly as if he expected this surprise. He gave a sly smile to both Bear and Hubie, then mashed his foot to the floor on the gas pedal. Christine rocketed forward toward the unknown as if her fuse had been lit.

24

The Pig

As Yolanda led the captive Lupita toward Alfredo's office and quarters, she abruptly shook off the grip the squat woman had on her upper arm. She squared back her shoulders, shook out her long hair with a haughty snap of her head, then looked down on the shorter woman as she raised one eyebrow in contempt. She put on her stage persona and her disgusting captor recognized the change. It seemed that the tigress had accepted her fate and would need no prompting. *Perhaps the restraints would not be necessary,* Yolanda thought.

Alfredo's double doors were open and the guard was nowhere to be seen. When the two women entered the office, Diaz rose from behind his desk and graciously motioned for them to enter. Enrique was present and also stood up. Lupita noticed the strange looking carved rock placed in the middle of Alfredo's desk. It seemed as if the two men had been ruminating over the stone idol. For some reason,

Lupita's attention was drawn to the thing as well. A glow emanated from within, although no change of color could be seen. She experienced a surreal sensation that the object was aware of her, as if it already knew who she was.

Lupita forced herself to ignore the stone. It was showtime, she knew it and so did everyone else in the room. The fact that Alfredo was wearing an evening robe only served to reinforce what was to come. The open robe exposed his hairy chest which displayed the evil looking claw suspended from a gold chain. Lupita noticed it for the first time as Diaz walked to the wet bar at the side wall of his office.

"*Señorita,*" Diaz said. "What is your pleasure? We have all manner of spirits on hand."

Enrique crossed over to the bar saying, "Allow me Uncle, I am thinking the lady might enjoy an aperitif that is sweet and smooth. Perhaps Amaretto Liqueur would be agreeable."

The younger man busied himself with the drinks as his Uncle stepped up closely to Lupita. He took her by the hand and turned her around in a pirouette as he appraised her closely. She felt herself tremble with a rage that was almost uncontrollable. Forcing herself to think of her brother and the remote possibility that they might come out of this alive helped her focus. As much as she hated the situation at hand, it seemed to be their only chance.

As Enrique turned away from the bar holding a silver serving tray with the refreshments, a long burst of rapid-fire automatic weaponry rang out. Hearing a muffled cry from above, Alfredo turned toward the balcony doors just in time to see a body fall from the parapet above and crash directly in front of the doors with a sickening thump. The next burst shattered the glass doors and windows on both sides. Enrique dropped the drink tray and let out a shrill screech as he ran from the room. Alfredo dropped to his hands and knees as he scooted for cover in front of the desk.

Yolanda regarded both men with disgust then yelled out, "The armory!"

She ran out of the room with a purpose, leaving Lupita alone with Alfredo Diaz as he cowered in front of his luxurious desk. Lupita absorbed everything during the few moments it took to develop. The loud reports of weapons being fired from above the office told her that some type of battle had erupted. Although she had no idea of what was happening, she saw her chance as the gunfire increased outside.

Lupita took two quick steps to where Diaz hid behind the cover of his desk and screamed, *"Tu puerco!"*

She kicked him sharply in the ribs and grabbed him by the hair with her left hand, forcing his head back as he gasped for air. With her right hand she grasped the claw and the gold chain easily snapped as she ripped it from his neck. Holding the sharp object between her fingers the enraged woman violently slashed down one, two, three times, opening up the forehead and fleshy cheek of El Diabolico. Then, before the stunned man could react, she plunged the claw directly into his left eye. The mutilated eyeball spewed blood and fluid down his cheek. Lupita savagely twisted the claw as she made a complete ruin of the man's eye socket.

*****

Gomez drove his Chevy like a madman until he slid to a stop behind Hubie's Cadillac. The large stone fountain provided some cover from the flashes of gunfire visible in the tree line beyond the cleared area in front of Diabolico's headquarters. Bear was trying to make his huge frame as small as possible in the front seat while Hubie ducked low in the back. Then, to their astonishment, Gomez Gomez calmly opened the driver's door, retrieved his sombrero from the seat beside him and calmly walked through the fusillade of gunfire and up the stairway to the building. Hubie and Bear could hear him chanting in his strange language as bullets struck all around him.

Hubie had a random, odd thought that he'd landed in the middle of some kind of Sergio Leone western film. Bear realized that Lupita must certainly be inside so he exited the vehicle and crawled up toward the steps, using the fountain and the automobiles as cover. He paused for a moment while crouching behind the cover of Hubie's Cadillac. Hubie suddenly found himself alone in the middle of a maelstrom.

*****

Manny reacted instantly upon hearing the rapid-fire weaponry. The Beretta appeared in his right hand as if by magic. He thought of his lovely Lupe and before he could stop himself, uttered her name. Pedro didn't miss a beat as he instantly realized the connection of how the Cadillac had arrived up at this remote mountaintop location. As Manny ran down the hallway toward the other rooms in the fortress, Pedro was hot on his heels. His new-found Christian serenity was forgotten as his only thought was of getting his hands on a weapon.

When they turned a corner leading to the other wing of the building they almost collided head on with Enrique who was wildly running in a panic from the opposite direction. Manny grabbed him and Enrique almost left his feet at the sudden stop.

"Qué pasó, Enrique?" Manny shouted.

"They're killing us!" Enrique replied in a shrill, high screech.

He shook loose of Manny's grasp and ran headlong through the door into Pedro's residence, then disappeared down the outdoor steps leading to the garden like a scared rabbit. Manny and Pedro continued toward Alfredo's office just up the hallway. Over the railing, Manny could see that the foyer below was empty but that the front doors were wide open. As the gunfire continued from outside and from the defensive positions above, Manny took a quick look into the office before he committed to entering the large vulnerable space.

What he saw upon entering the room stunned him. The fiery Lupita stood over a prone Alfredo Diaz wearing the red bustier and thigh-high stockings. She'd kicked the silly spike-heeled slippers across the room and was perched on the balls of her feet. Her hair was spread out in a fan around her shoulders and her chest heaved as she took in one rapid gasp of air after another. Blood dripped from the sharp object in her right hand onto the back of Diaz as he screamed face down into his lush carpet. Never before had Manny seen something so lovely, and so terrible at the same time. Lupita turned to look at this new threat with hate and rage, then she recognized her brother.

The claw dropped from her bloody hand onto the back of the sobbing El Diabolico and the siblings rushed to embrace. Manny lowered his weapon, then sharply brought it up again as the short figure of Gomez Gomez calmly entered the room. He nodded politely to the three stunned occupants as he walked directly to the desk and cradled the Artifact in his arms. It was apparent that nothing in the insane scenario he'd encountered surprised him in the least. He turned toward the door, then as he left the room he paused for a comment.

"My friends, it is time to go, is it not?"

Then he calmly walked along the upstairs railing, while holding the stone idol, toward the stairway. Manny, Lupe, and Pedro glanced at each other in astonishment. With unspoken agreement the trio decided to follow the odd little man. But first, Pedro stepped swiftly toward the shattered balcony doors and retrieved the AK-47 assault rifle laying beside the dead man outside. He momentarily released the long banana clip from the weapon and verified that rounds of ammo were ready for use. He slammed the magazine back into place then followed his sister and Manny out of the door.

*****

Bear knelt for a moment at the foot of the broad stairway, then when there was a sudden lull in the shooting he realized the attackers had to be in the process of reloading. The large man stayed low as he sprinted up the stairway then took cover inside the open doorway. He could see Gomez enter a room upstairs behind the railing. Not sure what to do next he took a moment to look around and evaluate the situation.

When the firing abated momentarily, Hubie took a chance and peeked up from the Chevy's back seat to take a look. He focused in on his beloved Caddy, which was parked nose to nose with a large black SUV that had been riddled with bullet holes. He could see that the SUV was in the line of fire of the front doors but in that position had protected the Cadillac. In a flash of realization, Hubie saw that with the Chevy Fleet Line parked behind his Caddy, there was no way to make an escape. Something had to be done immediately, otherwise when his companions came back outside precious time would be wasted moving the autos into position.

Suddenly, the shockingly loud gunfire resumed. Hubie dove back down to the floor consumed with overwhelming terror. His entire reality consisted of the terrifying gun battle and the worn, brown carpet one inch from his nose. He took a deep lung-filling breath of air and realized his fear would not miraculously disappear. In that moment, Hubie found his courage.

He peeked up again and could see the flashes of gunfire coming from the tree line. Hubie looked up at the fortress and saw rifles poked over the rampart as the defenders fired blindly while remaining low. In one fluid movement, Hubie rolled himself over into the front seat. His fingers found the ignition key as he moved upright behind the steering wheel. The gaudy fountain was directly to the left of the car, giving him some protection.

Hubie took another deep breath, then started the car and immediately jammed it into reverse. The Chevy shot backwards into the open and Hubie spun the wheel making the car slide into a three point one-eighty. He slammed the gear shift into neutral, set the brake, then killed the ignition but left the key in the slot. Now that the car was turned around, the driver's side was away from the firing. He rolled out of the door and left it open. On his hands and knees, Hubie crawled behind the cover of the fountain all the way up to the side of his bright red Cadillac. While keeping low, Hubie opened the driver's door and slid up into the giant car. *Damn!* The keys were not in the ignition. No matter. Hubie slid across the huge, front bench seat and reached up under the dash behind the glove box. He breathed a sigh of relief to find his hidden magnetic key box still in place. Without lifting his head up, Hubie started the car while using his other hand to operate the gas pedal. His baby started right up giving him even more confidence.

The convertible top was down so Hubie felt exposed as he sat up behind the steering wheel, but he was in the throes of action and nothing would stop him now. Once again, he hit the column shift into the reverse position and backed up rapidly. The rear bumper knocked over a large terracotta planter which gave him enough room to make the left turn alongside the fountain. Now the vehicle was pointed in the correct position for a getaway. Finally, he made a quick decision to back up closer to the building's entrance stairway. The rear bumper protested as it jumped over the second step. Hubie could think of nothing else to do, so he left the car running then slouched down and simply waited.

*****

Bear peaked around the corner of the open doorway in time to see Hubie position his Cadillac against the stairway. He also noticed that the Fleet Line Chevy had been reversed. *Good man*, thought Bear. Then he heard muffled cursing in Spanish and what sounded like something metallic dragging along the floor. The noise was coming from a downstairs hallway that connected with the entrance foyer at the bottom of the stairs. Bear quickly moved against the wall next to the open door and pulled it toward his chest for cover. He risked using his right eye to spy around the edge and was surprised to witness a short Mexican woman lugging a belt-fed machine gun emerge from the hallway. That she was wearing a short black skirt with spiky black heels and an off-shoulder bright red blouse made the vision seem more absurd than it already was. The metallic dragging sound was caused by a long belt of ammunition that slid along the tile flooring as the woman struggled with the heavy weapon.

Bear recognized it immediately as the familiar M-60 machine gun, the one his Marine buddies used to call *The Pig*. He had no idea of how the thing got into the possession of the cartel but he did know all about the deadly effect it could deal in the right hands. Bear could see that the first round was inserted under the breach which meant the charging handle had been pulled rearward and the weapon was ready for firing. As the ugly, squat woman moved toward the open doors, she cradled the heavy gun in both arms and Bear abruptly realized she intended to unload on whomever was outside, meaning Hubie and the automobiles.

The large man moved like lightning. Before Yolanda even realized he was upon her, he'd snatched the weapon by it's carrying handle and ripped it from her grasp. His giant right fist swung in a roundhouse punch that took the woman directly on the left side of her head. She was knocked off her feet and flew through the open doorway. The unconscious woman landed on the top step of the stairway then tumbled like a rag doll to the bottom. She came to rest against the rear bumper of the Cadillac and did not move again.

Gomez, Lupita, and the others witnessed this as they descended from above. Manny raised his handgun and began to aim at the back of Bear, below. Lupita instantly put her hand on Manny's arm and pushed it down.

He looked at her questioningly and she shook her head, saying, "*Él es nuestro amigo.*"

Manny took a look at Gomez as he held the stone idol. He could see that the Cadillac had been backed against the stairway into a position for escape. It was apparent by the way the giant in the foyer held the machine gun Manny had procured years ago that he knew what he was doing. In a flash he recognized that this was to be the manner of Lupe's salvation. He suddenly understood that he would not stand in the way.

Just then, heavy boots could be heard running down the same hallway Yolanda had previously used. Pedro, who was last in line on the stairway, leaned precariously over the railing and fired a long burst from his AK-47 into the hallway entrance from above. When the ear-splitting noise diminished, the sound of running boots could still be heard, but now moving in the opposite direction.

Bear spun around and positioned the heavy weapon for action on the stairway behind him. Recognizing Gomez and

Lupita instantly, he lowered the machine gun. He did not know the other two men, but that the four were together was beyond question. He waved them down.

"Come on, *God Damnit*, we are leaving." Bear roared.

The foursome gathered behind Bear as he cleared the area outside from the edge of the doorway. Still in the Caddy's driver's seat, Hubie waved then pointed ahead towards Gomez's vehicle. The gunfire had become sporadic so Gomez and Pedro swiftly moved down the stairs and headed toward the Fleet Line. Manny did not move.

"Go, now!" Bear ordered.

Manny held fast and looked into the eyes of his beautiful Lupe. She understood. As tears began to flow freely down the face of the normally impassive Manny, she pulled him down and kissed him on both cheeks then squarely upon the mouth. They hugged briefly, then Manny pulled back and nodded to Bear.

Without hesitation, Bear draped the lengthy belt of ammo around his shoulders while holding the weapon by it's carrying handle in his right hand. He stooped slightly and caught Lupita around her slender waist with his left arm then effortlessly took the steps with two leaps, landing on the trunk and stepping into the back seat of Hubie's car. Lupita found herself deposited into the front seat next to Hubie. The hood of the Cadillac got peppered with gravel as Gomez gunned his Chevy. That attracted the attention of the attackers and they began firing in their direction.

When Hubie floored it behind Gomez, Bear almost lost his balance. He remained upright in the back seat by bracing his tree trunk legs against the front seat and the rear seat back. Bear could see flashes of gunfire coming from the foliage on the right side of the car. He twisted to his right while holding onto the machine gun by it's pistol grip and draped the long belt of ammo into the front between Hubie and Lupita. Then he let loose.

The weapon roared while ejected casings flew everywhere. Hubie and Lupita were deafened by the brain numbing sound that came from directly above their heads as the spent, hot brass landed all over them. Hubie kept his resolve and mashed the gas pedal so hard he thought his foot would go through the floor.

Bear was in his moment. He fired with his right hand while his left forearm controlled the belt of ammo as it fed the gun. His mouth was wide open with teeth bared and he was unaware of the animal roar coming from deep inside. The muzzle flashes from the bushes abruptly ceased as branches and bark fell all over the commandos. For good measure, Bear twisted toward the rear and fired off a final long burst toward the front of the fortress. In the final fading light of the day, the front of the building could be seen erupting into a cloud of adobe dust. Then, the last round from the belt left the gun and there was silence.

From up front with Gomez, Pedro leaned through the open passenger window with his captured assault rifle at the ready. There was no resistance. As they passed beyond the open barrier and guard shack into darkness, they knew it was over. They were gone.

25

The Split

Hubie sat in the driver's seat of his beloved Cadillac listening to some extremely satisfying eighties alternative rock. The gentle motion of the ferry on the way back to La Paz was soothing after yesterday's chaos. He was still having a hard time absorbing how they had pulled off the impossible caper. Hubie breathed in the fresh ocean air on this cloudless, beautiful morning. He chose to ride along in the Caddy due to the crowded lounge area which smelled of diesel fuel mingled with the food vendor's vat of bubbling lard.

After last night's escape, the five lucky adventurer's drove in darkness directly to the ferry landing and waited for the early morning departure from Mazatlán. As they laid low throughout the long night, they all felt an elevated level of anxiety. They were still pumped up from the battle and didn't know if there would be a pursuit. Unbeknownst to them, the firefight ended abruptly when Bear hosed down the entire area as they escaped. Now, the empty machine gun was hidden under a blanket in the Cadillac's trunk. Pedro still had about fifteen bullets in the magazine of his appropriated AK-47 which he hid under the front seat of the Fleet Line, just in case. Another worry was that if local policía searched the vehicles, they surely would discover the military grade weapons. That would have been very bad, indeed.

After retrieving their hidden vehicles, Jorge de Jesus and his commando strike force had simply faded into the night heading eastward, further into mainland Mexico. He felt that the appropriate message had been delivered and did not wish to risk any casualties that a full assault might have caused. After arriving at the city of Durango, the group split up and began the journey back to Nogales. An early morning satellite phone call to Cesar Pastor confirmed he'd made the correct decision. Pastor had no desire for further death and mayhem. It was bad for business. If Diaz continued his shenanigans, then further action could be considered. For now, the man known as El Clásico was content to wait and see what would happen next.

As for Manny, he'd organized a feeble pursuit but it was only for show. He'd left the shaken Enrique to clean up the mess and arrange medical assistance for his uncle and mother. Yolanda had regained consciousness, but seemed vague about what had happened. Manny stuffed a wash cloth into Diaz's ruined eye socket and tied a strip of towel around his head to hold it in place. Nothing else could be done until the sobbing man could be delivered to the hospital in Durango.

Manny took his time gathering a few men to pursue Lupita and the rest. They took two vehicles with four armed men in each, but it was over an hour before they left the fortress. When reaching the little village of Chirimoyos, Manny took the small convoy east toward Durango rather than down to

Mazatlán. He wanted to give Lupe and Pedro as much time as possible to escape. As for the so called, Precioso Artefacto, he would be happy if he found out the rock ended up at the bottom of the Sea of Cortez. The thing was nothing but trouble as far as he was concerned.

Hubie opened his Magical Mystery Tour bag and sorted through his stash of personally mixed cassette tapes. The bag had been in the back seat when the leaping Bear had landed on it. A few of the tapes were smashed, but most survived intact. Too bad he couldn't say the same about his car. He got out and took another look at the damage now that it was full daylight. He leaned against Gomez's Chevy as he inspected the right side of his Caddy. Unbeknownst to him at the time, his car had taken several hits as they sped away from the gunfire. A stitch of bullet holes went diagonally from just behind where Bear was standing, up across the large pointed fender, and took out both tail lights on that side. Fortunately, the bullets impacted just above the right rear tire. A flat would have been most unfortunate at that moment. As it were, the spare tire mounted inside the trunk was shredded.

The trunk lid had a huge dent from when Bear landed on it after leaping from the fortress's stairway. The beautiful chrome rear bumper was smashed up into the rear sheet metal of the car from when Hubie had backed into the stairs. The left side of the bumper was held up by one remaining bolt. If that had let go, they'd have been dragging the thing all the way to Mazatlán.

As for the beautiful candy-apple red paint and flawless white interior? Forget it. The rocker panels and lower fenders were dented from uncountable rocks kicked up from the rough dirt roads. With the thick coating of dust all over the car, he could hardly tell it was red anymore. It looked more like a dull, matte-finish tan. Two of the front headlights had been smashed by rocks when Gomez peeled out the previous evening. The beautiful chrome on the massive front bumper was a mess and only one hubcap was still in place. The interior was a complete loss.

Even so, when Gomez suggested the car be abandoned before arriving in Mazatlán, Hubie protested. His thinking was that it could be found by cartel soldiers and put them hot on their trail. But, his real reason was that he just couldn't bear the thought of leaving it behind. After all, wasn't that why he'd put himself through all this god-awful mess.... to get the car back?

Hubie quit leaning against the Fleet Line and turned around to take a look at the other car. Gomez's Chevy didn't have a scratch on it. It didn't even look dusty. Hubie remembered how their enigmatic guide had simply walked through the curtain of flying bullets while chanting out loud. He reflected that something must be going on here that was beyond his range of understanding. Perhaps, did the Gomez magic bubble extend to protect them all? If so, Hubie's much loved 1959 Cadillac was certainly outside that bubble. Hubie looked back at his vehicle and sighed. At least they were alive and unharmed. The sparkling reflection from sunshine on the choppy water began to hurt his eyes, so he retreated inside the lounge.

His four companions were seated at a u-shaped booth. Bear and Gomez were on either end and Pedro sat close to Lupita in the middle. All were dressed with clothing worn the previous day, except Lupita of course. She'd borrowed a t-shirt from Hubie that was tied into a knot around her middle. His spare shorts wore a little snug against her generous rear but loose in the waist. A short piece of deck rope solved that problem. Bear's extra stuff was absolutely way too large for her and Pedro had only the clothing on his back. The diminutive Gomez had a few things but there was no way they'd fit Lupita's full-figured female body. He did have a pair of sandals that worked, however.

Hubie pulled up a chair and sat down at the outside edge of the booth. Behind the booth a row of portholes looked out upon the water. Passengers strolled by along the decking between the lounge wall and the ferry's railing. All in all, the crossing was going well and the ocean was flat compared to the previous day. In ten more hours they'd be back in La Paz. That was the subject of conversation, as they pondered what to do next.

Gomez was in a serious discussion with the other three as Hubie pulled up the chair and listened in. The reason all of this had happened was wrapped in Gomez's serape on his lap. He was not going to let go of the artifact until it was back where it belonged. The foursome greeted Hubie briefly, then Gomez continued.

"It must be returned, *mis amigos*, as soon as possible. Another must be found as protector."

As he said this, his glance rested upon Pedro briefly, then he continued.

"In it's resting place, it is calm. But in any other location it is capable of great mischief. Those that *think* they will be able to control it's power will be proven incorrect even unto their own doom."

"Do you think Diaz will attempt to retrieve it?" asked Hubie.

Gomez shrugged and shook his head questionably.

"I only know that it *must* be replaced. Other's have tried, and may try again, but Pedro Martinez is the only one to have succeeded."

Pedro looked down at the table top in shame, but Gomez reached over and gently lifted his chin.

"My friend," Gomez said as he looked closely into Pedro's eyes. "There is always redemption even for the most egregious sin. That you were successful in your endeavor tells me something very important. Your family has lived in the San Felipe area for many generations, no?"

Lupita spoke up, saying, "We are not sure of our lineage, *señor*, but it is said that the Martinez *familia* was among the very first to settle the fishing community of San Felipe. Before that it is unknown.

Gomez took a long hard look at both Pedro and his sister. He noted the dark tone of their skin and their high cheekbones. He began to put together the puzzle of how Pedro escaped the wrath of the mountain beast. He already knew a good deal about the tale of how the Artifact had been placed in Hubie's Cadillac, but the story of how Pedro avoided being torn to pieces was unclear.

He addressed Pedro directly, saying, "*Hombre joven*, it is clear that you entered the vehicle to hide the idol, correct?

Pedro nodded in the affirmative.

"So, is it also true that you came under the direct presence of the Beast?"

Again, Pedro shook his head, yes.

"*Con su permiso*, if you are able, can you tell us what happened in that moment?"

Pedro turned a shade of pale that was visible even through his dark complexion. He gathered his thoughts and took a deep breath.

"There was a great storm, such as I've never seen before. I crossed to the north by the open sewer known as the New River as many others have done. The thing followed and I sought to hide even while knowing there would be no escape. I entered the red car by cutting through the soft top, then hid it inside, hoping the Beast would pass me by."

Pedro paused for a moment, then took another deep breath and continued.

"The *thing* was not fooled. As I hid in the back, the

monster reached in through the opening I'd cut and caressed my forehead. After that, things are vague until I came to be at the Monastery. I do remember one thing, *mis amigos,* and it is most strange. I felt the touch of the Beast to be gentle. The sensation was as one of love, like the touch of *el amor de una madre.*"

"The love of a mother," Lupita repeated in English.

Gomez slapped his hand down upon the table, sending their silverware flying. He pursed his lips while thinking. As he did this, he looked closely at both Pedro and his sister.

"Pedro," Gomez said. "The only explanation is that you and Lupita carry the blood of the original people in your veins. We are relatives, the both of you are *Kumeyaay.*"

"OK, hold up," said Bear. "You said something before about a Chuakaber. Now you're telling us this is some kind of monster, a beast? I get it that you think that rock in your lap is some kinda special, but a *monster*? What the hell's going on here?"

"It is true *señor,*" said Pedro. "I have seen this thing, it touched me, the hand of *el Demonio* touched me, believe it."

Hubie and Bear glanced at each other with obvious disbelief.

"All I wanted was to get my car back and Bear's always in for something unusual. But, monsters? Magic rocks? Fountain of Youth? Cartel assholes shooting up my car? What the fuck, dude!"

Gomez said, "Speaking of your car, I must insist that you abandon it in La Paz and find another means of transportation north. It is most likely that members of the Diaz Cartel will be looking for it along the border crossings. Being found by them will not be pleasant for you."

Bear said, "Well, going north by any means might not be the brightest thing to do anyway. And what are you gonna do after we get into port?"

Gomez looked at Lupita and said, "The *señorita* will do as she pleases as she is one possessed of a strong free will. Pedro and I will drive Christine north and return what he has stolen to it's rightful place. He took it, he must return it. That is the only way to make amends and put things back to normal. Then, we will stay at the *Cerro de la Encantada* for a time, together. Only then may Pedro find his way to the future for which he was born."

There were a few moments of silence among the group as each of them reflected on the conversation. Hubie noticed that Lupita was resting her eye's upon Bear during the interlude. All of a sudden, Hubie experienced a flash of inspiration.

"OK, how about this. We'll split. You guys are going back to Magic Mountain, or whatever. We can head south. That way I don't have to ditch my car and the cartel jerk-offs might not expect that. Maybe I can sell it down in Cabo and we can get on one of those cruise ships. They come down from San Diego, right? I mean, that's where we were going anyway."

"*Señor* Hubie," said Lupita. "It will not be necessary for you to sell your automobile. Under the seat of your Cadillac is a large envelope. There are many thousands of U.S. Dollars inside. The one named Manny delivered it to me when I was compelled to take on this task."

Then, the beautiful young woman proudly raised her head and looked Bear directly in the eye as she reached over to place her slender brown hand upon his stout wrist.

"*Mi Gran Oso*, I plead that you understand I only sought to save Pedro. If there were another way I would never...."

Bear interrupted her as he held up his hand. "Forget it, Lupe. Those assholes needed a good whacking anyway."

"Fuck'n A," added Hubie, all grins.

Lupita smiled broadly at Hubie's comment while nodding her head up and down.

Still looking at Bear, she said, "Well, *mi grande amigo*, you came for me and I will never forget it. And, *Dios mío*, what you did with that large gun, I've never seen such a *cosa magnífica*. You saved us."

"Speaking of the guns," said Pedro, "It is not unexpected to be searched when arriving from the mainland. If the *federales* find those weapons we will be in *la prisión* until the end of time."

"Best you feed them to the waters, they are evil things" said Gomez.

Bear and Hubie got up to take care of it, but Lupita motioned for Hubie to remain seated.

"I will assist *Señor oso*, there is much that is owed to him."

Hubie watched the pair exit while ruefully shaking his head. Now that they had a plan, he immediately began to think of other things.

"Hey Gomez," he said. "You gotta phone number for that little Rosa gal?"

26

Revenge

Alfredo Diaz's remaining eye blazed with murderous rage as he sat behind his office desk. The doors and windows behind him were still covered over with plywood so the only illumination in the room came from his desk lantern. The light from the green lampshade cast a surreal glow upon his ruined face. Although his stitches had been removed, the wounds were still bright red. There were three deep gouges, one across his forehead and two on his left cheek. His open eye socket was covered with a black patch that could not contain the fluids which occasionally seeped from the hole. He kept a handkerchief close at hand to wipe away the goop.

"I want them, I want them all... do you understand?" he raged.

The other three in the room, Enrique, Yolanda, and Manny, shifted uncomfortably in their chairs. During the past six weeks no trace could be found of Lupita, Pedro, or the others. Even their parents in San Felipe were nowhere to be found.

"Enrique, you and Manny have been to that little whore's *casa* in San Felipe before. Where are they now?"

Enrique answered, "Uncle, our men have been to the place many times. It is abandoned and none of the local residents we have interviewed have any knowledge of where her *familia* has gone. Even the local *policia* have been unable to provide information.

Diaz abruptly stood and pounded his fist upon the surface of his desk.

"I do not care," he shouted as spittle flew from his mouth.

"They will be found, they will be brought here, and when that fucking cunt Lupita is located, I will make her watch as I burn her parents to death before her eyes."

"Give her to *me*, my brother," Yolanda said. "I will make her wish she'd never been born."

Manny was typically quiet during these exchanges and he stayed silent now. Because of the way things had played out during the gunfight, none of his compatriots realized that he was the one that let them all go. Diaz had his ravaged face buried into the carpet, Yolanda had been knocked silly, and Enrique had run screaming as he looked for a place to hide. Manny saw no reason to enlighten them and he planned to keep it that way. He decided to finally speak up.

"We have notified our associates along the border at Mexicali to look for the Cadillac. Nothing has been seen of it. In Tijuana we must be cautious to not offend the operation in control of that city. After the attack from Pastor's group, sending resources to Nogales is out of the question. Remember, their attack was one of revenge for the killings we performed when seizing their product."

"Do I care about Cesar Pastor? I will crush him!" shouted Diaz.

Enrique made another attempt to calm his uncle. It had often been necessary to do so ever since Diaz returned from the hospital in Durango. Even six weeks after the battle, the cartel leader's emotions were frequently out of control.

"Uncle," Enrique began. "Remember, we took the lives of three of Pastor's men. The two men killed at their guard post and the one that fell from above even the score. I think that for now, Pastor only intended to send a message. We must focus on the task at hand. If we are to retrieve the *Artefacto*, it must be assumed that the thing was returned to where Martinez found it to begin with."

"Yes," mused Diaz as he began calming down. "This must be our main concern. With the *Artefacto* in our possession, none of the other things have importance. Did you feel the *power*, Enrique? It is real and we must have it, once again."

Diaz automatically moved to finger the claw that had previously hung from around his neck. Then he remembered that because of it's gruesome reminder of what happened that day, he'd locked it away. Perhaps Enrique would like to wear it someday, but Alfredo would not be hanging that thing around his neck ever again.

"Yes Uncle, I felt the power and agree that no resource should be spared until it is found. We had it once and we will have it again. It is the destiny of our *familia* to control this tremendous gift."

Yolanda did not care one iota about the stupid piece of rock. Her only desire was for revenge on the one who'd struck her. She still felt vague and confused at times, and the headache that often visited her only increased her desire to gut the large man, if only he could be located. As for Manny, he hoped the idol would never be found. He knew it for what it was and wanted nothing to do with the thing. The time spent with Pedro had taught Manny invaluable things. Not Enrique, however. The infection of greed instantly took hold of him as soon as his uncle allowed him to hold it. That he had been infected with the fever was in no doubt and he had been forming a plan. Now seemed to be the right time to advance his strategy.

"We know this rock does not have feet. It can only go where it is taken and the first place to look would be back up on the mountain. That is where we sent Martinez to find it in the first place. If that little shit could find the place, so can we. Only this time we must not trust fate to the weak minded. We must accomplish this task ourselves, if we hope for success."

Diaz considered this opinion for a moment, then nodded in agreement.

"Yes, and perhaps that is where that slut and her brother are hiding. We will kill them all and take it."

"I will assemble a team," said Yolanda as she stood up. "My blade is hungry and will feast itself in the guts of the large man."

Enrique got up to leave with his mother when a thought occurred to him.

"Uncle, we still have product to move. As much as I would like to have him with us, perhaps it is best to leave Manny here. He is the only one that has the same detailed knowledge of day to day operations as we, and the men respect him. He is best suited to keep things under control until our return."

Manny nodded silently as Diaz looked at him questionably.

"*Si*, I will do this." Manny said as he kept his relief hidden from the others.

"Then *vamos*," Diaz declared. "We will leave as soon as the team is ready."

The meeting was over.

*****

* * *

At that very moment, Hubie was lounging on the beach with Rosa while he helped with her English and she in turn helped him appreciate the value of peace and relaxation. When the group split up after landing in La Paz, the impulsive Hubie had asked Gomez to enquire about her when they headed north. Apparently he did because within two weeks the happy young woman showed up with her meager belongings in hand. It seemed that although the net being cast by the Diaz cartel could not snag the fugitives, the underground network of the *Kumeyaay* knew right where to look.

They had been hiding in plain sight at the small resort town of Los Barriles on the east cape of Baja just forty miles north of Cabo San Lucas. It was not so hectic as Cabo and the beach house they rented was secluded and off the beaten path. Even though it was beachfront, there was a beautiful edgeless pool on the deck overlooking the Sea of Cortez. Rosa and Hubie used the luxurious upstairs master suite and Bear took the rooms downstairs adjacent to the expansive living room and fully stocked kitchen.

Lupita and her parents were staying one street up from the beach in a small condo. The first thing Pedro and Gomez accomplished was to move the Martinez family out of San Felipe immediately. This was done under the cover of darkness as soon as they had arrived. Gomez recruited plenty of help from his local group of *Kumeyaay* and overnight they were gone, as if they'd never lived there.

Of the thirty-five thousand dollars that Manny had delivered to Lupita, more than thirty-thousand remained. With the greenbacks it was easy to find a nice, hidden-away residence. Many *norteamericanos* came south with cash and without their wives. Ostensibly, these getaways were for fishing and recreation, but the locals understood the real reason. With cash, no questions were asked and no identification required. That would have been bad for business, for sure. Hubie and Bear, living with a Mexican woman and seen in the presence of another, was business as usual in this village. No one noticed, no one cared, no one gave it a second thought. The two gringos fit right in.

Rosa and Lupita took care of the shopping. *Señor y Señora* Martinez, Lupita's mother and father, were content to be hiding out with their daughter. *Señor* Martinez found great pleasure when Lupita accompanied him on a few fishing excursions. For him, it was like when she was a young girl, before leaving home to dance in the border towns. The beat up Cadillac was safely hidden inside the garage and the door was kept firmly shut. A rental golf cart was adequate for transportation in the small resort town and Lupita had procured a pair of quads for use on the beach and surrounding hills.

Lupita was very surprised when Bear appeared clean shaven. It had been so long since he'd seen his own face, he wondered who was looking at him from the mirror.

"*Hombre guapo!*" Lupita exclaimed when she saw his naked face. "You are very handsome, *mi oso grande!*"

Bear was eager to take Lupita out on the town, but that would have been foolhardy. That he was interested in getting to know her much better was obvious, however, she stayed with her parents out of respect which Bear completely understood. There might be plenty of time for those things in the future but for now, caution was in order.

That chance encounter back at Gonzaga Bay had been life changing for Hubie and Rosa. The pretty young girl had brought serenity and peace into Hubie's life. The man had always been wary of permanent romantic entanglements after witnessing the agony his father had experienced when Hubie's mother left them. Rosa changed all that with her smiles, love, and simple loyalty to her man. When Gomez and Pedro stopped overnight at Campo Papá Fernandez on their way north, Rosa couldn't wait to hear news of Hubie. When Gomez told her of their adventure and how Hubie had inquired about her, she made her goodbyes and left the next morning. Hiding out in paradise was wonderful for the pair and they made good use of it.

Hubie was happy as hell, of course. He was in heaven and if not for the anxiety of the Diaz cartel men finding them, he could stay in that place forever. Rosa agreed. If she was not fascinated with his long pony tail and twirling it between her fingers, she was in the kitchen doing her best to fatten him up.

She called him, *"Hombre rubio flaco,"* her skinny blonde man.

All was well..... for the time being.

27

Ayatatay

Pedro Martinez sat in the entrance way to the valley with Devil's Peak behind him as he looked out at the expansive Sea of Cortez to the east. It seemed like a lifetime had passed since the first time he had climbed the switchback trail arrayed below his feet. A lifetime and another life, it seemed. He recalled his futile anger and resentment from those days and was relieved to be rid of it. Now, he realized things could be different, with true meaning beyond the lure of greed and riches.

He had swung between two polar opposites of the evil represented by the cartels and righteousness as the Church saw it. Now he understood that the truth rested somewhere in between. He deeply felt his responsibility to a higher calling. Far below Pedro could see a lone figure negotiate the steep switchbacks leading upward. Pedro turned his back on the precipitous trail and walked back into the Enchanted Valley. The larger world was beyond his control, but this piece of ancient paradise was something that Pedro felt could be protected.   He would tell Gomez that someone was coming.

In the two months that Pedro had lived in this place, he had learned much from Gomez and the other members of the *Kumeyaay* that had been camping in the valley. Much in the same way Pedro had mentored Manny at the Fortaleza del Aguila, Gomez and the others had mentored Pedro in turn. He understood that he was being groomed to replace the ancient witch who's life he had taken.   There was no resentment or accusation in these people.   Existing in this place since before time was recorded gave them a different perspective on spirit.   A life was taken, it would now be replaced. Pedro's guilt and shame melted away.

The healing waters gave him a vitality he had not previously known. In the dark hours, Gomez would use the red powder as a means to open up alternative realities for Pedro. Gomez would apply a tiny pinch of the powder on the fire and speak with Pedro in the ancient way. At first, he did not understand the words but the images were clear. Now, after two months, Pedro was becoming accustomed to the dialect and shared it with his companions. They were patient, helpful, and considered him to be one of their own.

A man named Nemay instructed Pedro in the cultivation of the red flowers and how to process them for the mystic powder. The two men were of the same age and became friends, like brothers actually. More than anything else, their time spent together helped Pedro learn the ancient language. Nemay was skilled with the bow and tried to teach Pedro the art of spear and arrowhead making. Pedro just wasn't able to successfully apply the pressure needed to flake chips off the flint and obsidian rock. Nemay would just laugh at him and say he'd learn the skill in a hundred years or so.   Others showed Pedro the ropes of animal husbandry and maintaining the garden and groves. He learned much from these people but mostly he was struck by the good natured humanity and honesty they displayed.

Of the fifteen or so native people that came and went randomly, it seemed that there was always someone new to teach Pedro another craft. One woman walked directly up to Pedro and touched her forehead reverently against his in the traditional style.

Touching her fist to her breast, she said, "*Sunni.*"

After that, the young woman was never far from Pedro. Gomez explained that it is normal for the woman to choose her man. Additionally, she will take care of him for as long as he accepts her. If the man decides to keep her, then it becomes permanent and a new name is chosen for him. Sunni would sit apart from the men during the evenings when the spoken history was taught to Pedro. She quietly tended the fire and other necessities, but it quickly became apparent to Pedro that this woman was no shrinking flower.

Before sunrise one morning, she compelled Pedro to follow her up a cliffside trail that a lizard would not dare take. She had her bow slung with a small quiver of arrows on her back. Pedro watched as she took the life of a young female mountain goat with a well placed arrow shot directly between the ribs and into it's heart. With a small iron knife she gutted the animal, pausing to take a bite out of it's warm heart. Then, she cheerfully loaded the animal across her shoulders and led the way back to the valley.

During storytelling that evening, after the goat was roasted, she told of the look upon Pedro's face as she bit into the heart. They all had a great laugh over that one, but it was the laughter of love. Gomez explained that her name was taken from the great *Sunni* of the Melchor Diaz expedition. He also told Pedro that it was a great honor that she had chosen him.

Gomez was found with a group of men carrying rocks to

repair the pond wall. Pedro wanted to let him know that someone was ascending the trail.

"We know," said Gomez as he pointed to a great bald eagle circling high above. He is coming to tell us that Diaz is close. We have known since he left La Paz heading north two days ago. This is why the others are here."

"Why did you not tell me?" Pedro asked.

"I just did, *amigo*," Gomez laughed.

"So, now they will try to take *it*?"

"Yes Pedro, they will try, but we must fulfill our destiny, be not worried."

*****

Alfredo, Enrique, and Yolanda stopped for yet another break. Climbing up the interminable trail was not something they were used to. Yolanda, however, was in fairly good shape from her adventuring among the coca fields in Columbia as were the three men she had picked for the journey. The squat woman had ditched her silly heels and wore desert camouflage fatigues with sensible hiking boots. Diaz and Enrique were holding them back though, and they were drinking their water supply very quickly.

"Brother," Yolanda said in exasperation, "You will drown if you don't put the water away. That or we will starve to death before we reach the top. Get off your ass, both of you."

The group continued as it became obvious that they would not reach their destination until very late. Any idea of quickly getting the Artefacto and returning to their four-wheel drive vehicle the same day was not a realistic expectation. But Diaz was determined and would not be deterred.

Enrique looked high above and saw the rain clouds gathering. They were traveling as light as they could, except for their guns and those were beginning to become very heavy, indeed. Without rain gear, they were sure to be soaked if a downpour started.   Enrique noticed the clouds were becoming very dark. Ever upward they went.

Finally, as darkness fell upon them, they reached the granite notch at the very top of the switchback trail. Always cautious, Yolanda signaled to her three commandos to enter the valley.   The three men unslung their assault rifles and entered swiftly; the first to the right and second to the left, then the third man up the middle. They saw nothing but crops and groves. Yolanda was right behind the men then beckoned for Diaz and Enrique to follow. A light rain had been falling for some time, then suddenly it turned into a downpour.

In the faint light remaining, all of them were amazed to see the lush mountain shelf that was hidden from the desert below.   A huge flash of lightning accompanied by the thunderous report startled them. In the flash, they could see the sharp tip of Devil's Peak looming above.   The vision seemed threatening, as if the sheer granite peak might bend over and smash them flat.   Two of the cartel soldiers genuflected with the sign of the cross.

The third man cursed them and pushed ahead toward the trail through the grove. As he entered the trees he stopped suddenly and made a strange choking sound. His rifle fell from his fingers and dropped to the ground in front of him. It made a little splash in the swiftly gathering puddles. He seemed to be stuck in place so Yolanda flicked on her flashlight for better visibility.

The man slowly turned around as if to retreat, then fell straight back into the mud. Yolanda's light revealed three arrows sprouting from the man's chest and a forth protruding from his neck. Blood ran from his mouth, he was still. Before Yolanda could bring her weapon to bear, the other two men dropped to their knees and began spraying the grove with bullets. Diaz and Enrique fell flat on their faces without thinking.

After emptying their magazines, both men scrambled to reload. Yolanda admonished them to cease firing until she figured out what was going on. She quickly decided to avoid the grove and led the group around to the left where the garden and small corral provided some visibility in the gathering darkness. At least in the open, arrows would be less effective against firepower.

Yolanda gathered her little team in the darkness after turning off her flashlight. She kneeled down and motioned for the others to do the same.

"So, we are here and retreating in the dark is possible. Whatever asshole was shooting arrows is most likely hiding after all the bullets you *idiota's* wasted. So, Alfredo, do we proceed or do you want to run away? I care nothing for your silly rock."

"Uncle," Enrique said, "We have nothing but some indigenous cave men against us. Let us take what is our's and teach these *pendejos* a lesson once and for all."

Enrique was very much aflame with the fever of lust for the Artefacto. Alfredo Diaz only more so and the rage he was still feeling for his injuries tortured his soul. He wanted it more than anything, except perhaps to find Lupita hiding somewhere.

"*Si*, of course, we continue. It must be our's once again and that *perra* will feel my knife in both eyes!"

The group continued as silently as possible in the dark but were no match for the night eyes and ears of the natives. As they crept forward an occasional arrow would whistle by. Finally, one of the cartel soldiers was taken by a shaft in the leg. He howled in pain which pissed off Yolanda no end. She grabbed the man by his shirt and jerked him forward.

"Shut-up, keep moving or stay here and die."

She ripped off a quick burst toward the grove and the arrows ceased.

In the meantime, Gomez and Pedro returned from their task of hiding the rock. If the armed party gained control of the adobe casa, they would surely find its hiding place. They placed it on a rock ledge and covered it with stones. Pedro felt the strange sensation that it called out to not be left behind. Gomez felt it also, but both men continued forward with the goal of re-joining the native defenders.

The man with the wounded leg was unable to keep up with the others. He began to cry out for help. Diaz quickly returned to the man and pushed him down.

"You will betray us with your crying. Stay here, be silent."

Then Diaz turned and disappeared into darkness. Feeling the pain increase, he took the arrow by the shaft and tried to pull it out. That only made it much worse, so he sat still while whimpering in pain. It seemed like years had gone by, not minutes, when he heard soft footsteps.

He called out quietly, "I am here, do not leave me."

The footsteps quickly came in his direction, but he realized they were behind him. Suddenly a rough hand took him from behind and jerked his head back while covering his mouth. He felt a sharp heat across his throat as wetness flowed down his chest. He reached up and felt the open gash in his throat and tried to cry out, only to gurgle in his own blood. Feeling dizziness as he slumped over, his final thought was; *It is not so bad, I think I will sleep now.*

Yolanda, Diaz and Enrique reached the adobe structure built into the face of the Devil's Peak just in time to see the door open and shut quickly. Two men could be seen entering from the light of a dim oil lantern inside the casa. Enrique instantly recognized Pedro and sprinted forward to crash through the door before it could be barred from inside. With guns drawn, Yolanda and Diaz burst into the small room to find Gomez Gomez and Pedro reaching for a pair of spears stacked in the corner. With an assault rifle and two pistols aimed at them, Gomez and Pedro froze.

Diaz turned to the remaining soldier and said, "Remain outside as guard."

Before the man could protest, Diaz slammed the door shut and slid the lock bolt home. He turned toward his captured enemies with a vicious sneer on his face. A bloody red tear fell from under his black patch and ran down his cheek. Diaz looked all around the sparse room taking in the small kitchen and cooking pot to one side as well as the wooden frame bed on the other. A fireplace carved into the live granite of the cave was cold. The only illumination in the room came from an oil lantern shining dimly on the table placed in the center of the space. Hand woven tapestries hung from the rock walls.

"Where is it?" Diaz snarled.

Gomez let his arms hang loosely at his sides and stepped protectively in front of Pedro. His demeanor was serene and calm. Pedro felt immense fear but did his best to hide it while at the same time was amazed at the presence of his mentor.

"It is not yours, it is of the earth and soul of the world. You will not have it."

Gomez stared directly into the eyes of Diaz, then Enrique and Yolanda as he said this. Suddenly a sharp yell came from outside and several shots were fired. Sudden thunks against the closed wooden door told of arrows landing solidly. Their guard yelped with pain then fell quiet. They could hear softer thuds as the man outside was throughly feathered.

Enrique turned pale with fear and began to sweat profusely as he desperately thought of a way out. Diaz began to curse rapidly as his spittle flew around the room. He thought nothing of danger, the man was consumed with rage to find out where the idol was.

Yolanda remained calm as she stepped directly up to Gomez and thrust the barrel of her nine-millimeter automatic assault pistol under his jaw.

"Do you wish to live, *Señor?*" she asked. "If so, you will tell your companions outside to leave and lead us directly to this stupid rock that is wasting so many lives."

Gomez remained passive as he stared directly into her eyes. Diaz stepped up and began to shout incoherently.

"Where is it? And where is that she-devil Lupita, your whore sister? I will cut her guts out."

Yolanda realized that Gomez would remain silent, so she turned her gaze to Pedro standing to the side.

"Would you like a lesson my *pequeña cucaracha*? You will produce the thing and lead us safely out of here or *this* is what to expect."

She squeezed the trigger and a short burst of nine-millimeter bullets tore through the top of Gomez's head as pieces of blood, skull, and brains sprayed over all of them. He dropped to his knees and slumped to the side. Pedro stared in horror and disbelief at what had just happened. Yolanda smiled with satisfaction and aimed her gun directly at Pedro's midsection. The horrified Enrique was stunned at what his mother had done. He stepped back and felt the solid wooden door against his spine. Diaz seemed surprised as he looked down upon the dead body of Gomez Gomez.

Pedro felt something welling up from deep inside. His vicious hate knew no boundaries. From a place he never knew existed, a thing struggled to get out. Then he threw his head back and let out a piercing, screeching roar that penetrated everyone's eardrums as if the doors of Hell had been opened and every screaming demon was released. It was overwhelming. Yolanda, Diaz, and Enrique forgot their guns and covered their ears from the pain. Then, there was silence…. but only for a moment.

Even through the heavy rain and thunder, an answer could be heard. The stunned invaders of the casa looked at each other with confusion. There was another ungodly screaming roar, only closer this time. Suddenly, the wooden planks of the door burst into splinters knocking Enrique to the granite floor. He turned over just in time to see the Devil lift his clawed foot then tear his guts out upon the floor.

The thing whipped it's scaly tail back and forth, turning the wooden table into splinters and smashing the lantern into pieces as it spewed burning oil across the room. In the fiery illumination, Diaz watched as the horror advanced slowly toward him. The monster's tail continued to twitch as the grasping claws reached out to draw the horrified Alfredo Diaz inward toward its open mouth and slavering fangs. Wide open jaws clamped down on his left shoulder, shattering his collar bone and shoulder blade as its razor sharp teeth sank deeply. The screaming El Diabolico kicked his legs futilely as the monster carried him out into the rain and darkness.

Yolanda finally came to her senses and raised her gun to fire at the back of the Demonio when Pedro Martinez knocked her to the floor and threw her weapon to the back of the room. He was on her in an instant. Her rib cage collapsed inward from the full force of his knees as her breath escaped her lungs. She weakly scratched at his eyes to no avail. Pedro had her by the hair and began to pound her skull savagely into the granite surface.

As Enrique Moreno bled to death, he tried to replace his shredded intestines back where they belonged. He turned his head to the side and the last thing he saw was his mother's head being smashed viciously against the granite surface over and over as her skull turned to pulp while her brains and blood flowed toward his reaching hand.

*****

There was great sorrow as the group made ready for the rites of passage. What was left of Alfredo Diaz's consumed body was burned with the others. Their weapons were stacked upon the rotting pile at the end of the valley along with rusted Conquistador armor and blades. The dead of the people were washed and prepared for burial. Among them included the body of Nemay who had been killed at the first burst of gunfire in the grove. Two others were killed and three wounded. They would survive their injuries with the stoic acceptance of their kind.

Gomez Gomez was cleaned in the most gentle manner possible. Pedro insisted that he be included in the ancient ritual. The others understood and helped him with the ministrations of the body. The great man was gone.

After the tasks were completed, Pedro was astounded to find himself surrounded by the people as they brought the Artefacto to him and laid the idol at his feet. As they respectfully backed away from Pedro, Sunni came forward. She was wearing coarse-spun white linen from neck to ankle. She walked directly up to Pedro with head held high and proud. She lowered her eyes briefly, touched her forehead to his gently, then she turned to her people.

"His name is *Ayatatay*," she said. The Protector.

High on the mountain peak called "El Diablo," came a high and shrill shriek from beyond time itself. The rock-lava idol of the earth glowed with pleasure. The Sea of Cortez shined brilliantly under a cloudless sky.

* * *

Pedro Martinez was home

Epilogue

Hubie watched as his 1959 Cadillac was hoisted into place on the platform constructed above his new establishment. He was nervous as the large car swung precariously from a single cable suspended from the crane. The Mexican crew hired to get it up there seemed to know what they were doing. Two men on each end with ropes tied to the front and rear bumpers positioned the car perfectly, as it was gently lowered into place.

Below the Cadillac a large neon sign proclaimed, *"CADILLAC HUBIE."* It would be turned on the first time tonight for the grand opening of Cabo San Lucas' new blues club, bar, and grill. Below the sign, the entire front of the place was opened to the busy street. Outdoor seating blended to inside from the wide Malecon walkway directly across from the beach. The veranda was covered with a palm-frond shade that spanned the front. Inside was a long bar fully stocked with every beverage one could desire. Two bartenders were busy getting ready for the big night. In front of the bar were many raised tables surrounded with stools. Further inside toward the back a large stage was being prepared for the evening's entertainment. Posters of famous blues performers lined the walls. Billie Holiday was featured prominently along with others such as Bessie Smith, Blind Lemon Jefferson, Willie Dixon, and not to mention Howlin' Wolf and Elmore James.

Lupita insisted that Josephine Baker be included in the tributes. She admired the dancer and singer for elevating her art in Paris where the specter of racism would not hold her down. Lupita recruited some ladies she had made friends with from her dancing days in Mexicali. They were headlined as, *"Las Chicas de Lupita."* The women were choreographing routines taken from the classic days of burlesque, reminiscent of greats such as Gypsy Rose Lee, Blaze Starr, and the buxom Tempest Storm. There would be no stripper poles promoting acts that left nothing to the imagination. These were to be class acts only. Lupita's girls loved the opportunity to take their skills to the next level.

John Popper and his band, "Blues Traveler's," were warming up for the evening as the sound techs made final adjustments. Hubie had enticed his old friend to bring his new band all the way from New York. It was to be a big night for them as well and they were happy for the opportunity. Hubie had been relentless putting out feelers for other blues acts to make the journey south. He had acts lined up all the way from Chicago to New Orleans. Stevie Ray Vaughan and Double Trouble were on his list, but he had not yet made an arrangement with them.

During the five months since Hubie, Bear, and Lupita had come to "Land's End," the three had worked tirelessly to put it all together. When Lupita found the abandoned beachfront restaurant and inquired of the ownership rights, the attorney in charge of matters agreed to lease the building for a steal. When the big night was close at hand, Hubie realized that almost all of the money left over from Lupita's large manila envelope was gone. It was going to be sink or swim….. until an anonymous investor flooded the establishment's business account with funds, that is. Now they had enough operating capital to get the club on a solid footing.

Lupita had an interesting communication from her parents after they returned to San Felipe. It seemed that men of the cartel had been waiting for them. Instead of taking the elderly pair into custody, they were brought to a brand new beachfront Villa that had been purchased for them. The proud Señor Martinez absolutely refused to take any form of tainted money, beautiful home or not. He brought his wife back to the humble abode they had lived in all their lives. They wrote Lupita informing her that Pedro had come to visit often. This is how Hubie, Bear, and Lupita became aware of the demise of the Diaz clan. They were relieved to live without fear, although it was a mystery who might be running things now. Good riddance.

As the Cadillac was lowered into place, Hubie felt Rosa's arm encircle his waist. Hubie hadn't seen her emerge from her kitchen where she had been busy running the cooking and wait staff. She had found her niche while creating a menu guaranteed to please the guests. The woman was a master at producing a blend of traditional Mexican fare, along with many wonderful dishes she created from the abundant, fresh seafood brought in daily from the waters surrounding the tip of the Baja Peninsula.

"*Es maravilloso mi amor*," Hubie's gal said as she looked up at the red Cadillac prominently displayed over the large curved neon sign.

"Yes, it is. It's crazy how all this came together, *mi flor*."

Hubie and Rosa were stuck together like super glue. He called her his 'flower' and she named him 'mi flaco'. She kept trying to fatten her skinny man up, but it wasn't working. She didn't give up, though. Now that Hubie had learned enough Spanish, and Rosa enough English to communicate effectively, their feelings for each other grew ever more solid. The tall, blonde man from Philadelphia and his cute, smiling amor from Mexico were the ultimate odd couple. It never fazed them in the least. His acute business sense allowed him to run things efficiently and Rosa's magic in the cocina created the perfect partnership for the newly created establishment.

Bear and Lupita joined them as they watched the final positioning of Hubie's Cadillac. Hubie noted that they were holding hands again, something he'd seen more often nowadays. That Bear adored the beauty was impossible to ignore. It was plain to see that her attraction for the large man was difficult for her to conceal. Rosa often poked and prodded her for information to no avail. As far as Hubie was concerned, his friend was content and that was enough.

"So Boss, tonight's the big night, huh?" Bear said.

"Yeah," Hubie replied. "Did you hear Popper warming up his mouth harp? It's gonna be a good show for sure."

Two large, black SUV's stopped on the street right in front of the club. The foursome turned around to see what this was all about. They sure didn't need any trouble on opening night. The driver of the first vehicle got out and came around to open the passenger door. Three men emerged from the second vehicle, then positioned themselves to cover all angles from the street. The loose shirts hanging over their belt lines didn't hide the fact that they were heavily armed.

Lupita's heart skipped a beat when Manny got out of the first vehicle. Hubie had never seen the man, but instinctively knew this could be very bad. Bear remembered the scarred face and also how he had not tried to prevent their escape. When Lupita moved closer to Bear, he reached a long arm around her waist and pulled her in protectively.

Manny looked slightly sad for a moment, then his face

softened and he spoke quietly in Spanish. Lupita translated for her companions.

"My friends," he said. "Be not concerned. I am here to offer the services of these men for the security of your club. There is, shall we say, an interface between my organization and the local constabular officials."

Hubie understood instantly. Now he knew who the silent partner was and why there had never been any red tape or bribes that were considered a normal way of business south of the border. His brilliant business mind immediately considered alternatives and he wondered if the other shoe would drop now.

He spoke up, "*Señor*, is it Manny? I am sorry, I don't know your last name. I would like to know what the price of your security will be?"

Lupita rapidly translated, then Manny smiled while raising his hands disarmingly.

"The name is not important, but price?" Manny asked. "*Si*, I expect that your business will be a success, so the price will be waived. I may wish to visit from time to time and hope that I will be welcome. That is sufficient, if you agree to these terms."

"And the percentage?" Hubie asked, still unwilling to believe that there would be something for nothing.

Manny thought that over for a moment and wondered how he could explain to this skinny gringo that he wanted nothing but redemption for a thousand wrongs. He looked directly at Rosa and remembered the intelligence that reported her to be a first-rate chef.

"Alright, my friend. You will provide me and my men with dinner when we are present and if we are hungry. That is all."

Then Manny took a long look at Bear. There was no doubt who the man was, even though he was now clean shaven. He saw Lupe lift her head proudly as she stood next to her amante. Bear took his arm from around her as Manny stepped up to them. Manny had to look up at the large man towering above him. Bear returned his gaze with unwavering intensity. Manny looked away from Bear momentarily.

"Lupe, you are happy? He is a good man?" he asked.

She nodded her head in the affirmative. Once again Manny looked up at Bear.

"There is one small matter that must be attended too. You have not returned my machine gun and the damage you inflicted on the front of my headquarters has yet to be repaired. But, I actually like it that way. It looks dangerous, it is good for business."

When Lupita translated this, Bear began to wonder how much a belt-fed M-60 machine gun would go for down here, let alone how to procure one.

Manny spoke once again, "Perhaps I may be invited inside your beautiful club and you can buy me a shot of *tequila con limón y sal*. Then we will consider ourselves to be even."

"After all, will it not be showtime soon?"

Acknowledgments

This book was a delight to imagine and write. However, it was not created in a vacuum. I want to thank Jeff Fillbach for his insightful and lovely cover art. My loving wife, Rosemarie, was always present to endure proof readings and offer her welcome ideas. Hearing your work read aloud is a great way to visualize how a reader would imagine the story. Rosemarie's patient listening helped immensely. My daughter, Stacy Lynne Hunt, has been the best story editor any writer could hope to find. Her attention to detail and expertise in finding punctuation and other mistakes have made this work the way it should be. By that I mean she made it seem as if I knew what I was doing. The contribution these two women have made to "Cadillac Hubie," can not be underestimated. You guys are the light of my life, thank you.

I also must acknowledge the influence the marvelous land of Baja had on me, and this novel. I first visited the lovely beach town of San Felipe in the mid-eighties. I fell in love. That passion compelled me to build a beachfront adobe brick home overlooking the Sea of Cortez. It is impossible to describe the beauty of a morning sunrise or evening sunset, not to mention the silence and serenity to be found there. We can never understand the effects of civilization along with the constant background noise it produces until it is absent. Imagine a still day so peaceful you can hear the sound of the wind on the wings of a great ocean bird of prey as it circles overhead. Many might only see dry desert desolation. They would be wrong. Baja is full of life.

Sure, Cabo San Lucas has grown into a huge tourist destination. La Paz is a sprawling metropolis complete with noise and pollution. The Pacific side of the peninsula is rife with sprawling towns that did not avail themselves with any kind of community planning. So be it. But, when a traveler takes the plunge and steps away from the tiny ribbons of pavement, the magic is still there.

Although this story and its characters are imaginary, the locations and descriptions of that land are very real. Baja's Sierra de San Pedro Mártir, Baja's tallest peak, towers 10,154 feet above the Sea of Cortez. And yes, it is nicknamed, Pichaco del Diablo, or "The Devil's Peak." Tales of the ancient Chupacabra and evil Bruja's inhabiting this inhospitable region are infused in the mythology every child learns from an early age.

The Hawaiian Bar in the border town of Algodones is very real as is the expatriate community of Puertocitos, fifty miles south of San Felipe. The hot springs there bubble up from the heat of the earth where the crust is relatively thin. I'm not sure any mysterious artifacts have ever been spawned from those lava flows, unless you consider the entire area to be magical. I do. Descendants of the indigenous population that Spanish Conquistador's discovered in 1543 still live there.

Geologically speaking, Baja is very young, having split from mainland Mexico relatively recently. The waters of the

Sea of Cortez are a fisherman's paradise. While we maintain our lives in the facade of modern living, Baja remains the same as it's been for thousands of years. I would recommend you take a trip to Guerrero Negro on the Pacific side of Baja anytime from February to April to see the return of grey whales as they enter Laguna Ojo de Liebre (Scammons Lagoon) for breeding and calving, before they begin their long journey north. This migration is a mind-bending thing to imagine. Picture leaning over the side of a panga as a giant mother lifts her newborn calf up to the surface so the monkeys in the boat can touch her child. Are these creatures smart? I would submit they are every bit as intelligent as we are, and more so in many ways. I was compelled to write about this experience. I migrated there yearly, in order to see the creatures again and again:

"When I was a very young boy, perhaps six or seven, the world was so open and new. A kaleidoscope of images, odors, colors, and textures spread out for me to take in. I flew like the wind, gravity barely having a slight hold on me as I ran.... exuberant.

I remember a warm Spring day. Lying on the concrete sidewalk, I watched bees at work on the flowers planted in the park strip of my neighbor's home. So many fragrances mingled with the riot of color. I can still remember the manure, mixed with the soft perfume of open petals, giving their sex, welcoming their symbiotic partners, lovers, to do with them as they wished. No jealousy, no agenda, no manipulation, no selfishness... only nature, and life.

Young eyes, almost microscopic with ability, scrutinized the process. My nose and face intruded on nature's ritual as I rested, chin on hands. There was no fear on either side. The bees did their job, and I watched. The flowers ignored me completely, being absorbed with the sun above and the life they pulled from the rich soil beneath.

Mixed in was the soft hum of invisible wings. Some came so close that I felt the faint breeze upon my eyelashes. Dancing and flitting about, yet with purpose. Landing, working, and emerging, heavy with pollen. Abruptly leaving when the limit of cargo was reached, then replaced by another, intent on the task.

I wonder, sometimes, what happened to those days. Then I realize, nothing happened. It is always there, and always will be. The only thing changing was in me. As life crowded in, my eyes saw other things. Things just got bigger, more important, more complicated.

Baja brings that experience back, for me. Now, my bees have morphed and grown to impossibly huge swimming beasts. Buoyant and powerful, a flick of the huge tail propels the bulk with incredible speed and grace. These warm, caring, intelligent creatures follow their own path, winding along through nature's plan. As they make their long journey, they remember me, and I remember them. We see each other again. Proud, they show me their new, precious creation. The offspring, unafraid, sees us and learns. I imagine that one of these marvelous creatures was a baby I had seen, years ago. And now, as a proud mother, she presents her baby to me as her own mother did before. Without words I can hear the meaning, "Hey there, friend, nice to see you again."

And, I feel the same way.

*****

It strikes me that I must give credit to the late, great Robert E. Howard who tragically left us way too soon. His ability to blend larger-than-life characters with fantastic mystical creatures inside amazing adventures had me mesmerized as a teen. His influence is undeniable.

Finally, I would like to acknowledge you, the reader, for joining in on Hubie's adventure. I hope you enjoyed it and would very much appreciate your comments in a review. All reviews help, even less than stellar ones. I may be reached at: "radcrews@yahoo.com"

I would like to invite you to try another of my novels, "The Longest Road: Whole Lotta Love at Live Aid." It is available on Amazon in e-book format as well as paperback:

"It's 1985, no computers, no cellphones, only the largest concert ever conceived, Live Aid. Follow the MTV Generation, at its best, as Bob Geldof utilizes the finest talent of the times with the goal of relieving the starving people of Ethiopia. Young Mark, on his way to a once-in-a-lifetime chance to see Led Zeppelin, falls in with two stranded ladies, also on their way to Philadelphia. Follow the threesome on their journey as they enter into the world of Eighties music and self discovery. The world is changing rapidly, shrinking as satellite technology creates a smaller planet. Our trio experiences growth and tragedy in a world forever changed. As romance ensues, love blossoms as it only can for the young. A story of discovery, first love, loss and redemption, wrapped in those times, long gone and never to return."